Amelia's
DECEPTION

GG SHALTON

OTHER BOOKS BY GG SHALTON

A Previous Time – coming December 2017
Running From Past Roses – coming spring 2018

CHAPTER 1

R AIN POUNDED AGAINST THE WINDOW causing the glass to shake. Amelia sat up in her bed bringing the covers under her chin. Sleeping in the storm was impossible. Thunder rumbled through her room as the darkened sky lit up with lightning strikes. She inched to the side of the bed taking her robe to cover herself as she fumbled in the dark to light her lantern. Her stomach rumbled as she made her way down the stairs reminding her that she had skipped dinner. A quick snack may help her go back to sleep.

The stormed raged outside blocking out the noises of the night. Amelia searched the kitchen for the leftover apple tarts, but they had disappeared. Looking around for another snack, she settled on some bread and cheese. A lull in the storm finally brought some peace to her night. Faint sprinkles of rain were all she could hear. Relieved the storm was finally passing, she quickly finished her snack placing her plate in the empty sink. She reached for her lantern, hearing faint voices echoing in the hall. They were coming from her father's study. She tiptoed toward the study, shut off her lantern, and hid by the study wall to listen.

A deep, raspy voice vibrated by the door. "Your time has run out. Stop with the excuses. The debtor's prison will not save you from what you owe me." Amelia covered her mouth with her hand.

"What you ask is impossible. I have nothing left to give." The familiar voice of her father pleaded with the stranger.

The stranger's voice took a sarcastic tone. "Indeed? I believe if you try hard enough, you can think of many ways to pay your debt." He snickered before his voice changed back to a threatening tone. "For now, I will take what's left in the safe and the ring on your finger."

A whimper came from her father. "My ring? It belonged to my father and is a family heirloom—it's all the jewelry I have left. The ten pounds in the safe will barely put a dent in what I owe you. I have a family."

The stranger snorted. "You will be in prison within a month. Your family is not my concern. You have one week to find a way to get me the rest of my money, or you will pay with blood."

Footsteps came toward the door. Amelia jumped back and hid behind the settee, lowering to the floor. The door opened abruptly, and a man stormed out of the room, crossed the foyer and slammed the front door. She didn't move a muscle until she heard her father's footsteps exit the study and climb the stairs.

She waited a few minutes before standing. How could her father be so irresponsible? Trying to put her mind at ease, she rushed to the front door in the darkness avoiding any obstacles that may be in her way. Her stomach calmed as she reached the door unscathed and assured it was shut and now locked. Peeking out the window into the darkness, she saw no visible sign of anyone near their home. The stranger had left.

Amelia inhaled a deep breath and felt her way to the stairs thinking about the demise of her father. It was no secret that their London home was being repossessed for bad debts. Late night conversations overheard throughout the house was that her father would never make it through the move and would be in a debtor's prison by months' end. The family had to move within a month to the only residence they had left that was not being sold off—the entailed manor her father inherited. It would provide a small living space for the family although it was falling apart. Hardly a residence for a nobleman.

She lit her lantern and climbed up the stairs to her room trying to avoid being heard. The rain had stopped, and she wanted to go back to bed. She paused in the hallway and opened the door to her little brothers' room. The bed was empty, and she creased her brow searching every corner. Shadows from the windows danced on the walls as the trees swayed in the wind.

"John? George? Where are you?" she whispered loudly. Looking under the bed, she did not see them. She left their room and opened the door to her chamber. Two blond mops of hair peeked from underneath her blanket. A small tug of relief ran through her veins as she spotted both of her brothers lying in the middle of her bed fast asleep.

She blew out the lantern and crawled into the bed between them. They must have been afraid of the storm and went to find her. John was eight and George was seven. She mothered them, as her stepmother left their care to the help. Her stepmother felt children should not be seen or heard. Occasionally she would acknowledge them if certain guests were about, but she was mostly not involved in their daily upbringing. As their finances dwindled, many of their servants were let go causing their care to fall upon the housekeeper who was near being pensioned.

Amelia puffed up her pillows trying to fall asleep. She couldn't help thinking about her father. Dread filled her. Who was the man that came to visit to threaten him? Probably better she didn't know. Their relationship had become strained over the years. Her mother died when she was young. Rumor had it she was beautiful and an actress. Not exactly a proper wife of a baron. Actresses and singers made great mistresses, but one should never bring them home. To her father's defense, he was not a baron when he married her. Supposedly, his older brother was to be the heir, but with the carriage accident, her father inherited the title and her mother died soon afterward. A nurse and then a governess at her family's country residence raised Amelia away from the rest of the family. She barely saw her father through her childhood until he lost his country estate to bad debts. He had married her stepmother when she was very young although she was not invited to their wedding. They had two children together, and Amelia doted on her younger half brothers. She joined them at their London townhouse shortly after her twelfth birthday.

Unable to sleep she rose out of bed and lit a candle on her desk. She took some paper and ink out of the drawer to write some more letters to local employment agencies. The rejection of her other letters was making her desperate. It was hard to obtain a position as a governess with no experience or references. Amelia's stepmother told her there would not be enough room for her at their new home and she would have to be married soon without a dowry.

Her father was beginning negotiations with his second cousin who built a small living working as a merchant. Amelia shivered at the thought of marrying Edward—an overweight man with oily hair and a potbelly. His teeth had a dull color, and he spoke with a small whistle as he pronounced certain words. Her father's unscrupulous business practices caused many in the town to turn their back on her family. Most prominent business associates did not want to spoil their name with the association. Invitations to social occasions disappeared and Amelia's season was canceled. Her stepmother was devastated at their lack of fortune and took her frustrations out on her family. Most of society would not associate with her. Amelia's chances of making a suitable match were impossible.

She stopped writing the letter and began drawing instead. Smiling to herself, she realized she was drawing him. Her thoughts turned to Billy. Her friends had changed over the last year from fellow aristocrats to the working-class society. They were a guarded secret, especially Billy. Her family paid little attention to her Saturday outings.

Snickering to herself at her secret, she hid the picture under her mattress and blew out the candle. She crawled back into bed letting her thoughts take her to the first time she met Billy. Amelia's former maid, Tabatha, had also been a designated chaperone before her father dismissed her. She introduced her to a local girl she grew up with named Sally Collins. They met her one day at a local bakery. Sally worked at her uncle's stables and often invited Amelia and Tabatha over to their farm to spend time together. Her boyfriend Chuck worked at the stables renting horses and carriages. Chuck's group of friends took on odd jobs and traveled throughout England on adventures. Billy Johnson was their leader, and Amelia loved hearing stories of his days at sea. He was a rugged but handsome character with a scar on his right cheek and long disheveled hair. She kept her nobility a secret in the beginning and claimed to be an old friend of her maid's. Billy took an interest in Amelia and would often buy her trinkets for a smile. Those smiles soon turned to kisses. He seemed to enjoy her innocence and often filled her head with dreams. Amelia twisted in her blanket trying to fall back to sleep. Smiling at her thoughts of Billy, she closed her eyes hoping for a diversion. She knew tomorrow would come too soon.

The next morning Amelia was awakened by the housekeeper. The boys were out of bed, and the sun streamed through the window. Surprised that she had slept that long, she tried unsuccessfully to sit up. It must have been the late-night activity causing her to oversleep. Not wanting to face the day, she rolled over trying to pull the covers over her head to block the blinding light.

"Miss Amelia! Your betrothed is waiting for you downstairs. He is early, and your father demanded that I fetch you at once."

The butterflies in her stomach would not cease. Any mention of her engagement made her nauseous. Amelia groaned loudly, making herself get out of bed to get dressed. She had to hurry as her father did not tolerate tardiness. After combing out her hair, she twisted the ends so she could pin it up. Mrs. Brooks helped her with the barrettes.

Amelia checked herself in the looking glass one last time unable to force a genuine smile. If only she had the nerve to deny her father and live on her own. Perhaps she could find a governess position or become a servant, which would be better than marrying Edward.

Resigning herself to her fate, she dabbed some lavender perfume along her neckline. "Tell him I will be down in a moment." Mrs. Brooks nodded and left the room. Amelia sat down on the bed putting on her slippers. She looked around her room one more time, tempted to feign an illness and prolong the inevitable.

After a few moments, she took a deep breath and went down the stairs. Her father and Edward were waiting for her in the drawing room. Edward smiled when he saw her and walked toward her. He wore his hair slicked back trying to cover his balding circle that highlighted the center of his head. His black coat was a few sizes too small causing him to appear unkempt.

He bowed, "You look lovely, Amelia." He used her Christian name. After all, he was family, but the fact he was a suitor as well made her uncomfortable.

Looking at her father's stern face as a warning, she nodded at her betrothed. "Edward, how nice to see you."

Her father managed a smile and turned to the housekeeper. "They must be going, so you can hold off on the tea."

Amelia had hoped to spend a few minutes with her family before departing. She widened her eyes. "Who will chaperone us?"

Her father smirked. "You're engaged, Amelia. Hardly in need of a chaperone." Amelia wanted to protest but kept quiet.

"I have a driver who will be with us. I wanted to take you to my store to show you around and then back to my home for dinner. My family wishes to see you. Especially, my mother." Edward said.

Edward assisted her into the carriage. "I hope you like roasted chicken. I asked the servants to prepare a special meal this evening."

Amelia smiled not wanting to be rude. "I am sure it will be delicious." She noticed some sweat beading across his forehead. His nervousness was touching in an odd sort of way.

"I believe this is the first time we have spoken alone." He fidgeted with his handkerchief as he wiped his brow.

Amelia chewed on the inside of her mouth. "Yes, I believe you are correct." She didn't know what to say so decided to just agree with him.

He looked down at his lap. "I wanted you to know that I have favored you for years from a distance. I remember when you first came to stay with your family in London. You were a young girl, but so very beautiful. You have grown more beautiful as a woman if that is even possible." His eyes blinked a few times as he waited for her response.

Amelia's face felt warm and she was a bit embarrassed by his compliment. Not knowing how to respond she took out her fan, trying to hide her apprehension, and cooled her face.

He reached for her free hand and held it in his, rubbing his thumb across her palm. She had to hold back the feelings to pull her hand away. Being properly bred, she didn't want to appear rude and put her fan down on the seat beside her. Her chest felt heavy with guilt. He was not the man she wished to marry, but pushing down her bitterness, she would accept her fate. This man would help support her brothers and stepmother while her father was in prison. What else could she do? The silence was thick, and the air was hard to breathe. "Edward, tell me about your stores."

His face lit up at the prospect of speaking about his business. "I own two fabric stores and a candle store. I also sold some land that I owned to some wealthy merchants. I have enough money to buy a nice cottage. I can take care of us and provide a small living to your family. It was part of the deal I made with your father."

He put his hand in his pocket and pulled out a ring. "Amelia, I would like you to wear this ring. It was my grandmothers on my mother's side. It would mean a lot to me." His brown eyes met hers in a plea of desperation.

She closed her eyes not wanting to hurt his feelings and held out her hand. He slid the ring on her finger and kissed it. It was a small diamond surrounded by smaller diamond chips. The silver band was dainty and fit perfectly.

The carriage slowed at just the right time, as she was unsure how to respond to the ring. He looked out the window. "We are here at one of my stores. Please let us go inside." He stepped down assisting her out of the carriage. Amelia walked beside him taking his arm. He unlocked the door and they went inside.

The store was impressive and stocked with several varieties of material set throughout, covering the floor and shelves. He showed off the assorted styles and colors. He lifted his chin proudly. "My sister works at this store and my other sister manages the one in Bath. I work in the candle store down the street. I thought you would take the most interest in this store. You can have whatever kind of material your heart desires. I can have one of our seamstresses make you a dozen dresses. It's my engagement gift to you."

Her mouth fell open. "I couldn't possibly accept such a gift."

He walked toward her taking both of her hands. "Nonsense. You are my fiancée, and I own the store. I will send someone to your home for measurements this week." He bent down and kissed her hands. Her heart dropped as she tried to force herself to feel something for him. He was like a lost puppy, and she didn't know how to handle his affections.

He smiled at her showing his off-color teeth. "Are you hungry? Mother will be expecting us soon."

Amelia nodded. "Yes, I am a little hungry. Perhaps we should be on our way?" He escorted her out of the store and back to the carriage. He lived rather close to the store in a cottage he shared with his mother, father, and sister.

She looked over at him. "You live with your parents?"

He nodded his head. "Yes, mother said I should stay with them until I am married. When I turned one and thirty, I tried to move out, but mother took to her bed for a month, so I stayed with her and Father. She said she couldn't bear to be away from me."

Momentarily finding amusement in his story, she drew her brow. "What about after we are married?"

Edward straightened his cravat. "I am hoping she can adjust. I may need to stay a few nights with them each week until she can get used to the idea." Not that Amelia would mind him spending a few nights away, it just seemed like an odd attachment his mother had over him. She had seen his mother at a family gathering prior to her father's demise. She hadn't realized how dependent his parents were on their son. His father made no attempt to maintain a relationship with her father although they were cousins. The marriage request by Edward was a welcomed surprise by Amelia's father.

Edward helped Amelia out of the carriage and escorted her up the hill near the entrance of the cottage. The family was in the drawing room and stood as the two entered. His mother was a large woman and wore her hair in a tight bun. Her dress was colorful and matched her jewelry with green and blue tones. His sister Julia was equally as large in stature and wore spectacles, shying away from any conversation by looking down at the floor. His father wore a long face with gray hair and matching beard.

His mother smiled tightly, "Amelia! How nice of you to join us for dinner. Please have a seat." She studied her face scrutinizing her from head to toe. Amelia's arms wrapped around her torso trying to hide whatever flaw Mrs. Patton could find. She sat down beside her on the settee and accepted a cup of tea from Julia.

Mr. Patton cleared his throat. "I assume you are agreeable to the marriage contract as you are wearing the family ring." Amelia looked at Edward then down at the ring.

"The ring is beautiful." She carefully avoided the question.

Mrs. Patton narrowed her eyes. "Yes, it belonged to my mother. A pity my own daughters have not worn it yet. I would request that you pass it on if that time comes."

Amelia looked at the family's stoic expressions. "Yes, of course. I am sure that someday both your daughters will get a chance to wear it."

Mr. Patton rolled his eyes. "One could only hope." He muttered bitterly, "We may not have the same funds available as my son did to secure a wife. Given your father's circumstances, Edward could negotiate for your hand. My daughters may not be as fortunate." Amelia felt insulted that she was referred to as a poor relation that was given in to her circumstances.

Edward spoke up trying to defend his motives. "Father, I have already provided a small dowry to both my sisters to add to what you have saved."

Mr. Patton snorted, "Like I said. It may not be enough." Julia looked away and took a seat in the high back chair near the fireplace.

Edward raised his brow at his father regarding his comment. He turned to his mother. "Mother, Amelia likes to paint. Her brothers told me she has many paintings. I wish to frame them and decorate my stores and home with them." Amelia opened her mouth, surprised by his interest in her paintings.

Mrs. Patton took a drink of her tea. "Is that so? Well, we will need to see them first."

Amelia put on a guarded smile, hoping for a diversion. His mother seemed different than what Amelia remembered. Although, she never gave her much thought as a cousin's wife. Now she will be her mother-in-law.

Edward winced slightly at both women. "Yes of course." He took a sip of tea as the family sat in silence. Mr. Patton poured some brandy into a glass and took a drink.

Julia looked at Amelia. "I like to paint too. Have you been to the art museum?"

Amelia smiled at Julia's demure attempt to know her better. "Yes, I have on a few occasions, although I would love to go to Paris one day and look at the artwork. My mother lived in Paris."

Mr. and Mrs. Patton looked at each other with concern on their faces at the mention of Amelia's late mother—a subject not spoken aloud by family members. The past was buried, according to her father, along with any secrets that may be held.

Edward stiffened and tried to change the subject. He looked at Amelia trying to steal her attention. "Mother's favorite color is green. Do you have a favorite?"

Amelia put down her cup and looked at Edward. His effort at making conversation touched her. "If I had to choose only one color, it would be yellow."

Mrs. Patton puckered her lips in a challenging way. "On no. Yellow is too bright and gets too dirty. I hope you don't plan to wear yellow that often."

Amelia could not believe her rudeness. She cleared her throat. "Yes, I do have a few yellow dresses. They remind me of sunshine." A forced smile on Amelia's face shut down her retort.

Mrs. Patton grunted turning toward her daughter. "My dear, stop biting your nails. It's not ladylike." Julia looked away with a red face. Amelia felt sorry for her, with such an overbearing mother. She wasn't sure what was worse—having no mother or one like Mrs. Patton.

The footman came in and announced dinner. The family went into the dining room and took their seats. Amelia sat next to Edward who pulled out the chair for her. Mr. Patton pulled out Julia's chair and Edward rushed to pull out his mothers who gave him a stern look of disapproval.

The dinner was quiet with only pleasantries being discussed. They served plates of roasted chicken, asparagus, potatoes, and carrots. They served pudding for dessert. Amelia was full and enjoyed the delicious food. After dinner, they entered the drawing room once again and took their seats.

"Mother, I will need to take Amelia back to her home."

Mrs. Patton raised her hand. "Of course, dear. But don't be long. You promised me a game of chess before you retire. Would you rather your father drive her home?"

Amelia looked at Mrs. Patton, taken back by her suggestion. Edward pleaded with his mother. "But I wish to escort her home. She is my fiancée, mother."

Mrs. Patton put her hand on her chest. "I am your mother. I thought that meant something to you." She opened her fan forcing air on her face.

Edward looked at Amelia. "Would you mind riding home with my father?"

Mr. Patton protested. "Nonsense, you will escort Amelia home. I have no wish to see my cousin." Amelia swallowed her protest and tried to remember her manners. Edward's face turned nervously toward his mother. Unable to decide, he turned to his father who put up his hand to silence him.

Mr. Patton took a drink of his brandy. "If you leave now, you will be home in plenty of time to play chess." Amelia felt very uncomfortable at the exchange happening right in front of her. She spoke up hoping to end their argument. "I don't need an escort. I can manage with just the driver."

Mr. Patton lifted his chin. "Edward, escort Amelia home at once. Your mother can wait." Edward held out his arm obediently. "Yes, Father." He escorted her out of the house to the carriage. She felt like the consolation prize.

The ride home was quiet. Edward spoke of the weather and the new inventory he was expecting that week. Amelia welcomed the diversion to the scene with his family. A glimpse of her future life made her quiver.

She entered her home relieved to be away from Edward and his family. How would she survive another hour with them let alone a lifetime? Amelia stripped off her gloves and took the back stairs through the kitchen to her room. She wanted to stay clear of her family. Mrs. Brooks caught her in the hall and asked her if she needed assistance undressing. She shook her head and went to rest.

CHAPTER 2

THE NEXT DAY, AMELIA TOOK a walk in the garden trying to keep her mind off Edward. Fresh air would clear her mind and be a welcome change. After an hour enjoying the weather, Mrs. Brooks interrupted her thoughts.

"Miss Amelia, you have a guest in the drawing room. It's Lady Rachel. She is back from her trip abroad." Mrs. Brooks smiled giving Amelia the news.

Amelia's heart filled with excitement that Rachel had come to see her. She had been her closest friend when they had attended school together. Rachel had been out of the country for the last year during the scandal of Amelia's father.

She walked quickly inside practically running to the drawing room. "Rachel! I am so happy to see you."

Lady Rachel smiled at Amelia. She glowed in her yellow day dress accompanied by long white gloves, and her golden-blond curls were pinned up with sparkling barrettes.

"Amelia, you are a sight for my eyes. I missed you so." She hugged her as the girls broke out in laughter.

"Please come sit, I can ask my housekeeper to bring some tea." Amelia stepped outside, and Mrs. Brooks nodded as she went to prepare the tea.

Amelia walked to the settee and sat beside her friend. "Tell me how your trip was. I want to hear about all the wonderful places that you visited."

Rachel was beaming. "You shall, but I haven't much time now. I came by to extend a personal invitation to my coming-out ball tomorrow night. I know its short notice, but I only arrived home a few days ago and checked the guest list. My mother must have forgotten to invite you. I told her you were my dearest friend and I would not have my coming-out ball without you." She smiled and handed Amelia an invitation.

Amelia slowly took it and looked down at her lap. She knew that Lady Breconshire did not forget to invite her. Her family was shunned by the town. "Thank you, Rachel, but I couldn't possibly..." her voice cracked as her bottom lip quivered. She took a deep breath. "I couldn't possibly attend. Much has happened since I saw you last."

Rachel straightened her shoulders. "Nonsense. I heard the rumors and whispers. It's not your fault, Amelia. Did you know that last year people had you picked to be one of the most sought-after debutantes for this year's season? You are beautiful, Amelia. Many wonderful men will not overlook your beauty because of your father."

Amelia shook her head. "I wish it were true. My father is in negotiations for me to marry my cousin Edward. I am frightened at the prospect, but have no other means."

Rachel's face twisted in disgust. "Edward? The one I met at your birthday party a few years ago?"

Amelia dipped her head reluctantly. Rachel gasped. "That settles it. Meet me at my home tomorrow for luncheon. You can borrow a dress from me and get ready for the ball. You need some time away from your family."

Amelia looked frightened. "Rachel, I can't go. What if they are mean to me? You know how they will judge me because of my father." The thought of all those people taunting her with their haughty stares was unnerving.

Rachel shook her head. "You are my guest. I will not allow it. I want you there, and it's my ball. Please don't deny me this, Amelia."

Amelia resigned herself to accepting the invitation from her friend. "Very well. I will be there." Rachel smiled as tea was served. She accepted the cup from Amelia and began to tell her about all the preparations they made for the ball.

The next day Amelia hesitated before knocking on Rachel's front door. Her father was an earl. A very rich earl and came from old bloodlines. He died two years ago making Rachel's older brother Johnathan the new earl. Their family was well respected and active in the town's social life. Rachel's mother was a countess and friendly with royalty. She scrutinized those below her; looking down her nose was a common trait. Amelia thought about turning around and forgetting all of it, but she had promised Rachel and would not go back on her word.

Amelia made herself knock and waited until the butler answered the door. He greeted her properly and escorted her to the drawing room. Rachel was sitting with her mother, and her face lit up when she saw Amelia.

"Amelia! I am so happy you are here. Please come sit down. We are enjoying some tea." Rachel patted the seat beside her and poured her a cup. "You take sugar, if I remember correctly."

Nodding toward Rachel, she glanced at Lady Breconshire. The countess lifted her chin while examining Amelia. Her regal appearance beckoned her rank. Amelia's legs shook slightly as she sipped her tea.

"I am so excited you are here. The servants are preparing the ballroom. We can take a quick peek before we go to my room."

"If you two will excuse me, I must see the kitchen staff." The countess rose from her chair, dismissing herself from the girls.

Rachel turned to Amelia. "Don't mind her. She is nervous that something will go wrong with the ball. Come, let's go see the ballroom and decorations."

The girls left the drawing room only to be attacked by two young boys—Rachel's brothers who were twin eight-year-olds. "Melia!" Amelia turned to see the boys before they crashed into her, giving her a hug.

She laughed out loud. "I have missed you two! I am surprised you remember me. You both have grown at least an inch."

Ronnie, the bigger twin, wiped his cheek with his hand. "Of course. You helped us build our castle out of blankets the last time you were here. Can you still whistle?"

She lifted the corner of her mouth. "Did you say whistle?" Amelia whistled a tune swinging the boy's arms in an impromptu dance. The boys were laughing when she swung their arms in a circle, dancing around the room.

The giggles were infectious until they suddenly stopped dancing causing Amelia to bump into them. Unsure of their sudden cessation of movement, she turned toward the source of discomfort. The earl stood with his mouth opened with three men behind him staring at the group. Amelia looked down embarrassed by her childish behavior. Lady Rachel stood frozen as her brother took in the scene.

He cleared his throat. "Boys, go back to the school room at once." The boys let out a moan of complaint, but followed their brother's instructions. He turned toward his sister. "Lady Rachel. I am sure you and your *guest* have other duties to attend to." The use of the word guest was expressed as an annoyance. Rachel sagged her shoulders at the use of her title. His guests must be here on formal business.

Amelia looked away trying to find her feet to follow Rachel. The earl's look of disgust—one he shared with his mother—mortified her. He was a pompous man of medium build and had the same golden hair as his sister. His clothes were always of the height of London fashion, showing off his wealth. She had only briefly met him on very few occasions. He was usually away at school when Amelia visited attending Eton and Oxford. His stern voice and gaze made her legs weak. She tried to escape the room as quickly as possible.

"Wait!" A deep voice resonated behind her. Amelia turned around seeing a huge dark-haired man appear beside her. He was sharply dressed with broad shoulders and had a slight Scottish accent. He bent down to pick up a hair barrette. She must have lost it when she was dancing with the boys. He held a tight grin across his hard face. "I believe you dropped this."

Amelia's face turned red. Reaching out her hand, he dropped the barrette into her palm. She whispered slightly, "Thank you, sir." She could not make eye contact with him. Feeling humiliated by her clumsiness, her eyes locked on Rachel standing near the stairs.

He slanted his head trying to capture her attention. "Of course. You wouldn't want to lose it." She could hear traces of brogue in his speech.

Suddenly, he reached up taking a piece of her silky hair between his fingers running them down the strands. Her eyes widened at the impropriety. His rakish grin darkened the mood of the room. He let go of her hair and lowered his voice. "If you forgive my forwardness, I like your hair down. You don't need the barrette."

The man's throaty response made Amelia shiver. Everyone stayed still watching the exchange. Amelia swallowed and looked down at the barrette in her hand breaking his stare. *How dare he?!* They had never even been properly introduced, and his intimate touch was inappropriate. She fisted the barrette in her hand angrily and walked away without saying a word.

Rachel looped her arm around her elbow, and they climbed the stairs to her room refusing to look back.

She was a vision in his eyes. Unlike the usual pretentious English women, he couldn't stand, this beautiful stranger's demeanor seemed genuine and good-natured.

He turned toward the earl. "Who is she?" He had never found innocent girls attractive, but she was the type of girl that could change his mind.

The earl watched his sister disappear up the stairs before answering. "A friend of my little sister's. I barely know her."

"I believe I will accept an invitation to tonight's activities after all."

The earl's stoic expression was unmoved, "I understood that our business was completed and you have been paid in full, Mr. Baird. I see no reason to meet socially. You would be bored within minutes of my sister's coming-out ball."

Mr. Baird snorted. "Tsk, tsk my lord. Don't be rude. I will accept your gracious invitation on behalf of my party and we will be in attendance tonight. I hope your mood will be more courteous or I may be forced to take offense. Trust me, Johnathan. You would not like to offend me."

Johnathan flinched at the use of his Christian name—although he remained silent. Andrew enjoyed that the earl was a peer and knew it was rude to be addressed informally by a commoner. A commoner he may be, but poor he certainly was not. Money lending was only part of his fortune. He owned many gambling halls, and most of his businesses ventures were legal although rumor had it he was a blackguard who was the head of a criminal empire. One that allowed him to act as a gentleman through impeccable manners and befriend the exclusive elite of the town. One did not have to be a ruffian to be successful.

Johnathan took a deep breath turning red. "Of course, Mr. Baird. I will alert our staff of my personal invitation. I hope you will be discreet with our business today."

Andrew laughed at his presumptuous request. "I am not sure if I should be offended. All my business deals are kept discreet until I decide they needn't be." His grin faded as he looked seriously at Johnathan. "Good day, my lord." He left the house followed by two of his men.

CHAPTER 3

"That dress was made for you. I have never worn it, but it matches your green eyes perfectly." Rachel stared at her as she turned her around to see the back. "Exquisite, I have just the necklace to match."

Amelia tried to suppress her smile but was too excited not to gleam. "I couldn't accept anything more, Rachel. You already lent me this dress and the use of your lady's maid."

"Nonsense. Dressing you is as much fun as dressing myself. Don't take away my enjoyment." She opened her jewelry box and removed a pearl necklace. She helped put it on Amelia's neck. The girls giggled all afternoon as they made finishing touches for the party. They were served light snacks and hot chocolate to hold them over until the supper dance.

Amelia went downstairs when the guests started arriving. She left Rachel upstairs to make a grand entrance when they announced her. Amelia scanned the area choosing a chair by a few other girls who were not dancing. They smiled but were not speaking to her, feigning interest in their surroundings.

Amelia knew that her father's reputation and his upcoming trip to the debtor's prison would probably keep most dance partners at bay. But she enjoyed watching the guests arrive in style and admired the beautiful ball gowns displaying the latest London fashions. A few men nodded at her, but no one stopped to speak to her. She tapped her foot trying to keep herself entertained. A wallflower existence was in her future. Laughing at herself, she preferred that label than being married to Edward.

After a while, she went to the refreshment table and accepted a cup of punch from a servant. She wished for at least a chaperone to speak too. Anything was better than isolation. She walked back to her chair noticing that the announcement of Lady Rachel was beginning. Guests clapped as she descended the staircase. Amelia smiled at the beauty of her friend. The musicians started to play, and Rachel took her first dance with her brother. Amelia watched the couple, wishing she could dance.

"We meet again." A raspy voice came up behind her. She turned around noticing the massive man from earlier in the day. Her face turned red thinking of her embarrassment.

"Good evening, sir," she whispered, finding her voice yet trying to avoid his stare.

He leaned down, whispering near her ear, "May I introduce myself? I know the earl should formally introduce us, but he is otherwise engaged. Could we overlook propriety, so I can know your name?" His scratchy accented voice vibrated through her.

She smiled at his persistence. "I am Miss Abbott. And you are?"

He smiled back roguishly. "Mr. Baird. I am a business associate of the earl's. Now that we are acquainted, would you honor me with a dance later?"

She stared at him studying his face. The lines at the corner of his eyes showed he was a lot older than her. His risqué tones and shadowing height were a bit overbearing. His eyes held some mystery and a little danger. Although he was dressed fashionably, his features were rough. She noticed men following him around like protectors. Not knowing how to respond she nodded slightly, giving him her dance card.

He signed it, "I thank you, Miss Abbott." His gaze swept over her head lingering on her breasts and moving down to her toes. Appreciation combined with a bit of lust shined in his eyes. He whispered, "I will see you later."

Shocked by his brazen behavior, Amelia watched him walk away and then went to the lady's drawing room. Perhaps this was the way of men? Undressing women with their eyes. But truthfully, her experience had been limited. She took care of some private needs and made her way back out into the ballroom.

"There you are." Rachel's voice was out of breath. "I have been looking for you."

Amelia turned around to see Rachel's smirking expression. She had two gentlemen with her. They were both handsome with sandy hair and looked related. Her grin gave away her folly. "Amelia, these are my cousins from York. Thomas and Roy Martin."

She took Amelia's arm. "Cousins, this is my beloved friend Amelia Abbott." Rachel nodded toward one of her cousin's raising her brow.

Her cousin nodded back assuring that he understood her not so subtle request. "Nice to make your acquaintance, Miss Abbott. Would you care to dance?"

Amelia embarrassingly handed him her dance card trying to conjure up some dignity. She knew Rachel was only trying to be nice. "How nice of you, Mr. Martin."

He flashed his dimples in a big smile trying to put her at ease. "Please call me Thomas. After all, you're my cousin's friend."

Although she was embarrassed by Rachel's pity, she was grateful for Thomas' offer no matter how hard it was to admit. He chose a country dance and escorted her to the dance floor. Thomas was very charming and attentive to her. After the dance, he asked her to accompany him to the refreshments table. Rachel met them there with a gentleman named Lord Ryan, a viscount that took an interest in her. The earl stood close by their group talking to some of his friends.

Amelia began to relax as the group included her in their conversations. She smiled and enjoyed some laughter when she felt someone touch her arm. The group's enjoyment ceased as they were interrupted by a strong presence. Everyone stood still watching Andrew whisper to Amelia. "Lass, our dance is coming up. May I escort you to the dance floor?"

Rachel looked shocked, turning toward her brother to intervene. He tightened his hold on his glass taking a drink of his brandy and said nothing of the exchange. Hesitantly, Amelia raised her brow at Rachel as she took Andrew's arm.

He led her away from the group. She could feel his muscles tighten through his jacket as he guided her through the crowds toward the dance floor. Amelia felt so small compared to his bulky frame. She glanced up at her partner sneaking a look at his face as he showed no emotion. She wondered what kind of business he did with the earl? They seemed worlds apart.

The orchestra started playing a waltz and he put his hand on her waist. "Is this your first waltz? I hear some mothers find the dance scandalous." He raised his mouth to a half-grin watching her expression. His arms tightened around her pulling her closer to him.

She looked at his chest trying not to make eye contact. Her nerves were causing her head to spin. Taking a deep breath, she muttered, "I have practiced it on occasion, but this is my first ball. My mother died when I was small, but I don't think she would have minded." Amelia cringed after her admission, that was too much information to share.

He closed his eyes. "Forgive me. I didn't realize about your mother."

She lifted her head meeting his eyes. "No, please forgive me. I don't usually speak about it. I must be nervous for the dance. I do have a stepmother."

His eyes moved down her face as he pushed her around the dance floor and Amelia brought her attention back down to her feet. She didn't want to miss a step as he guided her across the floor.

"Are your parents at the ball?" He leaned over talking closer to her ear.

"No, they couldn't come." She did not want him to know the truth about her family. "They don't usually attend social engagements."

He waited a few seconds studying her face. "How are you acquainted with the earl's sister? Are you related?" He turned her around flowing to the music and changing the subject.

Puzzled by his interest, she shrugged her shoulders. "Not much to tell. We are only friends and went to school together. My father is a baron. He remarried when I was young. I have two younger siblings."

"Ah. So, your blood is blue and noble." His mouth twitched letting out a deep chuckle.

Not liking his reply, she tried to explain. "Hardly. Not all nobility is noble." She regretted saying it as soon as she said it. He was a stranger to her. She should not reveal too much about herself. The music was ending and she tried to step away, but he held on to her hand.

She looked up at him noticing his smoldering gaze. He took her hand to his mouth kissing her knuckles, not breaking his stare. "It was a pleasure, Miss Abbott." His words were smooth and suggestive causing uneasiness to course through her. He walked away not saying another word.

"A waltz?" Rachel's voice came up beside her. "You must have made quite the impression today with your missing barrette." She giggled as she covered her mouth.

Amelia shrugged her shoulders. "I am as surprised as you are."

Rachel turned toward her, biting her bottom lip. "My cousin has asked me a hundred questions about you."

Amelia blushed and walked with Rachel to the terrace for some fresh air. Her cousins joined them and they broke into conversations about the festivities. Thomas made a point to stand by Amelia and engaged her in conversations. Amelia's ego enjoyed his attention, which was not common among polite society. She knew he didn't know of her family's sordid past. Her heart ached knowing he would not acknowledge her in the same way again once he found out. But for now, she would relish in the moment.

"Would you like to take a walk in the garden?" He smiled showing his dimples again. Amelia was apprehensive to be alone with him and looked to Rachel for support.

She acknowledged her hesitancy. "It is a lovely evening. Why don't we all take a walk?" Amelia let out a breath of relief and accepted Thomas's arm as an escort.

She held his arm tightly following Rachel and Roy into the garden. He was very tall, but lanky and smelled of a woodsy cologne. Thomas guided her through the paths as Rachel and Roy walked several steps ahead of them.

"Are you having an enjoyable time?" Thomas slowed his pace, dragging his eyes over her face, searching for an answer.

Amelia looked up appreciating his interest. "I am having a wonderful time. It's my first ball."

He lifted his brow. "You're jesting? I would have thought you would be at all the balls. Your beauty certainly adds to them."

Her face flushed at his compliment. "I do believe you are jesting now," she said, looking away.

He patted her hand giving her a wink. "Modesty is a virtue." The corner of his mouth curled up into a satisfied smile. "I was hoping to spend some more time with you."

Rachel interrupted the couple. "Roy wants to play whist next week. A card party at Aunt Margaret's house. Should we plan it?"

Thomas looked at his brother. "If Aunt Margaret agrees, then I think a card party would be fun."

Roy looked at Rachel. "You must ask her."

Rachel put her hand to her chest. "Me? It was your idea." They all laughed and followed Roy through the garden.

Andrew watched the couples from the window. Remembering their dance, he could still smell the flower scent coming from her. The curve of her neck was so tantalizing he tried not to react to the smoothness of her skin. He wanted nothing more than to take her out of this ball into his carriage and have his way with her.

His jaw flexed, watching her with her friends. Trying to keep his anger controlled, he pushed back a tug of jealousy that touched his chest. A possessiveness came over him and he wanted no man to touch her. Glancing over at one of his men, he told him to get the earl.

Johnathan was playing cards with his friends but stopped his game after a heated discussion with the guard. He finally relented and made his excuses to quit the game. He found Andrew by the window. Andrew said nothing but took a long sip of his brandy waiting a few moments.

Johnathan let out a sigh. "You summoned me, Mr. Baird?"

Andrew focused his attention outside, waiting for the couples to reappear. "There is a man you were speaking with earlier with blond hair. I believe I overheard you introducing him as your cousin." His serious features showed his discomfort.

Bewildered, Johnathan squinted his eyes trying to understand. "Thomas?"

"I want you to engage him the rest of the night with someone other than Miss Abbott. He is getting in my way, and she is the reason why I am here."

The earl lifted his brow. "Miss Abbott? I don't understand."

Andrew cracked a sarcastic smile. "Come now, Johnathan," he said stressing the use of the earl's first name. "You went to Oxford. Surely you can understand what I am asking you. Out of respect, I am asking you to get rid of him or I will."

Johnathan appeared shocked at Andrew's blatant boldness but to appease his guest replied, "As you wish, Mr. Baird."

Andrew smirked. "Thank you, *my lord*. I knew you would catch on quickly. Now, what do you know about Miss Abbott?"

Johnathan hesitated and raked his fingers through his hair. "I don't know much about her. She is my sister's friend from school. I know her father is a baron and has had some problems. She doesn't socialize much with the town because of some improprieties of her father. I am actually surprised my mother allowed her to attend." His chin rose unable to keep his aristocratic manners at bay.

Andrew wanted to smack the pride from the young lord's face. He kept his calm. "What sort of problems?"

Johnathan shifted his feet peering over his shoulder, obviously uncomfortable with his request. After a few seconds, he stepped closer to him not wanting others to hear. "He lost all of his money and is on his way to debtor's prison is what I heard. He was involved in some unscrupulous business deals and accused of stealing investment money from a group of peers, although nothing was proven. He owes moneylenders as well. They are losing their London residence this week. Rumor is that he is a harsh father and husband causing many to not want to socialize with him. I don't know the extent of the abuse, but meeting the man on a few occasions, I can only imagine that it is not good."

Andrew's thoughts went to that beautiful sweet girl. The urge to protect her consumed him. "What is to become of Miss Abbott?"

Johnathan shook his head. "I heard my sister tell my mother that she is being given in marriage to an older cousin on her father's side. A merchant if I remember correctly. He has offered her father a piece of his business if he would give him his daughter. Apparently, it is not much but will keep the family from starving while he is in prison. Miss Abbott is devastated about it, but has no choice."

Andrew took a sip looking again outside. "Pity."

The earl took a glass of champagne from the footman. "Will that be all, Mr. Baird? I have other guests to attend to."

Andrew nodded his head not making eye contact with Johnathan. He walked toward the terrace doors. Johnathan took his leave carefully not bringing attention to others around him. Andrew knew if guests figured out their association, then he would have to explain to the town why he invited a crime lord to his sister's ball. He smirked at the discomfort he was causing. If the truth be known, a lot of guests in there probably had owed him money at one time or the other.

Andrew gathered from his conversation that nobody wanted to be associated with the baron. His influence could help the poor girl's family. Andrew glanced over watching Johnathan join his friends again at the card tables. He saw him whisper to a few footmen who took off toward the terrace hopefully taking care of the cousin.

Andrew walked outside to find Amelia. The wind was slightly blowing on the terrace cooling off the night. A smile crossed his mouth when he saw her appear. She was stunning with her luscious curves that filled out her light green gown. Her brown hair with golden highlights complimented her green-gold eyes. He wanted her. Her shyness challenged him and her innocence captivated him even more. Most of the women in his acquaintance could be beautiful, but they were damaged. Not the kind of woman you pursue for more than a few days. Miss Abbott was different. Not a typical spoiled debutante. She may be noble, but her life was not easy.

"Miss Abbott, may I have word?" He approached their group as they climbed the terrace stairs out of the garden.

A footman approached Thomas and whispered in his ear. He looked back at the group. "If you will excuse me. Johnathan needs me."

Amelia and Rachel waved goodbye. Andrew stood in front of the two girls as Rachel looked between them. She whispered to Amelia. "I will be over there by the terrace doors with Roy. I will see you in a few moments. I believe the supper dance will be coming soon."

Amelia nodded turning her attention to Andrew. "As you wish."

"Did you enjoy your walk?" Andrew tried to comfort her with small talk. He could sense her edginess and wanted her to relax.

"Yes." She was short and to the point.

Andrew gave her a crooked smile trying to break her indifference. "Very well. I wanted to know if I could have the supper dance if you were not already taken."

Amelia looked over at her friend. Hesitating, she shrugged her shoulders. "Let me check my dance card."

He took her dance card and wrote in his name. He cocked a grin and walked away leaving her alone on the terrace.

Amelia's hand shook looking at the dance card. His attention was unwanted and he was a bit frightening with his domineering features. The smell of his cologne lingered in the air filling her nostrils. He had stood so close to her brushing his thigh against her dress. It was inappropriate. Sheltered as she was growing up, she knew his attention to her was not honorable. The last thing she needed was more gossip about her family.

She had itched to have Rachel near her, but she was deep in conversation with some other guests. Why was he pursuing her? He must think she is an heiress.

Rachel approached her. "What was that about?"

Amelia shook her head. "It seems he wanted the supper dance. Although I am not sure of his intentions. Do you know him?"

Rachel looked concerned at her friend's hesitation. "No, but I will ask my brother about him." Amelia nodded watching the viscount approach and ask Rachel for the next dance. Amelia waved her away and went back inside.

She eyed some movement in the corner and saw little shadows dart underneath a table. She smiled knowing who it must be. Amelia stepped beside the table and casually took some tarts off a tray and handed them under the table. She felt little hands grab the tarts. She giggled as she lifted a corner of the tablecloth and whispered to the boys, "The footman just left. I will try to hide you while you go behind the curtain and scoot your way back up toward the staircase."

The little boys nodded, and she blocked their view as they hid behind the curtains. She saw their little shoes scurry around the wall and watched their heads poke out near the servant's stairs. She followed them upstairs to make sure they were safely back in the nursery.

"Thank you for your help, Melia," Ronnie whispered as he stuffed the rest of the tart in his mouth.

"I won't tell anyone, but you better stay clear of downstairs. You wouldn't want your brother to catch you." She couldn't help but smile at the mischievous twins.

"Will you play with us? We are bored staying in our room. Our nurse fell asleep a few hours ago." Luke looked at her with his big brown eyes.

Amelia hesitated. The truth is that she almost preferred to stay with the twins than face the town or Mr. Baird. She kneeled looking directly into their chubby faces. "I would like to play, but I am expected downstairs. Maybe I can come over another day and bring my little brothers. I think all of you would have a grand time."

Amelia went back down the servant stairs through the kitchen to the ballroom just as they announced the supper dance. She took in a deep breath as she looked around for Andrew. He surprised her when he touched her elbow from behind and escorted her to the dance floor. After the dance, he escorted her to the dining room and filled her plate with food.

He chose a table away from the other guests. Amelia had hoped to sit next to Rachel, but her table was full of other friends. She was in whispered conversations with her brother, and Amelia didn't want to interrupt.

The man stared at her as she took a drink of lemonade. It was unnerving how his gaze went through her. After a few moments, a smile teased on his lips. "Are you hungry?" He slowly bit into his food.

She took a bite of her biscuit not wanting to speak to him.

Andrew took a drink and seemed to study her reaction to his questions. She could see he was trying to engage her in conversation.

"What do you like to do when you are not going to balls?"

She finally made eye contact with him. He held his head in his hand propping his elbow on the table. Shifting his attention on her, she noticed that his eyebrows were perfectly shaped and his expression was astute holding many questions. He was hard to read. "I um… don't attend social events often. My father is a peer, but we are not connected, Mr. Baird." She wasn't for sure if he thought she was a rich heiress or not.

He curved his mouth into a half-smile. "I gathered that, Miss Abbott. My question was about you. What do *you* like to do?" His masculine tone was a bit provocative.

She looked down at her plate. "I don't have much time for myself. I help take care of my little brothers as they lost their governess. My stepmother has taken to her bed most of the time, so I help with household duties. A few months ago, I learned to bake."

He grinned taking in her answers. "You bake?"

She nodded and a smile slipped out. "I know most the debutantes here would *never* be caught in a kitchen. But we lost most of our kitchen staff and I missed apple tarts. Those are my favorite." A youthful giggle followed her confession. "Our housekeeper showed me how to bake and I have been doing it ever since."

She raised her chin, proud of her accomplishments. The moment passed as she attracted some unwanted attention from some other tables who whispered at her presence. She quickly paused then looked away not wanting to encourage any gossip.

He slanted his head oblivious to any onlookers. "You are an amazing woman."

Amelia's face flushed at the term *woman*. She was one and eight and most often was referred to as a young girl. But she didn't like the way he was staring at her.

Rachel approached the table appearing jittery. "Amelia, I need your help in the lady's drawing room." Clearing her throat, she looked at Andrew, "You don't mind if I steal her?"

Andrew's guarded expression flinched causing his annoyance to show. Although he tried to mask his frustration, he politely agreed, "Of course." He stood as Amelia walked away.

Amelia followed Rachel to the room and she quickly pulled her to the back area through a side door that led to a private sitting area.

"What's amiss Rachel. You seem distraught." She took a seat on a wingback chair facing the fireplace.

Rachel sat in the chair next to her and lowered her voice in case anyone followed them. "I spoke to my brother briefly about Mr. Baird. You can't speak to him again, Amelia. In fact, you may want to leave the ball. He is a *criminal* and operates many underground businesses. Unsavory businesses if you know what I mean."

Amelia covered her mouth with her hands. The gravity of her words fell heavy upon her chest. Visibly shaken, she muttered, "Criminal?"

Rachel let out an exaggerated sigh. "Yes, as you can imagine, I am very upset at my brother for allowing him into our home. He is known as the Black Baird, and many people owe him money. The men he is with are not friends, but work for him as guards and they do the dirty part of his business. My brother owed him money and he was here today collecting. No telling what would have happened if he did not pay them. It was just bad luck that he saw you."

Amelia's heart raced trying to digest what her friend was telling her. "What do I do?"

Rachel looked around the room studying the entryways. "We will take the side door to the kitchen and take the servant's stairs. You will wait in my room until everyone leaves and I will have my father's carriage take you back home. I think he will leave once he knows you have left the party."

Amelia hugged Rachel. "I am not sure why he would take an interest in me. He must think my father has money."

Rachel shook her head holding onto Amelia's hand. "That's what I said, but it's not true. Apparently, he is very wealthy and owns many estates. He has legitimate businesses as well. Probably how he hides a lot of his criminal activity. I can only imagine that he pays off many people. Besides, have you seen yourself, Amelia? You are beautiful. There could be no other reason."

Amelia did not feel beautiful and his interest in her was unwelcome. She snuck out the side door and took the servant stairs up to Rachel's room. She closed the door behind her and lay on Rachel's bed hoping that Mr. Baird would go away.

Andrew noticed Rachel enter through the side entrance of the ballroom. She scanned the room and approached a young lord. He walked closer to the couple to eavesdrop on their conversation. Rachel leaned toward her friend's ear and whispered, "Amelia had to leave." She looked away and made eye contact with Andrew. Trying to break her stare quickly, she stepped beside her brother.

Feeling confused and a bit agitated, he approached her while she stood behind her brother. Straightening his shoulders, he asked: "Did you say that Miss. Abbott has left?"

Rachel looked up at Andrew, "Yes sir, she had to be home early." Rachel turned away from him, continuing her conversation with other guests.

Andrew stared at Rachel's back and tried to control his temper. He did not like to be dismissed by a spoiled young chit. Her brother must have seen the discontent on his face and intervened before he could say anything to his sister. "Would you care for some more brandy?"

Andrew narrowed his eyes studying the earl. "Not tonight. I have other engagements." The earl seemed to breathe a sigh of relief at his statement and walked him to the front doors.

Andrew lifted his chin at his men who went out the door before him.

"Johnathan, I will need a word with you in the morning. Please be expecting my visit. I don't like to wait."

The earl forced a smile loosening his cravat. "As you wish."

Andrew stared at him for a moment and left.

CHAPTER 4

"**M**ARRIAGE?" JOHNATHAN TRIED NOT TO fall out of his chair. Taking a drink of water, he tried to calm his nerves. He wiped his mouth. "Are you mad?"

The earl could see that Andrew's patience was running thin. "Johnathan. Please watch your tone with me. I have been patient with your rudeness, but I can only be pushed so far."

The earl inhaled a deep breath. "Forgive me. I just don't think I could be more shocked. Miss Abbott is a young girl with no experience outside of the schoolroom. I don't see the attraction for someone like you."

Andrew lifted his brow blatantly annoyed. "Someone like me? Need I remind you that I could buy and sell you tomorrow and not blink twice? My associations are with far greater men than you."

Johnathan's face drained of color. He tried to recover. "I meant no offense. If you want to propose to Miss Abbott, then that is your business. You would have to speak to her father. Need I remind you that she is a peer's daughter? Are you sure you want the association with her father?"

Andrew wiped some lint off his glove. "Exactly why I am here. I need you to introduce me and would like an escort to the family home along with your endorsement. I understand that they are in the middle of relocating and selling their London residence. I would like to secure the offer today. I must leave town tonight and would like to wrap this up."

Johnathan stared at him with disbelief. "Today? You want *me* to introduce you to him? I am barely acquainted with him. Besides, it would also be unsavory if I went to his home. His business dealings are questionable and he is about to go to prison."

Andrew slowly stood up. He walked around the desk shoving the earl's chair against the wall. "Enough! I am not asking your permission." He grabbed his face squeezing his chin tightly watching the blood drain away. "We leave at once." He shoved his face back as he straightened his gloves, walking to the door.

Johnathan rubbed his chin trying to compose himself. He stood up, "As you wish Mr. Baird, far be it for me to stand in your way."

The baron's house was a bit drab and quiet. Andrew had heard most of the servants had been dismissed. The housekeeper led them to an empty drawing room and asked them to wait there until she could see if the baron was receiving. Looking around at the furnishings, it was obvious the baron had fallen on tough times. After a few moments, she reappeared and escorted them to a study. The sparsely furnished study included a desk and two old chairs with ripped cushions. The baron stood up to greet his guests.

"Lord Breconshire. Please come in. I hope you will excuse the state of our home as we are in the middle of moving." He gestured to the chairs.

"Quite all right, my lord. May I introduce you to an acquaintance of mine?" He looked at Andrew. "Baron Brayton this is Mr. Andrew Baird."

Andrew nodded. "My lord."

The baron narrowed his eyes recognizing the name. "Did you say Mr. Andrew Baird?"

Andrew smiled. "Yes, my lord." The atmosphere in the room grew silent. The baron shifted and sat back down in his chair.

The earl tried to lighten the mood. "My visit today actually concerns your daughter."

The baron turned and looked at Johnathan. "Amelia?" Johnathan nodded giving his attention to Andrew.

Andrew smiled taking in the conversation. "Yes, my lord. I came to present an offer for her hand in marriage. I have recently become acquainted with her."

The baron leaned back in his chair. "I must say I am surprised by this offer. But I am afraid you are too late, Mr. Baird. I have already accepted an offer from my cousin. They will be married within a fortnight."

Andrew slanted his head and rubbed his lips together. "In a fortnight? Then she is not married yet. You will simply tell your cousin that you changed your mind." He leaned back in the chair as his mouth twitched, challenging the baron. After a few seconds of silence, a thin smile snuck along his face. "For your trouble, I will pay your debts and you will not go to prison. I did some checking and I know about the men you owe money to. Those men are acquaintances of mine and they will not bother you anymore. But, just so we are clear, if you don't agree to my terms, you will go to prison and lose my protection."

Johnathan's mouth dropped open at the offer. Andrew heard a small moan coming from his mouth. He kept shifting in his chair looking toward the door. Andrew's annoyance showed at his demeanor. He knew the earl was brought up as nobility and he had heard that his own mother was personal friends with royalty. Facing the realities of gambling and their consequences was unfamiliar territory for the young man. Andrew would bet a fortune that he never engaged in any foul play or associated with anyone outside of the *ton*.

The baron rubbed his hand over his face. "I… um… Don't know what to say?"

Andrew lifted the corner of his mouth. "Say that you accept my generosity."

The baron studied his face for a few seconds digesting his words. He knew he had no choice. "Mr. Baird, I will accept your conditions and your offer."

Andrew smiled taking some papers out of his bag. "Very good. I will need you to sign this paperwork and go fetch your daughter. I request a private word with her."

The baron fumbled for some ink and signed the papers without reading them. He looked at Andrew still in shock. "I will speak to my daughter and then give you a private audience if that is agreeable to you?"

Andrew walked around the desk and shook his hand. "It is. I hope you understand that I need your support and encouragement for her to accept my hand." The baron nodded and excused himself.

Amelia was in her room with her siblings when her father entered. "Boys, I need a word alone with your sister." They looked at Amelia for direction and she nodded for them to leave. He walked over to the chair facing her bed, slowly taking a seat. Amelia's body tensed at his presence. Their relationship was not close and she could not remember the last time he came to her room instead of summoning her to his study.

A smile snuck across his face as he addressed her. "It seems I have wonderful news! Our dire circumstances have changed." He laughed out loud making a cackling sound. Amelia shifted in her chair wary of his mood.

He clapped his hands together. "I can hardly believe it!" He shook his head still recovering from the shock. "Amelia, we are all counting on you to do the right thing. Your little brothers will have you to thank for their legacy."

Amelia smiled wearily taking in the compliment. Her father's mood swings and usual condescending remarks caused her to hesitate before accepting his praise. "I don't understand. What must I do?"

He looked at her and slowly raised his brow. "I received another offer for your hand. I have accepted and he has agreed to pay our debts."

She examined her father's features trying to decipher his meaning. "What? I don't understand. Who would pay our debts?"

For a moment, there was no sound. He leaned back in his chair teasing her with the knowledge he wanted to share. With an elated tone he continued, "A wealthy man who took quite the interest in you." After another moment of torture, her father took in a deep breath. "A man named Mr. Baird."

Amelia felt dizzy. She stood up slowly from the bed. "No!" Grabbing her chest, she could hear a ringing in her ear as she replayed his words in her head. Mr. Baird?

Her father's demeanor changed and he stood up taking a step toward her. Gritting his teeth, he spoke in a threatening tone, "You will marry Mr. Baird and be a dutiful wife. The papers have been signed. You have no choice. Do you understand me?"

Tears filled her eyes. She reached for his arm as her fingernails dug into his coat, "Please, Father! You can't make me. I will run away." A sob escaped as she tried to catch her breath. "He frightens me and I will not marry him."

Her father lifted his arm from her grasp and smacked her in the back of the head. Amelia fell to the floor tripping over the rug as she pulled away from her father. He leaned over and grabbed her arm. "Do you want your brothers to live in poverty? What will happen if I go to prison? How long do you think they will last? They will be forced to work in unsavory conditions at their ages. All because of your selfishness."

Amelia pulled her arm out of his grip and ran away from him down the stairs. He ran after her pushing her to the floor at the bottom of the stairs. He lifted her up and hit her across the face with the back of his hand. Blood trickled from her nose and she laid in a ball on the floor weeping. Andrew and Johnathan ran out of the study watching the scene unfold.

Andrew ran over pulling the baron off his daughter. He kicked him in the stomach and her father backed away from the stairs. "If you ever touch your daughter again, I will kill you."

The baron spit blood on the floor. "She is my daughter and I will do to her what I wish."

Andrew moved back toward him when Amelia screamed. "No! Please leave him alone." She was holding her face as blood dripped from her hands.

Andrew stopped and looked back at her. He straightened his jacket and looked at the baron. "She is my fiancée, and the papers have been signed. I will be her protector, and you will not touch her again. Do I make myself clear?"

The baron stared at them. He narrowed his eyes but seemed to bite his tongue. "You are clear. If you will excuse me."

The earl looked at Andrew. "If there is nothing else, I believe I will take my leave as well." He turned on his heel and left out the front door.

Andrew leaned down to help Amelia. He gently touched her face. "Are you well?" He bent her head back and wiped the blood with his finger. Taking a handkerchief out of his pocket, he held it against her nose.

Amelia's tear stained face gazed up at him. "I am well." She took the cloth and held it against her nose. Andrew seemed to sense her hesitation, "Miss Abbott, please forgive me. This is not how I planned this conversation. Please, may we go into your father's study?"

She sat up touching her face wincing when her fingers hit a sore spot. He took her elbow and guided her into the study helping her sit in one of the chairs. He sat in the chair across from her taking her free hand.

Andrew softened his tone and spoke affectionately to her, "Miss Abbott, you deserve to be courted and spoiled. That was my plan until I was informed of the circumstances with your father. I knew you were promised to your cousin and would be moving soon. This has caused me to react differently and make an offer today."

She averted her eyes looking at her small hand being engulfed by his large fingers. Her nose throbbed with pain, but her vanity would not allow the handkerchief to cover her nose for much longer. She removed the cloth from her nose twisting her neck to look up at him. Even sitting down, he towered over her. His eyes held hers for a moment. She stuttered, "I..um.. don't understand. You don't even know me. How could you want to marry me and pay my father's debts?"

He brought her hand to his mouth kissing her knuckles. "You intrigue me. I will be good to you. You will want for nothing."

Amelia's head felt like it could explode. How can she deny his request? She would not allow her brothers to suffer.

Encouraged by her obvious contemplating he asked again, "Will you agree to the marriage?" He squeezed her hand trying to make eye contact with her.

Amelia took in a deep breath and looked up at him. Her bottom lip quivered. "I will." She closed her eyes pulling her hand from his to wipe the tears.

Andrew reached out to touch her face. "Don't cry. I promise I will take care of you." Amelia stood up causing Andrew's hand to fall away. She didn't want to be close to him or be touched. She tried to compose herself. "When am I to leave my home?"

He smoothed the edge of his jacket. "I have business out of town. I should return by Friday. A close friend of mine will help us obtain a special license and we can be married on Saturday at my London home. My main home is in Scotland, and we will leave the day after the wedding. I will visit you on Friday evening to go over final preparations. One of my business associates will take you to get anything you may need on my accounts."

Amelia was unsure she heard him correctly. "Scotland?"

A cunning smile dangled at the edges of his mouth. "Yes lass, you will love it." Andrew leaned over and kissed her on the cheek. Her whole body tensed at his touch. He sensed her discomfort and took a step away. "I will see you on Friday. Tell your father that my men will follow up with more details. Should I leave a guard?"

Amelia shook her head. "That won't be necessary." He gave her a soft look and left the room. Taking a moment to absorb the last hour of her life, she covered her face with her hands taking in a deep breath. She knew she had to find her father.

He was on the back terrace clutching his stomach spitting blood. She wavered before approaching him. "Father?"

He sighed loudly when he heard her. "Your insolence has caused unnecessary strife as usual. You are fortunate that he has offered for your hand or you would be on the streets with nothing." He wrung the rag out with water and blood pouring more water into the basin. "How dare you refuse my decision? You are but a woman that I have clothed, fed, and supported your whole life. You have been spoiled and this is the thanks that I receive?"

Tears dropped from her eyes. "Please, Father. He is a criminal and does many terrible things to people. Look what he did to you. I am afraid of him and don't wish to marry. Perhaps, I can still marry Edward? Or I can work as a governess and help support the family."

He scowled at her. "Are you daft? The papers are signed. He was overly generous on his terms considering the wife he would be receiving. He is paying my debts and keeping me out of prison. Would you suggest that I go to prison? You're a selfish girl. Who cares how he makes his money. If you can keep your mouth shut, you will be fine."

"Please, Father. Please don't make me." She fell to the ground in front of him begging him on her knees.

"Stop groveling this instant! You will marry him or you will never see your brothers again. Do you hear me? You will contribute to this family for once in your life and not be a burden that I have had to support for one mistake." He walked past her, leaving her on the ground.

CHAPTER 5

THE BARON GAVE THE NEWS to his cousin promising a monetary settlement once the marriage took place with Andrew. Withdrawing the marriage contract could have legal consequences and he wanted to keep the matter within the family. Edward refused the settlement despite his father's interference and advice. His only request was to meet with Amelia alone.

Edward and his mother came by to speak to her regarding the broken engagement. Amelia's stepmother was entertaining them with tea while her father disappeared claiming a business appointment.

Amelia was in the garden and came in a few minutes after their arrival. Her stepmother greeted her. "There you are darling. Our relatives have come to see you." Amelia cringed at the sound of her stepmother's voice. She only referred to her as *darling* when there was company around that she wanted to impress. Her stepmother was cunning and knew Amelia would be married to a wealthy man soon. She was playing her cards to be the dutiful stepmother.

Amelia noticed Mrs. Patton sitting on the settee. She wore a lavender dress that resembled a plump grape and a matching jeweled necklace. Her hair was in a long braid that was pinned up around her head. Her features were grim showing her disapproval when Amelia came into the room. Edward stood up from the chair when he saw her. He was wearing a tan coat that matched his deep brown breeches. He dropped his shoulders in defeat, walking up to Amelia. "May we speak privately?"

She nodded. "As you wish. Would you care to take a walk in the garden?" Edward held out his elbow and Amelia took it. Mrs. Patton warned Edward. "Don't be too long dear. We have dinner plans. I don't like to wait."

Edward looked down. "I will only be a few moments, Mother." Mrs.

Patton pulled her gloves tighter on her hands before reaching for her tea to take a sip. She sighed audibly with her impatience. Twisting in her chair with a "Humph."

Mrs. Patton had shunned Amelia's family in the past when her father fell out of grace with the *ton*. Amelia was perplexed at her accompanying Edward on his visit today. Thoughts of her rescuing her son from being too long in their home probably filled her mind. An inward smirk dangled in her mind.

The couple walked out the door and strolled away from the house sitting next to the garden shed. Edward turned to Amelia. "I canceled the contract according to your father's wishes. It is my understanding that your new match will keep him out of prison. I could take him to court, but it won't bring me you. It would only bring me money, and that is something I don't need."

Edward's words pulled at Amelia's heartstrings. Looking through her eyelashes, she paused trying to find comforting words. "Did my father give you back your grandmother's ring? He told me he would give it to you."

His brave persona started crumbling as his emotions showed a glimpse of moisture in his eyes. "Yes, he did give it to me. It was my greatest wish that we would have married, Amelia." He held her eyes with his and it was the first time she remembered him looking at her without turning away. Amelia's heart softened and she took his hand into hers. "You would have made a devoted husband. Thank you for your kindness and understanding."

He kissed her on the hand. "Can I ask you a question?" Amelia raised her brow.

He cleared his throat. "Is this marriage your wish as well? Is he a good man?"

Amelia looked away. "I hardly know him. Scarcely acceptable if you ask me."

Edward creased his forehead taking his smile away. "Will he hurt you?"

Amelia did not know if Andrew was abusive or not. Surely, there was hope that he was kind after he defended her with her father. She would not allow Edward to fret about her. Besides, his pride and reputation must be bruised at being replaced. Yet he showed more esteem than most men in her family. Trying to make light of the situation she sniffed a laugh. "It is not important for you to think about my welfare. Anyone who would pay my father's debts to marry me—a mere woman with no dowry—is probably mad."

He squeezed her hand. "I will always worry for your welfare. After all, you were not only my fiancée at one time but my cousin."

Amelia kissed him on the cheek causing him to turn bright red. "I know you will find a great wife one day."

He looked down shyly at his lap.

Amelia smiled. "Just don't let your mother influence you too much. You can do an excellent job by yourself." Edward shook his head and stood up. "Speaking of my mother, we should get back inside before she sends a search party."

Amelia laughed and took his arm as he escorted her back inside. Mrs. Patton was standing by the door waiting for Edward. He let go of Amelia's arm offering his arm to his mother. They waved goodbye and she watched them leave.

The next few days flew by for Amelia. She carefully avoided her father and stepmother choosing to spend most of her time in her room. On Tuesday, she made excuses and escaped to see Sally. Chuck was working in the stable and was surprised to see her in the middle of the week. Amelia usually went on Saturdays.

He was a large man with red hair and smelled of horses. "Sally will be back soon. She went to pick up some new horseshoes."

Amelia smiled. "I can only stay a minute. Do you know if Billy is in town?"

Chuck shook his head. "He left last night. Be back in a fortnight." Amelia's heart fell. She was hoping to tell Billy goodbye. It had been a few weeks since she saw him. Their last visit was interrupted by some of his friends. His kisses were getting more intense, and she was sure that he would ask for her hand soon. Although, her father would never allow them to marry. Billy lived day by day with no future or plan for his life. Amelia dreamt of running away with him even though she wasn't old enough to choose her own husband. Such is the fate of a woman.

"Amelia?" Sally entered the stable. "What brings you here during the week?"

Amelia looked down at her feet. "I was hoping we could talk?"

Sally gave the horseshoes to Chuck. Her brown frock showed specks of dirt from working on the farm. She wore her black hair in a long braid with loose pieces hanging around her face. "Come around back." Amelia followed her out the door, and they sat by an old tree that was losing most its branches. "What's amiss? You don't look well."

Shivering a bit at her predicament, she took in a deep breath. "Last weekend I went to a friend's ball."

Sally crinkled her freckled nose. "A ball? Sometimes I forget what side of town you live on. I wondered why you didn't come by last Saturday. I thought they might have kept you locked up." Sally found out about Amelia's nobility from her maid. It was by accident, but Amelia admitted it to her new friend a few months ago. A few close friends now knew including Billy, but for the most part, they didn't talk about it.

Amelia twisted her hands. "There was a man there who took an interest in me."

Sally raised her brow. "What about your cousin?"

Amelia shook her head. "My father had entered a contract for us to marry. This new man convinced my father to break the contract to marry me instead. He is older and rough looking."

Sally bit her bottom lip. "Is he like an old duke or something?"

Amelia smiled at her friend's question. Her limited knowledge of the *ton* was refreshing and amusing at the same time. "No, he is not titled. More of a sordid character with lots of money. He frightens me." She drew in a shaky breath as her fears came flooding over her. "My father accepted a hefty sum of his money and sold me." Placing her hands over her mouth, her eyes watered as a tear came down her cheek.

Sally shook her head. "Blast, that sounds bad." She stood up pacing in front of Amelia. "My family may be poor, but I can't imagine what it feels like to be bartered off." Swiping her brow with her dirty hand, she kicked a rock. "Can you refuse? Perhaps you can live with me and work on the farm."

Amelia admired her friend's simplicity in trying to solve her problems. "That is so kind of you. I wish I could, but if I refuse, my father will go to prison, and my little brothers will suffer. I have no choice." Startled by her own omission, she folded her arms around her torso, rubbing her arms for comfort, wishing she could curl up in a ball and disappear. The gravity of the situation was finally taking a toll on her.

Sally crossed her arms. "I bet they have no idea what you are doing for them."

Amelia wiped her face again choking back her tears. "I have to be strong. He says he is taking me to Scotland after we are married. I won't know anyone. My friend thinks he may be a criminal. He certainly looks like one. What if he beats me?"

Sally reached for her arm. "If you ever need me then send for me. I will do what I can to help you."

Amelia stood up. "Please tell Billy for me."

She widened her eyes. "He will be upset. Although he would never admit it to anyone, he was quite smitten with you." Amelia smiled and bid her goodbye.

The next day Amelia knew her time was running out. She had no gown to wear for her wedding and Andrew would be back on Friday. Two more days before her prison sentence. That is how she viewed it.

Andrew's business associate came by her home a few times to offer to take her shopping. When she refused, he offered her money. That was refused as well. Unwilling to be sold or controlled, she considered his money dirty. She would pay for her own gown. The less she owed Andrew, the better.

Shopping was not a normal pastime since her father lost his fortune. She had a little money left in her dwindling savings, but it would have to do. The dress shops were full of women looking for dresses to wear to their next social engagement. Balls, soirees, and musicales were the talk of the store. Most of them bought material and had their dresses specialty made. Amelia checked around the store trying to find a plain gown. No sense in dressing the part of blushing bride.

She considered wearing black.

After an hour of shopping, she settled on a plain white lacy muslin gown off the shelf that only needed to be hemmed. Rachel had sent a letter inviting her for tea, but she made excuses. She was trying to find a solace in her decision to marry Andrew. It would shame her if Rachel knew the truth although her brother may have told her. Amelia spoke to no one about the inevitable, except Sally. She did not run in the same circles as the town and had no one to tell. Besides, Amelia did not want anyone to know about her groom. The day proved exhausting, and her savings had almost disappeared. Hopefully she would not need any more money.

Later that night, Amelia tried to memorize her bed chamber as her time in her father's home was coming to an end. Her paintings from her childhood were still displayed on one of the walls. They told the story of her hidden feelings and were reminders of her past. Some paintings were like an escape although her father thought they were a waste of time.

Her thoughts always came back to her impending wedding. Dreams of meeting her perfect prince to rescue her from her father was a fantasy, her fate took her to a sacrificial marriage. She was the sacrifice, and her family was the recipients of the reward. Marriage scared her. Apprehension curled her stomach regarding her wedding night. She longed to have a mother. Someone to help her understand the duties of a woman and what to expect in the marriage bed.

Thinking of her mother, Amelia stood up from her bed and dug through a few crates in her wardrobe. Reaching for the one hidden between the others she pulled it forward. Opening it up, she spotted the familiar crinkled rose. A smile slid across her face as she looked at it more closely. Some of the leaves fell off as she picked it up. Not wanting to disturb it further, she put it back in the crate. Other items in the crate included a small empty locket and a rusted chain. They were all clues to her past—her most precious belongings. It was all she had of her mother. The items were found in a box in the attic with Amelia Rose written on the top. Her heart knew it was clues to finding out what happened to her mother.

Friday evening approached faster than Amelia had expected. Her father's new-found fortune added two new cooks to their kitchen staff. Andrew's money had started to come in and some of the original staff were welcomed back adding to the household's meager help.

Amelia dressed in her blue gown with cream colored gloves. She wore her hair in tendrils pinned up along the sides. Holding her stomach, she looked at herself in the looking glass trying to find the strength to leave her room. Her father demanded she be in the drawing room when Andrew arrived. He wanted to make sure she was not late or feign any reason not to attend.

Andrew arrived a few minutes late for dinner. Amelia secretly hoped he had changed his mind and wouldn't be coming. The new butler announced his name, and he was followed inside with two of his associates. Amelia wondered if he ever traveled alone. He was dressed formally with a perfectly tied cravat. His black waistcoat matched his custom fitted breeches. He filled the room with his presence intimidating her father. He smiled at her parents who seemed to forget his last visit. Although, her father was still spitting up blood because of his attack. The baron used his manners and made introductions to her family. After introductions, her little brothers were scurried off to their rooms.

Andrew took her gloved hand and kissed it. "You look lovely this evening."

He leaned near her, smelling of sandalwood and brandy. She felt so small in comparison to his immense frame. She tried to settle her nerves and found it difficult to make eye contact. She lowered her eyes and whispered, "Thank you, Mr. Baird."

He leaned closer. "We are to be married tomorrow, Amelia. Please call me Andrew."

The closeness of his warm breath near her ear made her tremble. She didn't think she could go through with it. Her knees were about to buckle at the realization that she feared her fiancé. She grimaced at the memory of his rage at her father and not to mention his reputation that Rachel had told her about. How would he treat her when they were alone? Would he ravish her and then beat her into submission? She tried not to swoon. Her voice cracked as she spoke: "As you wish."

Her father and stepmother were speaking with his associates as the butlers served them drinks. Andrew pulled her to the side. "I stopped by the Earl of Breconshire's today. You can imagine my surprise when he informed me his sister was unaware of our nuptials tomorrow."

Amelia tensed her shoulders as her heart pumped faster. He changed his voice to a patronizing tone. "I told him you were probably so *busy* preparing for the ceremony that it must have slipped your mind." He took a drink of his brandy as he studied her face for a reaction. She gave none and looked away. He continued, "I remedied it and invited them both. You told me she was an old and dear friend. You can thank me later."

He smiled with a half-grin trying to gauge her. She remained silent as he narrowed his eyes then changed back to a normal tone. "I also have some friends that will be attending. My brother is out of the country or I would have invited him. My staff has prepared a wedding breakfast and the vicar has agreed to marry us. The special license came through. All is set."

It was too much. She felt numb and placed her glass down on the table beside her. She took a seat on the new settee they had recently purchased with his generosity. He took a seat next to her touching her hand. "Now, Amelia, you must take it easy. Tomorrow will be a big day for you. I hope you have bought the perfect dress. My man said you refused my money." His jaw flexed holding back his displeasure of her refusal.

The strain in his voice made her throat tighten. She took a deep breath. "I did purchase a dress for tomorrow. I didn't feel right taking your money, so I bought it myself."

He held his head back and laughed. "Indeed? You didn't feel right taking my money. Not a family trait I gather."

She looked away, pulling her hand from him, feigning wiping her brow. She placed her hand back in her lap avoiding his glare. Their conversation was interrupted by the butler announcing supper. He stood and assisted her up, putting her hand in the crook of his arm. They walked into the dining room.

Amelia's family exchanged pleasantries with their guests. Her appetite had vanished and she was unable to eat. She chose to stare at her food, only nodding if addressed in the conversation. After dinner, she tried to make her escape, but Andrew insisted on a walk before she retired. Her family agreed and left her alone to fend for herself.

The night air was brisk and she was thankful to have her cloak. Andrew took her arm and walked around their small garden in silence. Several minutes passed before he stopped and turned toward her.

"Amelia?" He tried to capture her attention.

Amelia did not want to look at him. Her heart went into her stomach and she felt ill. She looked at her feet. "Yes?"

He touched her chin forcing her to look at him. "I want you to be happy, Amelia." He took his hand from her chin and cupped her face. He bent down and softly pressed his lips against hers.

Amelia's whole body tensed. His gentleness surprised her, but she did not trust him. He was like a wolf playing with his prey before the kill. She was embarrassed to look at him after the kiss. Unable to speak, she took a deep breath and stepped away from him.

She whispered trying not to show her fear, "I have yet to know you, Mr. Baird. This wedding has come quickly. I am not prepared."

He stepped forward and took her hand. Trying to ease her anxiety, he brought her hand to his mouth and kissed it. "We have our whole lives to get to know each other. My wish is to take care of you and be a good husband."

Amelia felt trapped by his sly words. He was a criminal and used his words to lie, cheat, steal, and manipulate. She would not fall for his charms although she could not refuse him. There would be dire consequences if she did not go through with the marriage. She looked at him trying to feel confident. "Please be patient with me, Mr. Baird. I require time to accept my circumstances."

He smiled taking his time to answer her. "As you wish, my dear. Let's get you back inside. You have a big day tomorrow."

He escorted her back inside and gathered his men for their departure. He kissed her one more time on the hand. The next time they met would be in front of the vicar.

Amelia stood in the room waiting for the announcement that they were ready for her. She arrived at Andrew's home a few hours earlier and was welcomed by his staff. It didn't feel like her wedding day. Her dress was not impressive, her gloves were old. The housekeeper helped her put some flowers in her hair as she wore a braid pinned up in a bun on top of her head. Her life would change after this morning and her childhood would be a memory. This is not the life she had envisioned and the tears threatened to fall. She closed her eyes trying to stop them as she gathered strength to get through the day.

A knock on the door broke her out of her woolgathering. She took a deep breath before answering. Relief filled her seeing Rachel's smiling face.

"Amelia, you look beautiful. Mr. Baird allowed me to come up as the guests are arriving. Is there anything I can assist with?" Rachel stepped farther into the room closing the door behind her.

"Rachel, thank you for coming." She walked to the bed and took a seat.

"Amelia, you should have told me. I am not cross with you, just concerned. Johnathan explained your predicament to me. I know you have no choice." She sat on the bed beside her.

"I hardly know what to do." Amelia could no longer pretend to be strong and let out a sob.

Rachel touched her arm. "Oh, Amelia. I feel so guilty. If you would not have been at my home that day, he would not have seen you." She hugged Amelia and held her.

"I don't blame you. It's not your fault. This is the burden of being a woman." She leaned back wiping her face.

Rachel squeezed her hand. "A burden of a beautiful woman." She smiled standing up from the bed. "Come let us stop crying and wipe your face with a cold cloth. We can't have you crying on your wedding day."

Amelia gave a slight smile to her friend. "It's not the day I am worried about. It's the night."

Rachel widened her eyes. "Blast! I had not thought about that. I would be frightened too. He is such a big man. A bit dangerous looking."

She watched Amelia's face fall. "Forgive me, I mean I am sure you will be fine. I heard it can be somewhat unpleasant for a woman the first time, but they say it's better after that. Some even enjoy it. Perhaps you will."

Amelia felt like she would vomit and held her stomach. "Oh, Rachel. I can't do it."

Rachel kneeled in front of her taking both of her hands and looked into her face. "Yes, you can. You are one of the strongest women I know. In school, I knew you would always find a way to help us if we were in trouble. Your family owes you a huge debt. You need to make the most out of this situation and find your place. Johnathan told me he travels a lot and has many estates. Perhaps you won't see him much. You can create your own life and be happy. I will try to visit you if he allows it."

Amelia took a deep breath. "Perhaps you are right. I will—"

A knock at the door interrupted the girls. Rachel stood and gave Amelia one last hug. "I will wait for you downstairs."

Rachel opened the door and let Amelia's father in as she left. "They will be ready in a few moments." He put out his elbow and she took his arm.

Amelia's brothers approached her as she came down the stairs and some of the guests welcomed her. The vicar stood close to the mantle and asked the guests to take a seat. Andrew smiled when he saw her and a few of his men stood beside him. The wedding was short and Amelia concentrated on her words. She accepted Andrew to be her husband agreeing to commit herself to him. The rest of the ceremony was a blur, and she did not come out of her stupor until she heard the vicar pronounce them husband and wife.

Andrew bent down and softly kissed her on the mouth. The well-wishers stood and congratulated the couple, and the wedding breakfast was served shortly afterward. Amelia barely tasted her food and kept quiet during the feast. Andrew bent down. "You need to eat something, Amelia. The staff went to a lot of trouble to prepare this for you. Please don't be rude."

Amelia did not like his tone with her. She did not answer him but forced herself to take a bite of the food. He gave her a satisfied look and turned his attention to a business associate.

Rachel and Johnathan approached her afterward and said their goodbyes. Rachel whispered her a promise that she would send letters soon. Amelia stood up to walk her guests to the door. Andrew stared at her, but didn't speak.

Amelia's father had some private words with Andrew after the breakfast and approached his daughter before his departure. "It's all set with the contract, and you will go to Scotland tomorrow. I wish you well, Daughter." That was it. She supposed he could have said some term of endearment, but wishing her well was more than he usually said to her. Her stepmother ignored her. taking her father's elbow and walking to the front door. Her brothers hugged her. Amelia's heart hurt, but she kept her composure. She bid farewell to the other guests until only a few remained—mainly Andrew's guards who lived at the residence with him. Amelia fidgeted with her gloves unsure of what was expected of her. Andrew finished his conversation with one of his men and came toward her.

"My wife, I like the sound of that. We will stay here tonight and leave early in the morning. It will take us five to six days to arrive in Edinburgh." He took her hand. "You will stay in my chamber tonight. The servants have moved your trunk in there. This home came with a small library, so feel free to make use of it. I need to leave to close some business and will return for dinner this evening. You have had an eventful day. I told the servants to prepare a bath, and you may rest if you wish."

Amelia nodded her head, and Andrew bent down and kissed her on the cheek. She walked toward the stairs and followed a servant to his chambers.

Brian, one of Andrew's men and closest friends, slapped him on the back. "I can't believe you're leg-shackled. I can handle Pruitt if you want to spend the afternoon with your new wife. It is your wedding day after all."

Andrew smirked looking over at Brian. He was a large man with red hair and a matching mustache. The big lug was more like his brother than an employee. "Our years on the street have come full circle. I am married when I told you I would never take a wife."

Brian snorted. "Better you than me. Reminds me of when we made a bet who would have a son first."

Andrew gripped his glass. "I always thought it would be you. Your family life was a lot better than mine. Based on my experience, I should run for the hills."

Andrew took a drink, thinking about the difference in their families. He had known Brian since they were young. Brian's family lived on the same street as Andrew's, and they were both poor. Yet their lives were completely different. Brian's mother worked in a factory and took in the laundry on the weekends. She would often feed Andrew and his little brother when his mother didn't come home. Brian's father was killed at sea. They had his memorabilia and awards throughout their home displaying all of his father's accomplishments. In contrast, Andrew's father was in an Irish prison the last he had heard. His parents were married only for a few months before he was locked up. He had a younger brother from a different father that passed away shortly after he was born.

"My family life was not perfect, Andrew." Brian chuckled. "But I guess it was better than yours."

Andrew laughed thinking about his mother. His uncle talked his mother into accompanying his family to Glasgow, Scotland to what was supposed to be a better life. The Irish were treated harshly and living conditions were cramped. His uncle died a year later from cholera leaving his mom to fend for herself with her two children. His uncle's wife moved to Edinburgh with his cousins shortly afterwards to live with her aunt. There was no room for Andrew's family, so his mother tried to support them with various jobs in the beginning.

Andrew took a seat in the chair and Brian sat in the chair across from him. He ran his finger over the rim of the glass staring into the fireplace. He glanced at Brian. "Yes, I guess I was a bad influence. If your grandmother only knew how much we capitalized on her lessons."

Andrew had no rules growing up and learned to work the streets at a very early age. Brian's grandmother taught them both to read and understand mathematics, an important skill in the life of crime. Growing up on the streets fending for himself taught him to trust no one. His mother eventually turned to other ways to make money. She ended up working nights in a popular gambling establishment often not coming home for a few days at a time. She told her children she was a serving wench, but rumors told a different story. Men would frequent their home often paying various bills and buying food. His mother told him they were friends that helped her out. One of her regular friends took Andrew under his wing and taught him the art of picking a pocket. He became very good at it. After a few years of mastering the art, his growing size led him to other ways to make money. After reaching a towering height at only fifteen years old, his mentor had him collect money throughout the neighborhood and spy on rival gangs. Andrew knew how to keep a secret and caught on quickly to the underworld.

Brian took out two pipes and handed one to Andrew. "Grandmother was a wise woman, and we were diligent students. Now, should I take the men with me alone? It's time you got to know you wife."

Andrew lit the pipe. "Nonsense. My new wife needs some time alone. I will be back soon and don't plan to miss my wedding night."

Brian laughed. "As you wish."

CHAPTER 6

THEY GATHERED THE MEN AND took two carriages to the Wild Boar private gambling establishment—one of three he owned in the city. The back of the building was a bit unsavory yet provided a bit of privacy for their entrance. The manager Harry Donavan welcomed them to the club, and a few other men stood behind him greeting the group.

"Mr. Baird, may I first say congratulations on your nuptials today." His toothless grin showed his years of hard living. Harry was a loyal employee and was always aiming to please his boss.

"Thank you, Harry. I appreciate your felicitations." He accepted some brandy by a scantily dressed female who brought drinks as soon as they saw his carriage arrive. He winked at her and looked at Harry.

Harry puffed out his chest proudly. "Tonight's business is breaking our previous records. The safe is overflowing."

Andrew grinned and looked at Brian who nodded and whispered to one of the money keepers. He took a few of the men to the private office upstairs to collect. Harry gestured toward a storage room, and a few of the men followed while the rest stood guard. They closed the door behind them, and Harry lit a lantern.

Andrew's good humor faded. "I received your message earlier. You can imagine my annoyance that Pruitt would steal from me. Brian said he checked the docks and a sack full of the jewels from the safe on Front Street was missing. One of the necklaces was found by you. Those jewels were collateral and belong to me. How did you find them?"

Harry's hands slightly shook, watching the anger rise on Andrew's face. "It was quite by accident, Boss. I remembered the piece you showed me with the anchor engraved in the gold stone. I ran into Pruitt's wife at a party and noticed she wore the same necklace. I asked her where she received it and she said Pruitt had it for a surprise for her hidden in her closet. She said she found it and he had no choice but to give it to her as an early birthday present. Pruitt looked nervous when she told me and began to stutter."

Harry let out a breath. "Some of the jewels are still missing. I had one of my men rip it from her neck when they left to go home. He ran off and feigned a robbery. Pruitt would never let me near his home because he knows I know. I gave Brian the necklace, but I don't know about the other jewelry."

Andrew kicked the chair and Harry jumped back. "Where is Pruitt?"

Harry's eyes widened. "He is in the storage room down the hall and tied up. We were waiting for you."

Andrew narrowed his eyes. "Good. I believe I will have a chat with him."

The guards moved to the side to let Andrew enter. He came in the door with a smile on his face. Two of the guards accompanied him into the room while the others stood outside of the door.

In his slyness, he chuckled sarcastically. "Mr. Pruitt, please forgive my tardiness. I was married today and detained at my wedding." Andrew walked toward the desk, sat on top of it, and watched the sweat drip from Pruitt's brow.

He liked to taunt his victims with feigned kindness. "You must forgive my men for their rudeness. We will untie you at once." He gestured toward Bull, a loyal guard. Bull nodded and untied Mr. Pruitt whose pale face looked like he was going to faint. He held his wrist. Afraid to move, he stared at the floor.

Andrew hopped off the table and walked near the desk to pour a glass of whiskey. He handed it to Mr. Pruitt. "Our hospitality seems to be lacking this evening."

Mr. Pruitt, a small man with bloodshot eyes, cautiously accepted the glass, fearful to drink it.

Andrew watched him as his smile formed a straight line. "Drink it."

Mr. Pruitt's hand shook as he tried to steady the glass near his mouth. His hard swallow indicated the liquid had gone down his throat.

Andrew turned away standing in front of the desk. "My time is valuable, Mr. Pruitt. I am a generous man, and you have taken advantage me."

Mr. Pruitt's breathing became labored, and his ashen skin made him look ill. "I was desperate. I owed McIntire money."

Andrew snorted. "McIntire? You stole from me because of him."

Mr. Pruitt looked away unable to make eye contact. "Please, Mr. Baird. I will pay you back."

Andrew studied his face losing patience. Lifting his eyebrow, he sternly asked, "Where is my jewelry?"

Mr. Pruitt shook his head looking away from him. Andrew lifted his hand and slapped him across the face, knocking him onto the floor. He gritted his teeth and spoke slowly: "Where is my jewelry?"

Pruitt spit out some blood from his mouth. A weakened reply revealed his confession. "Please, it's at my house. You can have it back."

Andrew started laughing. "How chivalrous of you to give me back my own jewelry?"

Andrew looked at Bull. "Tell Johnson to escort Mr. Pruitt back to his home to retrieve my jewels. Take all his valuables at the home and have him sign his mortgage over to me as well."

"No! Please. You can't do that—it will ruin me."

Andrew kicked him in the groin. "I own you now. Do you understand me? You have nothing. If you don't cooperate with my men, then you will die. You're lucky I am allowing you to live. No one steals from me and gets away with it."

Mr. Pruitt was coughing and gasping for air. Bull pulled him up and dragged him out the back entrance. Andrew straightened his jacket pulling his gloves on tightly. Brian came in the room and looked around at the mess. "Harry, have someone clean up back here." Harry nodded and went to grab a barmaid.

Andrew took a deep breath. "Let's go to the docks. I want to speak to McIntire." Brian agreed and took a few men with them.

The docks were abandoned, but Andrew knew better. His street smarts trusted his gut. He took out his pistol and gathered a few of his men outside the warehouse of McIntire Industries. A light sound of music could be heard when he put his ear to the door. Andrew kicked in the door, and the piano noise stopped. Two men flew out of a side door with pistols drawn. Andrew stood in front of his men pointing a gun. Royce Macintyre dropped the gun when he recognized Andrew.

"Are you mad? I almost wasted you." Royce quickly regained his composure, remembering who he was talking too. "Forgive me—I am just shocked to see you."

Andrew put the gun down and stood with his men. The door to a secret room remained slightly opened. Andrew slowly tilted his head and walked toward the door. He spotted around ten men and five women hiding by the back wall. Andrew cleared his throat. "What do we have here?"

McIntire shrugged his shoulder trying to appear nonchalant. "Just a small party."

Andrew laughed mockingly. "A party? You didn't invite your business partner? I think I feel offended." He looked over at Brian. "Brian, were you invited?"

Brian lifted the side of his mouth. "No Boss, he must have lost my invitation."

Andrew grabbed his chin. "Hmm, it doesn't look like a party. Just look at all these unsavory characters playing the tables. Some may say you were running a side business in here. Certainly, that can't be the case. Would you try to compete with me?"

McIntire shuffled his feet. "Please Mr. Baird, I know we are business partners with McIntire Shipping. I would not cheat you. I always pay your percentage on time. Tonight, is only a bit of fun, a group of friends playing cards." His nervousness caused him to stammer. "I uh … uh… invite you to play."

Andrew grunted his disapproval. "I don't gamble, Mr. McIntire. It's not good odds."

McIntire looked away as his men stared at him. Unable to mask his apprehension of his punishment. He began to sweat profusely wiping his face with his sleeve.

Andrew leaned toward Brian and whispered in his ear. Brian was followed by two of his men and looked for the money box. They located it behind the bar and took it. Andrew looked back at McIntire and his men. "My patience with you is at an end. I will be taking tonight's profits and any future profits if you don't close this little operation down. You know how I feel about competitors. If you lie to me again, you will suffer the consequences and my commission will go up. Do I make myself clear?"

McIntyre nodded his head willing to agree to any demands. Andrew smiled. "Good. I will let you get back to your guests. It's my wedding day and I am anxious to get home to my bride."

The men left with the money box and boarded the carriages. With business out of the way, he couldn't keep his mind off the night's future activities.

Andrew sat in his study after arriving home enjoying his brandy. He notified the maid to inform his wife he would be up soon. He took longer than he had wanted at his business meetings and missed dinner. Thoughts of her all day stirred his desire. Seeing her walking to him in that dress that accentuated her womanly curves drove him mad. She was a vision with her beauty and innocence. He would enjoy teaching her the art of seduction and lovemaking. She was worth every penny.

The chamber door squeaked when he opened it. He saw her wrapped in a robe sitting on the edge of the bed with her back facing him. Her long hair had been brushed and cascaded down her back. She turned her head slightly when she heard the door, but quickly turned back toward the fire that roared as it warmed the room. It was eerily quiet as the night winds howled against the window. Andrew took off his cravat and slowly removed his clothes putting on a robe that was lying on top of the chair. She kept her attention on the fire not acknowledging his presence behind her. Andrew sat on the side of the bed crawling toward her, the mattress sinking down with his weight. He sat behind her straddling his legs around her and pulled her back against his chest. Her body stiffened at his touch, and he rubbed her arms trying to comfort her. "I apologize for my delay." He moved her long hair to the side breathing near her neck.

His strong muscular legs held her in place as he rubbed her tense shoulders. Moving his hands gently, he played with her hair, placing feather-light kisses across the back of her neck. Amelia trembled trying to cover herself with a blanket as she was only dressed in a thin shift. Tears were falling as she winced at his touch.

Andrew grew frustrated as he continued to feel her tension. He whispered in her ear. "Do not fear me. I am your husband."

The silent crying caused her back to shudder. Andrew finally sighed loudly backing away from her. How could he make love to a woman that was sobbing and shaking with fear? His night of passion was replaced by coldness. He wanted to punch something but reined in his temper.

He stood up beside the bed and kneeled in front of her. Her eyes were swollen and she was visibly shaken. He reached over and took her hand. "Amelia, look at me."

Amelia looked at him trying to wipe her face with her hand. "Forgive me."

He reached for a piece of her hair and put it behind her ear. "We will not consummate our marriage tonight. We will wait until we reach our home in Scotland. I want you to get to know me so you are more comfortable. I wish to share the same bed, but will not touch you intimately until then."

She stared at him, speechless. He stood up and kissed her forehead. She shivered as she waited for him to leave. He didn't and instead got into bed beside her. She gasped as he pulled her towards him.

"Shh. Relax. I am a man of my word. I only want to hold you." He breathed her in and couldn't help but notice the flower smell in her hair.

"Your hair smells good. You have such beautiful hair." He reached over and turned off the lantern.

"Thank you, Mr. Baird," she said weakly as she hiccupped.

He sighed with annoyance. "Amelia, you are my wife. Please call me Andrew. It makes me happy. Please don't call me Mr. Baird again."

She didn't answer but feigned sleep.

CHAPTER 7

THE NEXT MORNING AMELIA WOKE up alone. One of the servants was packing her trunk. Amelia sat up, "Hello?"

The servant curtsied. "Hello, Mrs. Baird. You were sleeping soundly this morning. My name is Wilma. Your husband hired me to accompany you as your new lady's maid. Will you want some hot chocolate?"

Amelia shook her head taking in her surroundings. "Pardon me. I didn't know that he hired anyone. We didn't discuss it."

Wilma looked coyly at her. "It was your wedding day. I am sure discussing the servants was not important."

Amelia's face burned with her implications. Wilma was tall with golden red hair, and she guessed her age around five and twenty. Freckles on her nose reminded her of Sally. She rubbed her eyes trying to adjust to the light in the room. She didn't think she needed a designated lady's maid, but would not take the opportunity away from the woman. Not wanting to tarry too long, she sat up and washed her face in the basin preparing for the day. Wilma chose her apricot traveling dress for her to wear and helped her brush her hair. She told Amelia that she used to work at one of Andrew's factories in Glasgow. She didn't like it, so she took a job as a maid in his London home. Her mother was the cook and recommended her. She was excited to be promoted to a lady's maid. This new job gave her the chance to see her mother again.

Amelia's head spun with all of Wilma's chatting. The woman seemed nice enough, but she would be guarded with her trust. She would not disclose any secrets until she knew her better. A knock on the door interrupted the women. Wilma opened the door to the main housekeeper.

The housekeeper was very stoic and nodded. "Mr. Baird has requested his wife's presence in the dining room to break her fast."

Wilma curtsied. "As you wish. We are finished now." Amelia stood and thanked the women walking past them toward the stairs. She took in the rich decorations of decadent proportions that were displayed in the corridors. The dining room was a few floors from her room and she was determined to find it on her own. After a few wrong turns, she finally found it. She hesitated before entering the dining room. Andrew was chatting with his man Brian and they both stood as she entered.

Andrew smiled walking to meet her in the entryway to escort her to the chair beside him. He pulled out her chair. "You look well rested, my dear. I hope you slept well."

Amelia smiled. "Yes, thank you."

Brian stood. "I will see to the final preparations before we leave. If you will excuse me." He left them alone in the room.

Andrew kissed her on the cheek. "Let me make you a plate. What do you like to eat?"

Amelia was not hungry. "Just some bread would be great and some tea."

Andrew took some bread and a few pieces of cheese. "You may want some cheese too. We have a long trip ahead of us."

Amelia took the cheese and bit into it. The salty, creamy taste was delicious. She took a few bites of bread and sipped her tea. He watched her as he drank some coffee. She was lost as to what to say to her new husband and chose to fill her mouth with food instead.

He grinned with amusement in his eyes. "That is the most I have seen you eat."

Amelia's face blushed. "I guess I was hungrier than I thought. Is there anything you need me to do for you before we depart?"

He raised his brow. "No, the servants have packed everything. Is your new maid acceptable? If not, we can hire someone else."

Amelia shrugged her shoulders. "I don't really need a personal maid. I have never had one, and I can prepare myself."

He took her hand and kissed it. "It is my wish that you have the help that I can provide. Come now—let's see if we are ready to leave. I have a carriage just for us. I will ride some of the journey with you in the carriage and other times I may ride a horse with my men. The other carriages are for luggage and servants."

Amelia nodded. "May I visit the library? I thought I would select a few books for our journey."

He touched her face. "Amelia, this is your home now. Of course, you can take books from my library. You can buy any book that you wish. Which reminds me that I have asked Brian to set up an account for your personal use. I will put pin money in there for you."

Amelia looked down. "I have some savings and should be fine for a while." She lied because she didn't want him to know she hardly a shilling to her name.

Andrew snorted. "You are the only woman I know that would not jump at the chance to spend my money. Keep your money and spend mine. It's my duty and joy to provide for you."

He bent down and kissed her on the mouth. Amelia's body shook in surprise. It was a quick flutter in her belly. "Let's get you in the carriage."

The day was long for Amelia trying to get used to the motion of the carriage and the rough roads. She tried to find solitude looking out the windows, but that only lasted a few hours. Reading her books provided her some entertainment yet reading caused her motion sickness. All the idleness gave her time to reflect on her circumstances. She glanced out the window and spotted Andrew on his horse laughing with Brian. Who was this man that was her husband? He demanded respect and most people feared him. Yet he had different sides to him. He was gentle and polite to her, and she had not expected that.

Although, it didn't make her favor him as a husband. After all, she was sold and bought without anyone considering her feelings. He was a master at manipulation and did not come into money by honest means. She secretly loathed him.

The door swung open causing Amelia to jump. She must have been woolgathering and didn't realize they had stopped. Andrew laughed touching her arm. "Did I frighten you?"

Amelia took a deep breath. "Forgive me, I must have been asleep." Andrew held out his hand to assist her down from the carriage.

"We are taking a break to acquire some horses to continue our journey. Are you hungry?"

Amelia nodded and looked for a place to take care of her private needs. She excused herself and headed for the small structure down the hill. On her way back to the inn, she noticed a few other riding parties had arrived. The crowd ascended on the small inn causing hordes of people to stand outside. Amelia headed toward the crowds and was stopped by an older man. He was a big burly fellow and smelled of rotten vegetables. Amelia tried to go around him, but he stood in her way blocking her path.

"What's a pretty little thing like you doing all alone?" He grinned and rubbed his beard.

"Let me pass, please." Amelia took a step away from him. Unsure of his attention she chose to avert her eyes and not look at him.

The man was unmoved and took a step toward her. "You work in that inn? With those fancy clothes you are wearing, I bet you could fetch a high price. Lucky for you, I have money to spare for a tumble in the hay."

Amelia dropped her mouth open. He thought she was a trollop? She raised her chin. "I am not a prostitute, sir. I am a baron's daughter."

He crossed his arms. "You can call yourself whatever you want, sweetheart. You're all alone and I am a paying customer. You want me to speak to the manager. I know Ron personally."

She tried to storm off from him, but he grabbed her arm. "What's your hurry?"

A panic of desperation rose through her when he squeezed her arm. He was rough and was hurting her. She tried to jerk her arm away when he twisted tighter. She felt herself being dragged toward some trees as she pleaded with him to stop. She opened her mouth to scream when she felt his hand rip away from her arm. She fell back onto the ground losing her balance. Drops of blood sprayed onto her dress. A scream came out of her mouth as she wiped the dirt from her hands. The man was being beat into the ground as blood was everywhere. Andrew was hitting his face with his fist tearing his flesh. She cried for him to stop. Three men dragged Andrew off the stranger as he lay in a heap with a raspy breathing sound coming from his mouth. Andrew's eyes were dazed and clothes disheveled. Blood dripped from his fist.

Brian showed up with a group of his men to intervene in the situation, but it had all happened so fast. One of the three men recognized Brian, and he held up his hand. "Forgive us, Mr. Burns. We didn't realize it was you.

If you will allow us to take charge of the man. He is my wife's brother, and I will pay for any damages he may have caused and hope you will allow any misunderstandings to be dealt with by us."

Brian looked at Andrew who was assisting Amelia up from the ground. She was pale and shaking. Her dress ruined with bloodstains. He motioned for a guard to take her to Wilma and told him to pay the innkeeper for the use of a room so she could freshen up. He waited for her to leave until he looked at the group.

Brian cleared his throat. "Mr. Baird. May I introduce Mr. Keeling? We had a few business meetings in London a few weeks ago. He spent the last few years in America and would like us to invest in some cotton factories in the colonies."

Mr. Keeling's voice faltered at the recognition of the man they call Black Baird standing in front of him. "Nice to finally make your acquaintance although under unsavory circumstances."

Andrew tried to control his breathing. He raged inside as his voice rumbled. "Mr. Keeling, your brother-in-law touched what is mine. One of my most precious possessions—she is my wife."

Mr. Keeling's eyes widened at the admission. "I make no excuses for him. A relation only by marriage. I give him no defense and ask to make amends because he is with my party. Please accept our apologies."

Andrew's breathing slowed, his face drawn in a scowl. "What compensation would you propose is fair?"

Mr. Keeling looked at his partners. They whispered among each other. "We propose to pay you his portion of the two factories we built in the states. He owns ten percent of Wallington Cotton."

Andrew looked at him and tilted his head. He smirked. "Mr. Keeling, that is how he will compensate me. How are you going to compensate me?"

Mr. Keeling pulled at his cravat. "I don't understand?"

Andrew lifted the corner of his mouth dissecting the men with his stare. "Come inside to the inn. I have my solicitor with me today. We will draw up the paperwork. You will give me fifty percent of Wallington Industries."

Mr. Keeling gasped and looked at his partners. He shook his head. "Impossible. Mr. Baird."

Andrew raised his brow. "Your brother-in-law insulted my wife. Practically absconded her. You are traveling together and are responsible for his actions as he is with your party. You can either bring him home in a box to your wife, or you can sign over fifty percent of Wallington Factory to me. Don't insult me, Mr. Keeling. I will ruin your name, and no one will do business with you ever again."

Mr. Keeling's partners shifted nervously as Mr. Keeling ran his fingers through his hair. He was trapped and knew he had no choice. "Be reasonable, Mr. Baird."

Andrew looked at Brian who called the guards to circle the group. "Don't insult me, Mr. Keeling. I am losing my patience. You are lucky all of you are still alive."

Mr. Keeling turned red, unable to breathe properly. "I hardly know what to say. I must confer with my partners."

Glaring at the man, Andrew's face lacked emotion. "Be quick about it. I must tend to my wife."

Mr. Keeling walked away from the group and whispered to the two men by their carriage. One of the men was lifting his arms visibly upset. The other took off his hat and wiped his brow. After a few moments, all three came back to the group. "We agree to your proposal, Mr. Baird."

Andrew slapped him on the back. "I am a great business partner, Mr. Keeling. Have no fear."

Mr. Keeling's face was red as some sweat trickled down his brow. "Can I take my brother-in-law to my carriage? He may need a doctor."

Andrew motioned for one of his men. "You do understand that he cannot leave here unscathed." He whispered to his man loud enough for the group to hear. "Break his arm. The arm that touched my wife."

He looked at Mr. Keeling with all seriousness. "If he comes near her again, I will kill him."

The men looked at each other suspiciously, emotions playing havoc as the air grew heavy. Accepting their fate, they followed Andrew aimlessly into the inn. Hesitantly, accepting some brandy, they drank with him. His personality completely changed and he was well-mannered and humorous to be around, a common trait of his after an altercation. Mr. Keeling signed the paperwork and said his goodbyes. Andrew went to find his wife.

Amelia finished soaking in a tub that the innkeeper's wife had prepared for her. Wilma had helped her into a new dress, and she sat drinking tea by the fireplace. She asked Wilma to leave her alone to calm her nerves. Pictures of the unconscious man kept coming into her mind. Although he had hurt her, she could not help but to wonder of his welfare. Her arm still stung, but she thought by tomorrow the redness would go away.

A knock on the door brought her back to the present. "Come in, Wilma."

A deep voice sounded, "It's me. Wilma is eating lunch."

From the corner of her eye, she saw Andrew enter. Shivering, she held the shawl closer to herself. He came beside her and knelt on the ground in front of her. "I have taken care of the man who hurt you. Please don't worry anymore. Have you eaten anything?"

Amelia shook her head. "I am not hungry. But I put an apple in my reticule for later. Andrew, I am curious. It's just that the man… Will he die? There was so much blood."

Andrew touched her face. "You're my wife. I know that you have an aversion to this marriage, but I made a vow to protect you. You are mine, Amelia and no man will hurt you. The man is being taking care of by his brother-in-law. I don't think he will die. Unless, of course he touches you again."

Amelia trembled. "Are we leaving soon or staying here tonight?"

Andrew looked around the room. He spotted the tub and smiled. "We will leave within the hour. I am going to wash up. You can stay if you want. But if you prefer to meet your maid, she is in the dining room."

Amelia's face turned pink at his jest. Refusing to acknowledge his implications, she answered, "I will leave you to your privacy and find Wilma. Perhaps I will get a bite to eat."

He laughed out loud. With a sheepish smile, he countered, "We are married. One day we will bathe together. You may enjoy it." He loosened his cravat and began to undress in front of her.

Amelia's eyes widened, not wanting to see him naked, she hurried out the door as he was removing his breeches. He was laughing as she closed the door behind her.

The party traveled several more hours before stopping for the night. The Peacock was a popular inn that was much larger than the other ones they had come across. The owner knew Andrew by name and welcomed him with open arms.

Amelia was escorted to a huge room with a four-poster bed. The innkeeper's wife told her it was the best room they had available. Amelia appreciated her kindness and freshened up before dinner. Their servants delivered the trunks to their room and Amelia went downstairs to inquire about getting some food. She had skipped lunch and was famished.

She eyed Wilma eating with the other servants. Amelia gave a hopeful glance to the group longing to join them, but Andrew insisted she sit with him. He sat at a table with some of his men that were dining alone in a secluded area away from the others. She stayed quiet beside him and did not participate in the conversation. Admittedly, the roast beef was simply delicious and the buttered asparagus melted in her mouth. She topped it off with pudding for dessert. Unbeknownst to Andrew, she snuck a few bites of his pudding as well when he wasn't looking.

Andrew ordered her some wine to drink. The warm fruity liquid burned as it went down her throat. She was not used to drinking alcohol and only had champagne one other time in her life. A warmness came through her veins as she asked for another glass.

The conversation was limited and she concentrated on her food. And of course, the wine. When dinner concluded, Andrew walked her up to her room.

Her balance was a little off as she stood up. Not wanting to admit that she may have had a little too much to drink, she made no mention of it. He suggested she retire for the night as they had another full day of travel early in the morning. He kissed her cheek and told her he would meet her later.

Alone in their room, Amelia was bored. She wished to stay downstairs a little longer, but obeyed her husband and stayed in their room. Wilma came up a few minutes later to help her undress. She was talking nonstop about a piano player that was going to be there later that night. She knew him from London and was excited to dance. Amelia listened with interest and feigned exhaustion so Wilma would leave her alone.

A few hours later, Andrew had not come back to their room. Amelia shifted in the bed unable to sleep. Not that she exactly wanted to see him. Curiosity of the fun going on downstairs took a toll on her. She could hear the vibration of the music and an occasional scream of delight coming from the inn's main dining area. After contemplating several minutes arguing with herself, she sat up and put on a dress determined to find some entertainment.

The music filling the hallway became louder as she neared the stairs and walked down. A quick look around the room showed many women sitting on men's laps. Drinks were covering the tables, and people were singing out loud. The piano music was lively, and a few patrons were playing cards. She spotted Wilma hugging a man that she didn't recognize. Brian was kissing the neck of a serving girl and Andrew was nowhere to be found. Amelia went to find the innkeepers wife. She was trying to stay clear of the drunken men who seemed to watch her. The innkeeper's wife was surprised to see her.

"Mrs. Baird, this is no place for a lady at this hour. You should not be down here. Can I assist you?" She fumbled with her apron trying to guide Amelia back up the stairs.

Amelia was annoyed at the way people treated her. She was not a child and pulled away from the woman. "I assure you that I will not break. If I could trouble you for some warm milk?" She had no idea what to say, but could only think of what could help her sleep.

The woman raised a brow questioning her request, "Milk?"

Amelia knew it sounded absurd but nodded. "Yes. If it's not too much trouble."

The woman shook her head. "No trouble at all, Mrs. Baird. I will have Clinton escort you back to your room, and I will be up shortly with the milk."

Amelia shook her head, "I will wait." The innkeeper's wife whispered to Clinton and he nodded and walked away. A few minutes later Andrew came up behind her.

"Amelia? I heard you were down here. You must go back up to our room at once." He took her by the elbow and tried to guide her toward the stairs.

She stopped and looked up at him. "I don't understand why I can't come out of the room. Am I being punished? Why are you not staying in the room?"

He looked surprised at her question. "If you would like me to join you, all you have to do is ask. I am sure I can find something for us to do." He winked and raised his brow suggestively. She closed her eyes regretting her outburst and the implications.

Pouting, she lifted her chin. "I only wanted some milk. I apologize if that upsets you." She stepped away from him crossing her arms.

Sternly, he touched her face. "Watch your tone, little one. I understand that you had a dreadful day. However, you will not be insolent with me. When I tell you to do something, I will not be questioned."

She stared at him for a minute. Without responding she turned away from him and walked back up the stairs. Hearing the whispers of the people behind her. She felt humiliated and the hatred for her new husband grew inside her.

Andrew watched her climb the stairs without acknowledging him. He had to remember her youth. Such innocence needed to be protected. One day things would change between them, and they could build a relationship together. She would learn her place and act more maturely.

He took a seat beside Brian and ordered another brandy. A serving girl with a plunging neckline approached him and took a seat on his lap. She rubbed herself against him. Andrew smiled and whispered in her ear. "Not tonight, sweetheart. I am here with my wife." A disappointed look came across her face. But not before many servants witnessed the flirtation. The serving girl took the glass from his hand and licked the outside rim suggestively. "Is that the woman you sent upstairs?"

Andrew took the glass from her and set it down. "Yes, she is my wife and who I will be sleeping with tonight."

She shrugged her shoulders. "If you change your mind, I am in room ten. You seem like a man that likes variety in your appetite." She got up from the table and planted a kiss on Andrew's lips before walking away. The exchange shocked Wilma and a few of the onlookers. Andrew stood up and excused himself. He retreated to his room finding the atmosphere of the inn getting too heated.

Amelia shifted as he opened the door, but her eyes remained closed. Andrew took his time to disrobe and crawled into bed next to her. He heard her breathing and pulled her close to him. She never made a sound. He kissed her head and wished her a good night.

CHAPTER 8

THE FOLLOWING DAYS FELL INTO a routine. Andrew avoided the carriage and chose to ride with his men. The servants whispered behind her back and always stopped talking when she got close to them. She was lonely and hated her new life. Andrew would walk her to their room and then spend the evening carousing with his men. He joined her late at night and kissed her on the cheek while she feigned sleep. She was repulsed by his touch.

On their last night of travel, Amelia went out to the carriage to retrieve her book alone. She knew she might face Andrew's wrath for leaving without an escort, but she couldn't find him and didn't want to wait. On her way back inside, she heard whispers and stood by the corner of the inn hiding near some bushes. She realized she had lost all propriety and good breeding by eavesdropping while hiding in shrubbery. But she didn't care. This is how far she had fallen from who she used to be. When she heard her named mentioned, her curiosity peaked and she wanted to hear what they had to say.

"It's a shame is all I am saying. It's obvious he married her for her nobility. He spends most nights with the help. He grew up like the rest of us and isn't like her or her kind. He can barely stand to sleep with her." The female's voice carried across the lawn.

"I know. Did you see him at the Peacock? The serving chit sat in his lap in front of everyone. He didn't look like he was hurting none. No wonder he sent the misses back to bed." A male laughed then broke out into a cough.

"Did you see that kiss? I know who was a very happy man that night." The laughing continued.

"You all have nothing more to do than gossip. Who is it about this time?" The new voice was familiar and she recognized it as her lady's maid. Amelia strained her ears to see if she would defend her.

"Miss Innocent. Your lady." The female's voice paused and there was silence.

"Hardly a lady. At least not anymore. I almost feel sorry for her." The whole group laughed. "But not quite. Those types deserve what they get. The Black Baird will never be husband material. Miss High and Mighty will soon learn."

The group left and Amelia's eyelids burned with tears that she fought to hold back. She entered the side door and walked through the kitchen unnoticed. When she approached the chamber door, Andrew stood in the room waiting for her.

"Where were you? I was looking for you." His arms were crossed and his face was serious.

Amelia held the book in her hand. "I went to get my book. Forgive me, I couldn't find an escort."

He stepped toward her wrapping his arms around her waist. Amelia tensed at his touch. He pulled her against his chest and she laid her cheek on his chest feeling his heartbeat. He stroked her hair running his fingers through the silky strands. "I missed you today. It seems I didn't see much of you."

Amelia remained quiet hoping he would release her soon. She didn't like him to touch her, yet knew his patience was running thin. Perhaps he would not remember his promise to wait for Scotland?

He stepped away slightly to look down at her face. She was afraid to look up. "Look at me, Amelia." She had no choice but to look up at him.

She watched his eyes close as he brushed his lips against hers. His experienced mouth played with hers as he teased her to open to him. Without realizing it, he had opened her mouth and was rubbing his tongue against hers. He pulled her closer to him as he passionately kissed her.

Her head was spinning and she was trying hard not to enjoy it. Her body tingled and she felt out of breath. When he released her, he moved his mouth to her neck placing light kisses down her throat and carefully caressing her back. Amelia felt weak and he had to help hold her up. She was experiencing feelings she had never felt before and it scared her.

He whispered in her ear. "Oh, Amelia. Our time is close. You belong to me and soon I will make you mine."

Amelia's heart pounded in her chest. Not wanting to encourage any more affection for the night, she remained silent. He rubbed her arms and kissed her forehead. "I will be up shortly after attending to the staff. I told them we would dine in our room."

Amelia nodded and readied herself for bed. She wanted to be fully clothed by the time he came back upstairs. Andrew's attention to her comfort was evident. She always had the best room in each inn they stayed in. He always assured she had plenty to eat.

They traveled most the following day arriving at Andrew's estate the next evening. The massive home was surrounded by a stone fence and driveway. Huge stables could be seen beside the home with horses running freely. A large lake sat far behind the property surround by woods. There were servants standing outside to greet the party. Andrew was approached by his steward with urgent business, so Bull escorted Amelia into the home. She was greeted by a chambermaid who escorted her to a chamber. Andrew had insisted they share a chamber to sleep but have separate rooms for dressing.

Amelia sat on a chair by her window. Her dressing room had a beautiful vanity with several soaps and perfumes. Her trunks were soon delivered by the servants, and Wilma ordered her a bath.

After a bath, she took time to study her reflection in the looking glass. She stood sideways, backward, and forward. Her body was no longer a child. Would she feel the same after tonight? She would no longer be a girl, but a woman. He would exercise his husband rights and take her innocence away.

Her thoughts turned to Andrew—a man she did not choose but was forced to marry. He may have bargained for her body, but she was determined he would never have her heart. That only belonged to the one she would choose. Closing her robe, she moved away from the looking glass.

Hearing movement in the sleeping chamber, her body tensed. Trying to mask her nervousness, she resolved herself to her fate and opened the adjoining door. He stood without a shirt beside the bed. Her eyes locked on his bare chest and bulging muscles that were chiseled into his skin. Quickly, she looked away taking a seat by the fireplace.

"Did you like what you saw, Amelia?" A cynical laugh escaped his mouth. "It's okay love, you don't have to answer that." He poured two glasses of wine. Andrew took off his pants and put on a robe while she stared into the fire. He took the chair beside her and handed her the glass. Amelia accepted it not speaking.

"I hope you like your new home. I wish I didn't have to leave tomorrow as I wanted to give you a personal tour, but I have an urgent matter I must resolve. I will be back in a few days." He finished his glass of wine and placed it on the table. He stood up and knelt in front of her.

She had not touched her wine. He took the glass from her hand and put it on the table. He lightly touched her face. "Relax. I promise I will be gentle. I want to do nothing but please you tonight."

He took her hand and placed light kisses on the inside of her wrist. The move gave her chills, and she looked away not able to concentrate. He gently placed kisses up her arm until he reached her lips. Not pressing too hard as he skillfully nibbled on her bottom lip before opening his mouth and searching for her tongue. Her body tensed but she did not move away from him. He placed his arm underneath her legs and braced her against his chest lifting her from the chair without breaking his kiss. He carried her over to the bed placing her in the middle. He broke his kiss to crawl up beside her and placed light kisses along her jawline while softly touching her throat. She arched her back in response as he pulled her closer to him.

The intimacy of his touch as he explored her body immersed her into feelings she had never experienced. He moved his kisses down her neck to her chest as the smell of sandalwood and masculinity intoxicated her. He untied her robe and pushed her arms gently to the side. Her resistance finally broke and it began to feel natural to be giving herself to this man. Allowing him access to her most private areas of her body no longer embarrassed her. Her modesty was lost as their bodies intertwined and became one.

Andrew's body shook as he took her to be his true wife. The possessiveness he was feeling was new to him. He desired her with his whole soul and it felt different than a tryst. He never wanted to let her go. The knowledge that she belonged to him made him want her more and explore the feelings he was encountering.

Their breathing subsided, and he turned over in the bed taking her with him as he tucked her next to his side. He kissed her neck wanting to make sure she was okay. "Amelia, that was incredible, sweetheart."

Her body stiffened at his words as her breathing began to slow down. He squeezed her tightly a little worried. "Are you well? Did I hurt you?"

She seemed apprehensive by his closeness and lack of modesty. "I am well," she answered not looking at him. Carefully avoiding his stare, she covered her body with a blanket shifting in his arms.

Andrew was hoping for more openness about her first encounter with making love. But he didn't want to push her. Her affections were guarded and he longed for her to initiate his touch. She had been a virgin and he knew he must be patient. He kept awake watching her until he felt her breathing deepen and he knew she was asleep. Amelia was a bit of a puzzle to him and he wanted to spend more time with her. They lay in each other's arms for the rest of the night until he had to leave. Not wanting to disturb her, he kissed her head and left the room.

CHAPTER 9

THE NEXT DAY AMELIA WOKE up alone. Andrew told her he would be gone in the morning. Her body ached and was sore—all she longed for was a warm bath. She pulled the bell for her lady's maid and wrapped a robe around herself. Tears welled in her eyes showing an emotion that she could no longer control. Weeks of frustration overwhelmed her. Unable to make her own decisions and being passed around like a pawn in a game between men came to a head. She sobbed thinking about her own will being ripped from her and how her future was looking bleak.

Amelia tightened the robe around her as a chill ran through her body. The way she felt last night was confusing and any enjoyment was temporary. She was married to a man that would never love her. A broken man that loved only himself. Her whole life she was either a burden or used by people that could never love her back.

She wiped her tears walking to the basin looking for a cool rag to wash her face. If only she had a mother who could teach her the things women should know. Was her mother dead? One of the servants told her a story when she was little that her mother ran off and was not dead. When she told her father, the servant was dismissed. The story was denied.

Her maid entered the room and curtsied. Amelia quickly tried to hide her tears. Wilma tried to approach her, but Amelia lifted her hand. "I desire a bath. If you could ask the footman to bring up some water." She turned away from her maid and sat on the chair near the window.

"May I assist you with your bath, Mrs. Baird?" She asked inquisitively, not showing any sign of her earlier folly with the other servants.

Amelia thought back to her cruel words a few days ago. She didn't trust her. "No, you may not. I will not need your services today." Her sharpness was evident in her words.

After a long pause, the maid answered back. "As you wish." She left the room and a few minutes later the footmen appeared with buckets of steaming water. Amelia thanked the footman and readied herself for the day.

The house smelled of pine oil as she walked along the corridors. Woodwork and marble decorated the home throughout all the floors and walls. Huge carpets lay in various rooms matching the tapestries and paintings. The house was exquisite. Amelia could hardly believe the furnishings—detailed and expensive. She heard voices in the kitchen and felt her stomach growl. She craved some tea and bread. The voices went silent when she entered the room.

"Are you lost, Mrs. Baird? We can send a tray up to your room or you may dine in the dining room." A heavyset woman with a gray bun who she guessed was the cook and somewhat in charge gestured toward the door behind her. The kitchen servants looked at each other in shock. A few others were enjoying their breakfast at a table inside the kitchen. They were smiling and whispering.

Amelia shook her head. "I thought I would just serve myself a piece of bread from the kitchen."

The woman shook her head with a repugnant stare. "That won't do at all, Mrs. Baird. Allow me to introduce myself. I am Miss Haughton and I am the head cook. I know you were otherwise engaged last night with your husband so proper introductions were not made. The kitchen is not for the mistress of the home. We will gladly provide anything you may need within our capabilities. If you will please take your leave to the dining room, we will bring you some bread and tea."

Amelia's face burned with the implications of her being engaged with her husband. She had never been addressed in such a way from a servant. Not knowing how to respond she chewed on her bottom lip. "Should I go over menus with you?"

The housekeeper snorted. "I have been providing the menus for Mr. Baird and his associates for over five years—every meal including his dinner parties. I am more than capable of continuing to plan on my own."

Amelia's mouth fell open. She was being treated like a child and an outsider. The other women snickered in the kitchen. She didn't have the strength to address the insolence of the staff. She had hoped they would be kind to her. Feeling her discomfort, Wilma stood up from the table.

"Mrs. Baird, if you would like to sit in the dining room. I will bring you your bread and tea."

Amelia left the room. Only hunger forced her to go to the dining room. Wilma served her and a footman stood in the room ready to assist if asked. The bread was good but not as good as hers. Amelia liked to put a touch of honey in the dough making the bread sweet. Perhaps one day she would be allowed to use the kitchen. She thought Andrew might like to try her bread. After finishing her meal, she decided to spend time in the library. In the future, she would take a tray to her room for her meals. She didn't have the stomach or willpower to go near the kitchen. Eating alone in the dining room made her feel even lonelier.

The next few days went by slowly. Anytime she left the room the servants were obedient but often made her feel uncomfortable with all their secrets. No one tried to get to know her. She wished Rachel was there and hoped to write her soon. Her solace each day was her walks outside. Although never alone, as guards would watch her from afar.

The gardens needed some attention and she decided to ask Andrew for some garden tools. Playing in the dirt would be a welcomed pastime. She knelt on the ground by a stone fence and ran her hands over mounds of soil. It was moist and could probably produce beautiful flowers. She thought about painting the landscape—another favorite pastime she engaged in growing up. The ground was wet with dew and beginning to soak through her gown. She stood up and wiped the dirt off her skirt. Her new home was growing on her. After exploring more of the garden, she headed to the house.

She ordered her daily bath to soak in the bathtub.

"Wilma, I will need your assistance today. I would like to wash my hair." Amelia stood in her robe handing Wilma some rose soap.

"Of course, Mrs. Baird." She retrieved a ceramic pitcher to help rinse the soap from her hair. Amelia disrobed and stepped into the steamy water. After washing her body, she leaned her head back with her eyes close allowing Wilma to lather the soap down her hair.

Amelia could sense Wilma's distraction. She felt her stand up and move away from the tub. A few seconds later, she heard the door close and Wilma return to the tub and rinse her hair. Amelia was a little annoyed at her inattentiveness with soap in her hair and eyes, "Wilma, where did you go?"

There was no answer.

"Wilma?" Amelia pulled away from her and rubbed her eyes with her hands. Looking up she gasped. "Andrew!" She was mortified at being so exposed.

He laughed at her expression. "Good Morning, sweets. I sent your maid out of the room so I could help you instead."

Amelia was dripping with water realizing she was naked and quickly tried to cover herself with her hands from his prying eyes.

He grabbed her hands. "You're beautiful, Amelia. Please don't cover yourself up." He picked her up out the bathtub and held her in his arms.

"Andrew, don't carry me. I will get your clothes soaked. I am dripping wet." She tried to push away from him, but he held on tighter.

"Nonsense. I don't care if you get me wet. I don't plan to have my clothes on that long." He grinned as he placed her on the bed and took off his clothes. He kissed her and joined her on the bed.

He whispered between kisses, "I missed you while I was gone and couldn't stop thinking about you." He touched her face gently. "I wrapped up my business a day early and traveled all night so I could be with you sooner."

After making love, he held her, wanting to know how she liked her new home. "So, tell me about your week. Are you getting familiar with your staff?" Andrew held his head up with his elbow rubbing her arm. Her hair was tumbled down partially covering her. He had never seen anyone more beautiful.

Amelia was unsure how to answer him. "I guess you could say I am now familiar." She looked away biting her lip unconsciously.

He frowned with concern. "What is amiss?"

She shook her head trying not to cry. "Nothing really." Not able to hide her emotions her breath caught in her throat. Her eyes watered threatening tears to drop onto her cheeks. He touched her face. "What is it? Tell me."

She rubbed her lips together. "I don't wish to upset you. I can handle it."

He pulled her close to him and buried his face in her neck. "Amelia, please tell me why the staff displeases you. I will terminate all of their employment if that is your wish."

After a hiccup, she closed her eyes. "They don't like me. Mrs. Haughton said I wasn't allowed in the kitchen. She told me my help with the menus would not be needed and she would decide what you would eat. The rest of the staff talks about me behind my back and often laugh at me, whispering when I walk into a room." Tears escaped and she quickly wiped them away.

Andrew's jaw tightened and his face turned red. "I will address this immediately. No one will treat you this way. Especially servants."

Amelia's eyes widened as her voice trembled. "Oh no! Please don't say anything. I will handle it. If they know I came to you it will only be worse when you leave."

He held her close to him. "Shh. Don't fret, sweetheart. I only want to speak to them. I promise all will be well. What about your lady's maid?"

Amelia leaned back to make eye contact. "Wilma? She is the worst one of them all. She laughed with them regarding… Never mind. She can't be trusted."

Andrew tilted his head holding her eyes with his. "Regarding what? Tell me." Amelia looked down to fidget with her hair. Taking a deep breath, she looked away to answer his question. "It was about that night at the inn. The servants were saying you were improper with some of the help."

Andrew's nostrils flared. "Lass, look at me. I was not improper with any serving wench. She sat in my lap uninvited, and I told her my wife was upstairs and I refused her services." Amelia didn't know how to answer. She looked at him as he kissed her on the nose. "Get dressed, and I will meet you downstairs."

The servants were gathered together in the entry hall. Andrew stood in the middle of the staircase. He held out his hand to take hers when he saw her come down the stairs.

"I would like to formally introduce my beautiful wife as I was unable to when we arrived a week ago. She is now mistress to all my estates. The staff will ultimately report to her and she will make all staffing decisions. Mr. Charles will return in a few weeks from taking care of his mother and will remain as the butler. He will also report to my wife." He squeezed her hand pausing for a minute to look at her. "She likes to bake and will have full run of the kitchen, and I have asked her to personally plan all my meals." He kissed her on the hand giving her a wink. "As my wife, she is to have the same courtesy that you give to me."

He turned to Mrs. Haughton. "If you would be so kind as to make a picnic basket for us as I plan to take my wife riding. We will be dining out this evening."

Amelia's face burned at his acknowledgment. She saw the shocked faces and angry looks from the staff. He wasn't finished and called for Wilma. "Yes, Mr. Baird?"

"My wife will be interviewing for a different lady's maid. She will no longer need your services, and there will be no letter of recommendation. Because of her generosity alone, we will provide you one month's severance. You can thank my wife for that, as I would have dismissed you with nothing." He turned and kissed Amelia on the cheek. "Please meet me in the stables in one hour. I have a surprise for you on our bed." He walked away leaving a stunned Wilma and Amelia.

Amelia climbed the stairs back to her room. When she arrived, a package was sitting on the bed. He must have had someone put it there for her. She couldn't help but smile as she opened it. It was a riding habit. The material was beautiful and golden in color. She dressed in a hurry, asking the chambermaid to help her.

Andrew was waiting for her by the stables. Two horses were saddled, and he carried the basket and a blanket. He helped her mount and she followed him into the countryside. The estate was beautiful and the scenery was breathtaking. There was a lake nearby on his property and they stopped to put the blanket beside the water. He helped her sit down and took the fruit and wine out of the basket. She smiled and accepted a glass of wine. Taking a drink, she relaxed as the warmth of the liquid filled her body. He took a small box out of the basket and handed it to her. She slowly took it, confused by his grin. The box was red silk and when she opened it, a diamond necklace welcomed her. Her mouth fell open at the sparkling beauty. "Oh, Andrew. This is beautiful."

He took it from her and put it around her neck. "I noticed that you have very few jewelry pieces. A problem I hope to rectify." He turned her around and kissed her lightly on the mouth. "It looks great on you."

She felt her necklace with her hand. "I am almost afraid to wear it."

He laughed, taking her hand and kissing it. "Nonsense, it pleases me to see you wearing it." He sat back down seeming happy that he surprised her. Looking over the water, he sighed. "I love to look at the lake. It's home to many fish, but I have not the time to go fishing. I can't wait to take my sons." He leaned back on his elbows watching Amelia as she drank her wine, glancing over the lake.

She smiled and looked down at him. An infrequent site indeed for her to smile in his presence. "What about your daughters?"

He chuckled, amused at her defense., "Of course. They will learn to fish as well." He reached over touching her face to kiss her. He had hoped she was now more accepting of him as her husband. Her melancholy was taking a toll on him. He could command many men and hundreds of employees were at his beck and call. But having his wife indifferent to his affections had bothered him more than he wanted to admit. She responded to his touch and he held her close drinking in her kisses. He laid her down on the blanket caressing her neck. Her surrender excited him and he wanted her more than ever before.

Sounds of a horse coming near interrupted their embrace. Andrew sighed in frustration. He looked up to see Brian dismount. "Forgive me. I would not have come if it was not urgent. We received word that our business deal is ready to be signed and they need you at the warehouse as soon as possible."

Andrew took Amelia's hand. "Forgive me, my dear. I will escort you back to the house and take care of this business quickly. Please dress in the dress I bought for you. I want you to meet some of my friends this evening. They invited us to their home for a dinner party." He stood up assisting her onto the horse as they rode back in silence.

Andrew arrived home later than he wanted. He quickly bathed and went to look for Amelia as they were running behind. He ordered two carriages for the night. One for them and one for his men. He caught a glimpse of her in the doorway, and his eyes took a moment to adjust to her beauty.

She was stunning.

The dark burgundy dress fit her womanly curves tightly making him weak in his knees. He had known beautiful woman all his life, but his wife stood out more than any other woman he had ever known. She wore the diamond necklace he gave her that accentuated the sparkle in her green eyes. He did enjoy spoiling her.

"You are beautiful, my dear." He walked over and kissed her on the cheek. "I will be the envy of every man there." She looked away blushing.

CHAPTER 10

THE HOME WAS OF MODEST size in a busy part of the city. It was an hour's ride away by carriage. Andrew explained to her that the woman hosting the party was a childhood friend who grew up on the same street that he did. She worked in some of his establishments and was loyal. Her husband was introduced to her through Andrew and he ran one of his factories. The other guests were either close friends or business associates of Andrew. Amelia twisted her hands as nervousness took over her body. Meeting actual friends who may judge her made her worry.

A pretty woman with dark hair opened the door. "Andrew! You're over two hours late. We almost started without you." He kissed her on the cheek and took Amelia's hand. "Better late than never. May I introduce you my lovely wife, Amelia?"

The woman smiled admiring Amelia. "She is lovely. I am Jean and so glad to meet the woman who brought Andrew Baird up to scratch. Many women have tried and failed. You must be very special, dear."

Amelia was not sure how to take the woman's comment. How many women had Andrew been involved with? Was he still seeing any? Amelia pushed the thoughts out of her mind. "Nice to make your acquaintance." She gave her a guarded smile and looked away.

Jean must have felt some of the tension and looked at Andrew with a raised brow. She then looked at Brian. "Come here you stranger. I missed you the last few dinner parties. Give me a hug."

Brian hugged her and walked with her into the drawing room where guests were drinking and conversing before dinner. Andrews's men followed close behind. A few of the couples came over to greet Andrew. He introduced Amelia to many people and left her by the fireplace as some of the men led him away for a brief private chat.

A scantily dressed woman approached Amelia as she feigned interest in a painting. "So, you are the newest?"

Amelia gazed over at the woman who had a painted face. She tried not to stare at her but was distracted by the redness of her cheeks. She raised her brow. "Pardon?"

The woman snorted proudly lifting her chin. "I am Sophie. I am sure you have heard of me. I knew that he would marry someday. But you're nothing but a child playing dress-up. That innocent look does nothing to stir a man's desire. He will grow tired soon."

Amelia was sure the woman had just insulted her. She was confused by her slurred speech and insinuations. Part of her wanted to tell the woman to go hang. But she decided to just walk away from her. The woman followed her to the other side of the room. "You don't walk away from me. I know your father is a baron. That doesn't make you better than us. We have known Andrew for years."

Jean came to interrupt the conversation. "Sophie, that's enough. Leave Mrs. Baird alone."

Sophie looked at Jean. "Mrs. Baird? This is ridiculous. Look at her. He won't be satisfied with only one woman."

Amelia tried to steady herself grabbing onto a table. Jean took Sophie by the arm and pulled her away from the scene. One of Andrew's men approached Amelia. "Mrs. Baird, are you well?" Amelia's eyes widened. "Yes, thank you."

A young woman approached Amelia. "Never mind Sophie. She is just jealous and had her heart set on Andrew for years. She wasn't even invited tonight but showed up knowing Jean wouldn't send her away. They used to work together by the docks." She laughed while taking a drink of wine. "I am Josephine. I am married to Georgie who works for Andrew."

Amelia nodded not saying anything. Josephine stepped closer and whispered. "The truth is we are all a bit shocked. Andrew had a reputation of a lifetime bachelor. The fact that he married an English woman from nobility has surprised us all. He didn't seem the marrying type. He lives for his business and has always wanted to build an empire. He had a woman in every city. Forgive me. Perhaps I have had too much wine and shouldn't be telling you all of this. Please don't tell my husband." She walked away in a nervous hurry and joined a group of other women.

Amelia stood speechless. She never met such ill-mannered people in her life. She would remain silent the rest of the evening hoping for a quick escape after dinner. Andrew joined her a few moments later and escorted her to the dining room. The dinner conversations were different than what she was used to. It was obvious many of them wanted to please Andrew, often talking about their accomplishments with his business interests. Andrew called them his friends, but they were more of his cronies vying for his attention and acceptance. It made her nauseous. He would never own her despite his thoughts on the matter. It was obvious to her that he must have many indiscretions. He only saw her as a conquest and someone to have his children. She would close her heart no matter how much he tried to open it.

After dinner, Josephine went to the piano to play music. A few of the men moved some of the furniture out of the way so they could dance. Amelia did not want to stay and sat alone near the corner of the room trying to avoid the constant stares from Sophie and the other women. Jean approached her trying to get her to join the others.

"Hello. Are you not well?" Jean took a seat next to Amelia's chair. "I hope you enjoyed dinner. Did you know that roasted goose is one of Andrew's favorites?"

Amelia shook her head politely not speaking. She didn't want to be there any longer and propriety forbade her to voice her opinion. Instead, she looked down into her lap.

Jean looked with sympathy at Amelia. "Can I call you Amelia?"

Amelia looked up and made eye contact with her. She would prefer the woman didn't call her by her first name. Amelia suspected that she may have had a past relationship with her husband given the familiarity of their greeting. It made Amelia feel awkward. Not knowing how to answer without appearing rude, she nodded her head with acceptance.

Jean smiled. "Amelia, I had hoped we could be friends. Andrew is like a brother to me. We grew up together, and he has always been my protector until I married one of his close friends. I want him to be happy, and I hope you can both find happiness together."

It was hard for Amelia to believe anything that Jean was saying to her, so she gave her a guarded smile and said, "If you will excuse me." She stood up dismissing Jean to look for her husband.

Jean stood up beside her and touched her arm again. "Amelia? Did I say something to upset you?"

Amelia pulled her arm out of her grasp straightening her shoulders. Remembering her manners, she decided to act in a manner appropriate of her station. A baron's daughter. "Not at all. If you will excuse me, I must find Mr. Baird." She turned on her heel and walked toward the staircase where she saw Andrew. When he saw her, his face lit up. "There you are. I saw you speaking to Jean earlier and left you alone to get to know each other."

Amelia nodded and whispered in his ear. "Is it possible to leave?"

He looked at her with concern. "Are you not feeling well? You look a little pale." Amelia nodded her head and looked away from him. He put his hand around her waist and whispered in her ear. "I will tell the groom to fetch our carriage and we can say our goodbyes."

Andrew approached Jean and told her Amelia was not feeling well and they would be leaving. Jean nodded her head. "Of course. I hope she feels better."

Andrew asked the servant to fetch Amelia's cloak. They were standing by the front doors getting ready to leave when Sophie approached them. Jean tried to grab her, but was unsuccessful. Sophie stood by Andrew rubbing up against him in front of Amelia. "Are you leaving so soon? We didn't get a chance to dance, Drew. Remember how we use to dance?" She eyed him seductively and giggled.

Amelia removed her hand from his arm and turned to walk out the front doors. Andrew looked back at his wife and scowled at Sophie. He unattached her hand from his arm and left her standing there as he ran after Amelia who was walking briskly toward the carriage.

He caught up with her. "Wait!" She was holding back tears and kept walking. He walked beside her until they reached the carriage.

"Don't cry, sweetheart. She is nothing to me." He wiped the tears from her eyes and helped her into the carriage. Amelia felt a chill and looked around the carriage. "I forgot my cloak."

He touched her face. "Wait here, and I will go get it." She nodded leaning back against the cushions. Her mind raced with thoughts of the night. It was not exactly jealousy that she was feeling but humiliation. That woman flirting with her husband in front of her. The gossip would be relentless.

Andrew stormed through the front door grabbing Sophie by the hair in front of all the guests. No one dared stop him. She screamed out as he pulled her until she fell onto the floor. He knelt and grabbed the back of her neck. "If you ever show disrespect to my wife again, I will ruin you. You don't ever speak to her again. Her name will never be on your lips. If I find out that you even looked her way, I will make you pay every day for the rest of your life. Are we clear?"

She nodded and screamed out again. "Let me go!" Jean rushed over and stood between Andrew and Sophie. She grabbed his arm. "Let us talk for a minute. I will assure she understands."

He shook his head. "I have to go. Amelia is upset and waiting for me. I only came back for her cloak." The servant handed it to him. He looked at Jean. "I will come to the Tree Lounge tomorrow. Meet me there and we can talk then." Jean nodded and watched him walk out the door.

Andrew entered the carriage and took the seat beside Amelia. He took her hand and kissed it gently. He slid his arm around her and held her next to him the entire way home. She fell asleep in his arms and he carried her upstairs to their bed. He undressed her and tucked her in beside him. She stirred a few times but stayed asleep until he snuggled close to her.

"Andrew? Did you carry me?"

He kissed her on the cheek. "Yes, you were very tired and I didn't want to wake you."

She closed her eyes. "I am very sleepy." He smiled as she drifted back to sleep. The next morning, he left her sleeping as he went back into town.

Jean was waiting for him at the Tree Lounge—a tavern that Andrew owned and Jean managed for him. She saved a private table for them in the back.

She laughed as they ordered a few drinks. "It's not a party if someone doesn't get hurt." Andrew smiled, loosening his cravat. "It's warm in here."

Jean pressed her lips together trying to find the right words. "How is Amelia?"

Andrew took a long breath. "She slept most the way home and was still sleeping when I left this morning. She will be fine, just probably exhausted."

Andrew shook his head. "Why did you invite Sophie? Were you trying to make me angry?"

She puckered her lips. "Are you mad? I didn't invite her. She just showed up. I made her promise to behave if I let her stay."

Andrew creased his brow. "No matter. I don't wish to speak of her. What did you think of my Amelia?"

She lifted the corner of her mouth. "Darling, it doesn't matter what I think. You're already married." Jean smiled, wiping some crumbs off the table.

Andrew leaned back. He studied his friend's face and accepted a glass of brandy from the server. He took a drink enjoying the sting that went down his throat. "What does that mean?"

She took a drink of her wine. "Oh, stop Andrew. She is obviously very easy to look at and I know her beauty is why you married her. I doubt you really know much about her."

Andrew tilted his head. "Of course, I know all about her. She is my wife and we are intimate."

She snorted. "That is just like a man to say something like that. There is more to women than their bodies, Andrew. The poor girl is so frightened and untrusting of her surroundings that she barely speaks. It's like she suspects everyone and holds secrets if you ask me." She took a drink of wine looking at Andrew who didn't say anything back as he thought about her revelation.

Jean cleared her throat. "Has she ever had an actual conversation with you? Honestly, she probably only answers your questions. I challenge you to pay attention and see if she asks you anything about your life? Or is she just obedient and agrees with what you say not ever telling you her true feelings."

Andrew drained the rest of his drink and gestured toward the waitress for another one. "That's ridiculous. Of course, we have conversations."

Jean shook her head. "Andrew, I am your friend. Trust me when I tell you that you don't know the girl at all. You are so blinded by her beauty that you fail to see that she is miserable. It's clear to me that you are smitten, but does she return your affection? I have never known you to fall for any woman. Not even Loren who you were with on and off for years."

Andrew looked away at some patrons who just entered the tavern.

He recognized an old friend and turned back to Jean. "I appreciate your concern, but we are good. If you will excuse me, I want to speak to Bartley. I haven't seen him in a long time."

CHAPTER 11

Amelia finished up her last interview for her new lady's maid. Beatrice was her favorite and just a few years older than her. Her references were limited, but she felt at ease with her. She could start right away, and Amelia jumped at the chance to have someone to talk to. The rest of the staff only gave her customary greetings keeping their distance. Some of them were upset over Wilma's dismissal especially her mother who remained the head cook. Amelia was hoping to convince Beatrice of her good nature before the others had a chance to poison her reputation. She walked Beatrice to the front door after she accepted the position just as Andrew came home.

Amelia smiled and made introductions. Andrew seemed very pleased with her choice. "I am happy you will be joining our staff."

Beatrice curtsied. "Thank you, Mr. Baird. I am looking forward to the opportunity." Andrew held the door for her as she waved goodbye to Amelia.

Andrew kissed her on the cheek. "I see you have been busy."

Amelia took in a deep breath, "Yes, your solicitor sent five applicants. Beatrice was my favorite." Amelia walked with him toward the drawing room. She poured him a glass of brandy and a cup of tea for herself. Andrew thanked her and patted the seat next to him on the settee.

Struggling with his words, he stared at her curiously. He reached for her hand rubbing circles on her skin with his thumb. "I spoke to Jean briefly today." He made eye contact with her as if measuring her reaction.

She stared at him blankly waiting for him to continue.

Andrew continued, "She thinks you're lovely. It's just that…"

Amelia narrowed her eyes and pulled her hand away. "What did she say?" A nervous feeling came over her. She reached for her cup of tea and took a sip.

Andrew reached for his glass and took a sip of brandy. "She wants to have tea with you tomorrow."

Amelia was suspicious. "Just tea?"

Andrew stared into his glass contemplating his response when he finally looked up at Amelia. "Do you have any questions about me? Something maybe a wife should know about her husband?" He observed her closely waiting for her to respond.

She paused for a few moments and began to chew on her bottom lip. She shrugged her shoulders. "I hardly know."

Andrew touched her arm. "There has to be something."

Amelia took a moment before replying, "Very well. I guess I have wondered how old you are."

Andrew chuckled at the irony of the question. "Of course. That is something most wives know about their husbands. I am two and thirty."

Amelia accepted his answer and sighed, debating within herself. She finally looked at him with a raised brow. "There is one more thing that I can't get out of my mind."

Andrew tilted his head in amusement. "Ask me."

Amelia looked down at her hands and closed her eyes. "How much?"

Andrew seemed confused by her question. "How much what?"

Amelia opened her eyes looking straight at him. Her voice sounded slightly unsteady, "How much did my father sell me for?"

Andrew was taken back by her question and didn't want to answer and hurt her feelings. She was priceless to him. But how could he deny her an answer when he insisted she ask him anything? His voice was gentle. "Amelia, I will tell you only because you asked me to. But before I do, I want you to know that I would have paid double. You intrigued me from the moment I saw you. Please know that it was never about the money for me."

Amelia looked at her lap. "I want to know how much?"

He let out an exhausted breath. "Fine. With the payment of all the debts including the rest of the mortgage, in addition to bringing all other accounts up to date, it was around twenty thousand pounds."

Amelia's mouth dropped open gasping. "Are you mad?"

He smiled at her and shrugged his shoulders. After a few seconds, he bent over and cupped her face. "Not mad. Just captivated by you." He brushed a soft kiss against her open lips.

Amelia turned her head breaking the kiss, trying to compose herself. She pulled away from him. "Thank you for telling me. If you will excuse me, I have to attend to some private needs." She ran out the door and up the stairs. The tears flowing as he watched her exit.

Andrew stared at the door his wife just left and decided to give her some space. It was a lot for her to digest knowing the price her father had set for her. If he could only make her see that they could have a good life. He would shelter her from his business and reputation. The dinner party incident would not be repeated. His life with her would be separate from his other life.

Jean came by the following day for tea. Amelia wore her yellow dress and a pearl necklace. She welcomed Jean into their home. The cook made small cakes to serve with the tea. Jean spoke to the staff with familiarity making Amelia uneasy. What exactly was her relationship with Andrew that she knew his staff by name?

"Amelia, I am so happy to get a chance to speak to you alone." Amelia smiled hoping her request was of a friendly nature.

She took a sip of her tea. "I welcome any female company that I can find."

Jean laughed. "Yes, you must tire of all of Andrew's companions. How are you settling in? I hope all is well? I am anxious to see the changes you will make to the home. It definitely needs a woman's touch."

Amelia blushed. "I hardly know what changes to make. Although I do like to look at artwork. Some of it can be expensive."

Jean swished her hand. "Money is no problem with Andrew. He will give you your heart's desire. Trust me, I have never seen him more smitten."

Amelia looked away, uncomfortable of where the conversation was leading. Did Jean think she was a fortune hunter?

Jean finished one of the cakes and stood up from the settee to pour herself some more tea. "I am so happy Andrew found you. He has had a hard life and deserves to have a nice family."

Amelia realized she knew very little about her husband's past. "I am not aware of his past."

Jean sat back on the settee. "Our families lived near each other when we were children. Andrew stood out from most of the boys on the street—always brawling with the other kids in the neighborhood trying to prove he was tough." Jean laughed shaking her head. She took a drink of tea.

After a few seconds of silence, she leaned over and whispered. "Amelia, maybe it's not my place, but I want you to understand why your husband is the way he is. My hope is not to scare you but just to help you. You see, many Scots disliked the Irish. They had it rougher and faced a daily struggle to adapt to life in Scotland. My mother was Scot, so I was more accepted than most others on my street. Some made fun of Andrew because he didn't have shoes that fit him, so he used to take them off and go barefooted until winter was too unbearable. His mother was not home often, and when she was there, she always had a drink in her hand. Some of the men that visited his home were not kind to him, and he used to try to protect his mother and brother."

Amelia shifted in her seat. "He never speaks to me about his childhood or his family."

Jean shook her head. "One of his mother's boyfriends used to whip his little brother. Andrew protected him as much as he could even though he was a child himself. That same year he grew at least five inches. He was around one and three and ended up taking the belt from the man and beating him to near death. The man disappeared and no one asked about him again. After that, Andrew's mother was introduced to another man who took Andrew under his wing. Andrew learned to fight and be quiet—important attributes when you live on the street."

Amelia bit into her cake as her mind thought about Andrew and his mother. Jean shivered after swallowing her food. "He closed his heart and mind to feel nothing but survival. That scared a lot of people. But the other side of Andrew was loyalty. He always looked out for me growing up. I would like to return his kindness someday."

Amelia looked away from Jean and stood up uncomfortable with the conversation. "Andrew must have many sides to him. I am not sure that I know the man you describe."

Jean lifted her brow. "Perhaps he buries his past when he is with you—

waiting for a time to share the man behind the mask. Like I said, I am happy he has found you. His happiness means a great deal to me."

Amelia smoothed her dress and gave a guarded smile, not sure how to answer. She may not know the circumstances of their marriage.

"Jean, thank you for coming by today. If you will excuse me, I must attend to some duties. Should I see if Andrew is at home?"

Jean must have realized she was being politely dismissed. "I must go. I hope we can have tea again soon." Amelia smiled as she walked her to the door.

CHAPTER 12

THE NEXT FEW WEEKS FLEW by for Amelia as her life fell into a routine. Andrew spent most of his days building his empire, attending meetings, and making backroom deals. Most nights he came home late, often waking Amelia so they could make love. He was very passionate and enjoyed showering her with small gifts. Their conversations were brief due to the late hour and he was usually gone by morning. Amelia fulfilled her wifely duty while protecting her heart from any emotion.

She preferred to fill her days spending time with Beatrice, and the two became fast friends. One of their new favorite pastimes was going shopping. Andrew was generous with pin money allowing Amelia to buy anything she desired. Her favorite items were art supplies and books. She even took some art lessons from a local artist in town. Andrew assured she had guards with her always. She and Beatrice would often try to dodge them making it a game of wills on occasion. The guards did report some of the mischief to Andrew, but he chose not to confront her. The reports indicated that the two of them had become thick as thieves, often whispering to each other. Andrew wished he could spend more time with Amelia. A tug of jealousy at her new friendship went through him, but he quickly dismissed it.

The staff was leery of Beatrice. Amelia took her meals in her chamber so she could have Beatrice as company. Propriety would not allow them to eat together in the dining room. Beatrice was guarded with her mistress and protected her from the rest of the staff. Amelia had tested her trustworthiness over the last few weeks and she had proven to be a loyal friend. Ms. Haughton complained about Amelia to other servants in the kitchen often referring to her as the mundane mistress. They could not understand what Andrew saw in her as she was practically a child and a spoiled aristocrat. Beatrice would counter their attacks speaking of her husband's protectiveness and obvious devotion. After many groans and scowls from other kitchen maids, Beatrice put salt in the sugar bowls causing Andrew to send the tea cakes back with complaints.

On another occasion, Beatrice put a mouse in the stew pot giving Mrs. Haughton a huge scare early one morning. Her shenanigans did not end there. Beatrice got up early before the servants rose and rearranged all the spices taking the labels off causing a flurry in the kitchen. With every negative comment that was made about Amelia, a prank in the kitchen could be expected.

Amelia was kept constantly entertained with Beatrice around. She never met anyone with so many funny stories about her childhood. She wished they would have met under different circumstances when they were younger because she knew they would have been the best of friends. Beatrice grew up with seven siblings that were always jesting with one another. Her oldest sister married a doctor who had inherited a nice living. Beatrice was his mother's lady's maid before she died, giving her some experience before coming to Amelia's.

Amelia looked forward to Beatrice's birthday. She planned to take Beatrice to the dress shop in the city. She convinced a few of the guards in letting her go into Edinburgh instead of the local village. Andrew was out of town and couldn't deny her. The guards had tried to persuade her to put off the trip until Andrew could be consulted, but Amelia got her way.

She was so excited to give Beatrice her surprise when the day arrived. The carriage ride was rough and Amelia was thrown twice from her seat. Beatrice ended up sitting on the floor of the carriage. Both girls were looking forward to their day and tried not to complain about the muddy roads.

The seamstress recognized her and showed her the latest fashions and fine fabrics knowing that her husband owned a fortune. Amelia enjoyed looking at all the materials but was secretly looking for colors to match Beatrice's skin tone. The seamstress had a few pre-made dresses that only needed to be hemmed. One was a beautiful yellow color.

"Beatrice, what do you think of this yellow fabric?" Beatrice's eyes grew large as she touched the garment. "Oh, Mistress. You would glow in a dress this color."

Amelia looked coyly at her lady's maid. "True, but you would look better."

Beatrice shook her head. "I have never worn such fine material."

Amelia grabbed her hand. "I insist you try it on. It is my present for your birthday."

Beatrice's face turned red. "How did you know?"

Amelia giggled. "I have your references, you ninny. The agency gave me your date of birth." She made Beatrice change in the dress shop.

Amelia watched one of the guard's eyes when he saw Beatrice. She had noticed his interest in her and Beatrice's sly glances at his attention. Her heart pulled when he gave Beatrice a wild flower he picked from an open field earlier in the day.

Amelia made Beatrice wear the gown as they continued shopping. The guard, Alfred, kept close attention on Beatrice. He made sure to open all her doors and escorted her to each store. Amelia made excuses to leave them alone after a few hours of shopping. She went without a chaperone into the bonnet store leaving Beatrice to sit outside with Alfred. John and Aaron, the other guards stayed with the horses. Not trying to intrude on their privacy, Amelia found herself unable to resist peeking from the window. Alfred leaned against the side of the building shielding Beatrice from the patrons walking by on the sidewalk. He touched her face placing a stray piece of hair behind her ear. He smiled as he leaned down to whisper to her. Amelia saw Beatrice blush and smile back at him. Her heart ached to know what they were saying. She dreamed of romance. Suddenly thoughts of Andrew came into her head and she quickly dismissed them. Andrew was her husband, but their relationship was not based on a courtship. It was a business deal like most of his interactions and relationships. Amelia shivered thinking about their life together. Pulling herself away from the window, she finally chose a blue bonnet and paid the woman behind the table.

Beatrice broke away from Alfred when Amelia exited the store. "Are you finished, Mrs. Baird?"

Amelia smiled wanting to give them some more time together. "Not quite. I think I will go next door and look at some jewelry."

She winked at Beatrice who looked away from Alfred. "Should I accompany you?"

Amelia shook her head. "I think I can manage. If you could hold my bag and wait for me outside, I would be much obliged."

Amelia spoke to the store manager about some necklaces. After a while, she decided it was time to go. She told the man that she would bring her husband to see a few pieces of jewelry when he was back in town. The man thanked her and Amelia left the store empty-handed. It was getting later and Alfred suggested they head back before it got too dark. Amelia agreed and they walked to the carriage.

"Mrs. Baird?"

Amelia turned around to a familiar face. Unable to recognize the woman at first, she smiled at the greeting. "Yes, I am Mrs. Baird. Are we acquainted?" The woman's face was obscured by her bonnet.

The woman smiled. "From Jean's dinner party. I am Sophie."

Amelia's face went pale. Sophie was not painted the way she was at Jean's party. She hadn't recognized her at first. Not wanting to appear bothered, Amelia tried to hold her composure. "Oh yes. I do remember you now. I was just on my way. I hope you have a pleasant day." Amelia turned to board the carriage.

The woman stepped closer to her. "It's a pity you know."

Amelia turned to look at her. "Pardon me?"

She smirked coyly trying to patronize Amelia. "I said it's a pity that we met under unpleasant circumstances. We could have been great friends. After all, we do share the same taste in men and have much in common."

Amelia's eyes narrowed. "Indeed? I assure you that we have nothing in common."

Beatrice stood in front of Amelia while she stepped into the carriage. Beatrice dropped her smile and brought her chin up looking at Sophie. "I know your kind. And you're correct, it is a pity."

Sophie looked at Beatrice. "Pardon?"

Beatrice smiled again. "I said it's a pity if something happened to you due to your ill-mannered words. Mrs. Baird may be genteel bred, but I am not."

Sophie smiled at Beatrice and walked away. Beatrice climbed in the carriage with Alfred's help. He whispered to her, "Remind me not to ever make you mad."

Beatrice winked at him and took the seat opposite of Amelia. She hugged her friend. "Thank you. Who needs a guard when I have you?" They both let out a laugh. They giggled in the carriage all the way home.

The next day they went into the local village to buy some sweets as an afternoon treat. They took a seat at a table near the cobblestone sidewalk.

The guards were on the other side of the street conversing with each other keeping an eye on the women. "How are you and Alfred?" Amelia smiled taking a bite of her apple tart.

Beatrice looked over at him and wrinkled her nose. "He is always staring at me. I haven't kissed him yet."

Amelia let out a chuckle. "I think he is in love."

Beatrice looked over at the guards. "He is one of your guards and doesn't want to lose his position. Do you think Mr. Baird would mind our relationship?"

Amelia shrugged. "I don't think my husband pays attention. Alfred is smitten. The question is if you are interested in him?"

Her face turned red. "He is handsome, gentle, and kind."

Amelia smiled hoping to help the two. She lifted her shoulders giddy with excitement. "He could be your match. You must spend more time with him."

A deep voice came up beside them. "Who must she spend more time with?" Both girls jumped looking up to see Andrew cracking a smile. Another man she did not recognize stood behind him.

He chuckled. "Did I frighten you?"

Amelia was shocked to see him in town. She shook her head. "Just surprised is all."

Andrew sat beside her and kissed her on the cheek. "The staff told me you were probably in the village. I have wonderful news and didn't want to wait. May I introduce my brother Ian? He came to visit."

Amelia looked up at the large man who held out his hand. She took it and he kissed her knuckles. "So glad to meet my new sister."

She smiled. "I am honored to meet you, sir." His eyes held familiarity and reminded her of his brother.

"Sir? Oh no, please call me Ian."

She nodded. "Of course, and please call me Amelia."

He took a seat opposite of the couple next to Beatrice. "Are you going to finish those tarts?" He eyed the pastries.

Amelia pushed them toward him. "Help yourself."

He took the tarts and winked at her.

She laughed at his expression as he ate.

It was a flirtatious laugh in Andrew's opinion. He watched their exchange. His wife seemed more at ease with his brother than she did with him. Andrew cleared his throat watching his brother evaluate his wife. "He is only staying a few days. Ian could never settle anywhere more than that. My brother is a wanderer."

Ian laughed looking at Amelia. "I am not a wanderer. Just looking for a reason to settle down. It looks like my brother has found one. You are even lovelier than he described. He is a lucky man."

Amelia blushed at his compliment. She looked over at Andrew who was scowling at Ian. "Will you be staying for dinner?"

Andrew nodded. "Yes, I thought a family dinner would be nice. I will invite Jean and her husband, Greg. Brian can bring Julia."

Amelia looked surprised by the mention of Brian having a partner. "Julia?" she questioned.

"Yes, a local woman he sees on occasion. Her brother is one of my solicitors and I introduced them last year. She is widowed."

Ian snorted. "That sounds grand. To be surrounded by a bunch of couples. Can you have Jean bring one of her girls?"

Andrew shook his head with amusement. "It's a proper dinner with my wife. We can go to the Tree Lounge afterward."

Amelia looked away as she lost her smile. "We should go so I can alert the staff about the dinner." She looked back at Andrew. "If you will excuse us?"

Andrew stood. "I will escort you back."

Ian stood and held out his arm for Amelia. "Allow me, brother. I want to get to know my new sister."

Andrew sighed but knew his brother meant well. He is probably the only man on earth who he would allow to slight him and escort Amelia home.

CHAPTER 13

THE SERVANTS PARADED A FEAST for the impromptu dinner party. Andrew sat at the head of the table with Greg on one side and Amelia on the other. Ian sat next to Amelia whispering jests into her ear. Amelia chuckled and whispered back a few times laughing. Andrew narrowed his eyes annoyed at their childish behavior. His other guests tried to capture his attention by speaking of a new factory, but he found it difficult to concentrate as his attention was pulled toward his brother and his wife.

His jaw flexed in frustration. "Ian?" He said sharply to get his attention off his wife and to acknowledge the other dinner guests.

Ian looked at Andrew innocently. "Yes, brother?" He grinned back at Amelia as though they shared a secret.

It infuriated him.

Andrew took a drink of water studying them both. Tension rang throughout the dining room. He tried to calm himself as his jealousy consumed him. "Tell us about your plans."

Ian smiled sarcastically enjoying his brother's discomfort. "Of course, brother. My plans are to live off your generosity for the next few days and then go to London. I hear London women are something to see and I may need to check it out for myself." He winked at Amelia.

Turning his attention back to his brother, he leaned back in his chair. "I do have a few friends I want to visit. Which reminds me—may I stay in your London residence?"

Andrew rolled his eyes. "I will let you stay, but I have some work for you to do while you are there. I won't have you living there for free."

Ian laughed out loud. "Of course, Andy." Ian turned to Jean and started asking her about the Tree Lounge. The guests began to speak as the tension in the room faded and they moved on to more pleasant topics.

Andrew took a bite of his chicken not looking at Amelia. He was angry at her banter with his brother. She was his wife and he would not allow that type of behavior. It was rude to him and his guests. Furthermore, why was it so easy for his brother to make her smile? She enjoyed Ian's company more than she ever did his. He had never seen her so relaxed and happy.

After dinner, Ian suggested they play charades. Andrew excused himself and took Brian and Greg into the other room. He would not play a child's game. It surprised him that Ian played with the women. Ian was at Amelia's side and Andrew could hear them laughing from the study. After his conversations with the men, he joined the others. He was unable to sit by his wife because Ian sat beside her on the settee. They were in whispered conversations as they played their turns. Jean approached Andrew as she excused herself from the game.

"Are you well?" she whispered as her brow creased with concern. They walked to the other side of the room toward the fireplace unnoticed by the group.

"Of course." His mouth formed a straight line. Jean touched his arm. "Stop it. I know you better than you think. You're upset."

He sighed. "Why is it so easy for Ian to make her happy?" He looked away trying to mask his emotions. Andrew hated looking weak in front of anyone. To his business associates and everyone else, he was powerful and feared. With his wife, he was anything but.

Jean shook her head. "Andrew, I think you are too hard on yourself. She is very young and is in a world that is hard to understand. Ian is immature and she relates to his childish side. They mean no harm to you. She will favor your strength when she needs to. You will be her protector and the father of her children. She will learn to care for you in time."

He looked at Jean whispering through his teeth. "I don't like it."

She took a drink of her wine. "It's harmless. All you will do is push her away if you insist on being a brute."

He shrugged his shoulders. "If I had my wish, I would steal her away from the world and keep her all to myself." He walked away and poured another drink. The couples stopped their game and claimed fatigue as they left the party. Andrew said good night to all his guests and escorted Amelia up to bed.

The next day Andrew organized a picnic for his friends. He hoped to interest Amelia in some activities to show her a different side of him—he was not all business and could have fun. He decided they would go riding and eat a picnic by the lake. The men wanted to do some rowboat races, and Ian was like a little kid challenging any of them to race.

The group mounted the horses and Andrew helped Amelia onto her sidesaddle. Brian had brought Julia, and a few of the guards came with them. Amelia dressed in a dark orange gown that brought color to her cheeks. Andrew could smell her floral scent. He stayed near her as they rode on the property near the lake.

Most of the men organized the boats to compete in the races. Andrew took a seat beside Amelia on the blanket. She cheered for Ian and Andrew joined her as the tension of the race proved to be competitive.

She smiled. "Are you racing today?"

He laughed. "I prefer to watch with you." He took her hand and held it as they watched the race.

Brian and Ian were the finalists, and both were disqualified for rocking the boats and wrestling each other into the water. They both came to shore dripping from the fall into the lake.

"He cheated," Brian yelled, trying not to laugh.

Ian patted Brian on the back. "It's not a problem, old man. We can call it even."

Brian picked Ian up. "I will show you an old man." Ian laughed as Brian put him back down. Amelia seemed to enjoy the teasing and the mood of the atmosphere. Everyone was having an enjoyable time. A few servants served chicken, cheese, bread, and fruit.

Andrew kept her close to his side for the rest of the afternoon not wanting to share her with his brother. Even if their acquaintance was harmless, he wanted to keep him at bay. As the afternoon dwindled to evening, the group went back to the house and Ian left to go out to Tree Lounge with some of the guards. Andrew stayed with Amelia ordering a tray for dinner to their room.

"Tell me, my dear. Did you enjoy yourself today?" Andrew loosened his shirt removing it and stayed in his breeches. Amelia looked away not wanting him to know that she was watching him. She turned toward her wardrobe looking for a nightdress. "It was fun to be outdoors for a change." She went behind her dressing screen, uncomfortable to change in front of him. He smiled at her shyness.

She came out from behind the screen and saw him lying on the bed. He had a bowl of fruit and two glasses of wine. He handed one to her and she took it sitting on the chair and not the bed.

He tilted his head. "Amelia, join me on the bed." She hesitated but obeyed.

"Do you think Ian would like to go to the art museum? He said he likes paintings." She took a bite of fruit.

Annoyed that she would bring up Ian, he shrugged his shoulders. "Probably not. I have never known him to like art. He said he liked paintings because you paint. If you want to go to the art museum, then I will take you."

She wrinkled her brow. "I didn't think you would want to go."

He took a drink of wine. "If it pleases you, then I will not deny you a trip there."

She shrugged her shoulders. "I just thought we could do something with Ian being that he is our guest. You both seem so different from each other."

Andrew studied her face, growing weary of the conversation. "We are *very* different. I always protected Ian, and was forced to provide for us when I got older. He seems carefree because he never had any responsibilities."

Amelia shook her head. "He just likes to have fun and people like being around him."

He snorted. "It may seem like he is fun to you, but he is irresponsible, impulsive, and rash. Honestly, is that what you want? Someone that floats through life?"

She rolled her eyes. "That is ridiculous. I was only trying to be nice and take your brother to the art museum."

He took her hand. "Amelia, don't you know that I would do anything to make you happy?"

She looked down at their hands. "I don't know what to say."

Andrew let go of her hand, upset from her fascination with his little brother. "I will be in my study." He grabbed his robe and went down the stairs.

Andrew kept Ian busy the next few days carefully keeping him away from Amelia. She withdrew to her room spending time with Beatrice. After a few days, Ian said his goodbyes to go to London. Andrew announced that he would be leaving as well for at least a week or two to attend to some business out of town. Amelia never asked questions on his whereabouts, she gave no reaction to his departure.

He insisted on having dinner with her the night before he left. Determined to please her, he tried to gauge her attention. "Amelia, I asked the cook to make apple tarts for dessert. You seem to favor them."

Amelia smiled briefly. "Thank you." She offered no other words, looking down at her plate and shoving her food around.

Andrew tried again to get her to converse with him. "I thought we could take a wedding trip when I return. Just the two of us. I was overly busy when we returned from London and would like to rectify that."

Amelia looked up eagerly. "Can we go back to London?"

Andrew was leery of her question. After all, Ian was on his way to London. He raised his brow. "London? No, I thought maybe Ireland or other parts of Scotland. We could even sail somewhere if you wish. We could stay along the coast and enjoy the sea air."

Amelia's face fell. She took in a deep breath. "I don't think a wedding trip is necessary. We have already been married over two months."

He was angered by her rejection and chose to remain quiet. Bitterness, combined with antipathy fueled his anger, making the rest of the evening intolerable. They ate in silence.

After dinner, Amelia excused herself to her room and he went to his study. Later in the evening he left to go to one of his clubs leaving her to sleep alone.

The next morning Andrew awoke to an empty bed. He was annoyed Amelia was not there to say goodbye. He dressed quickly and gathered his men to finish packing the carriages. He excused himself to go find her.

She was painting in the field by the lake. He thought she looked beautiful sitting under a tree with the sun streaming through her hair that was loose along her back. His body ached for her.

"Amelia, I was looking for you. We are ready to leave." He got off his horse and walked to her. Her maid walked away carefully looking the other way to give them privacy.

Amelia turned from her painting with a guarded smile. "I wish you a safe trip."

He took her hand and pulled her up off the ground. "I will miss you."

She tensed at his words. He felt her resistance and pulled her closer to him. He took his hands and wrapped them around her waist and placed his forehead on top of hers. "Please say you will miss me."

She closed her eyes unable to say anything. He sensed her hesitation and chose to kiss her instead. He pulled back and cupped her face. "If you only knew the thoughts I have of you." He smiled and kissed her again on the forehead. "I will be back in a week or two."

She nodded. "Goodbye, Andrew." She sat back down and started painting.

CHAPTER 14

THE BUTLER MR. CHARLES CAME back to work a few days after Andrew left. He was an older gentleman with good manners and took an immediate liking to Amelia. She admired his direction with the staff members. He was the only one who could control Mrs. Haughton. Beatrice's antics ceased at his return causing some order to come back to the kitchen and mealtime. The staff respected his orders, and it made Amelia's job easier. The staff had resented her, but now she had a partner.

Mr. Charles was amusing, often teasing her in a good-natured way. He helped her hang her paintings and organized workers to hang new tapestries that she chose. She enjoyed her new freedom in her own home and worked hard redecorating parts of the house. Mr. Charles helped her plan menus and even baked apple tarts with her despite Mrs. Haughton's silent protests.

Mr. Charles often went to the library in the evening. He agreed to play chess with Amelia at her insistence. He thought it was improper, but when the rest of the staff had retired for the evening, Amelia would sometimes find him in the library and they would play a game of chess.

"Mrs. Baird, I believe you are letting me win." He smiled as he won again. Amelia scowled at him. "Nonsense. I never let anyone win. I want you to teach me your secret."

He grunted. "Then it wouldn't be a secret." The old man chuckled. "Oh, Mrs. Baird, you do make an old man smile. Your problem is that you wear your emotions on your face. I know the move you are going to make. A lot of chess is studying your opponent. You are easy to read, Mrs. Baird."

She smiled back. "Nonsense. It's part of my strategy to make you think that is the move I am going to make. Perhaps I will let you win for our real game tomorrow evening."

Mr. Charles shook his head. "You do have some wit. Mr. Baird is lucky to have you. You're not only beautiful but a challenge."

He took a drink of his tea and started cleaning up the pieces of the chessboard. He glanced up at Amelia. "I have known him for years, and you are the only woman that I ever met that he took a fancy to. I know he has had woman acquaintances before, but not one he wanted to marry. I can see how he surrendered to your charms, Mrs. Baird. Forgive me if I have spoken too frankly. I heard a rumor that he is very tolerable since he met you."

Amelia smirked unsure what to say about his kind words. "Honestly, Mr. Charles, it's no secret how we married. I can hardly take credit for anything Andrew does." Wanting to change the subject, she took a deep breath. "Tell me again how you came to work for my husband. You're so different than the other staff."

He nodded. "I worked for a family in London. Most of the children were grown and married. The man was a viscount and borrowed a lot of money from Mr. Baird. When he couldn't pay, he collected the collateral. Many of the staff members lost their jobs and I was on my way out. Mr. Baird spoke to me at the residence before he sold it and offered me a job at his own residence in London. After a few years, he thought I did an excellent job and made me the head butler at his main residence in Edinburgh. He is a fair employer and pays well. He is feared by a lot of people and has a ruthless reputation, but I find him honest and generous. He helped me out financially when my mother took ill."

She thought about the kind words regarding Andrew which was not a common occurrence. "I am happy he could assist you and that you work for him." She stood up from her chair to put the chessboard away. "In fact, I believe it was probably his smartest decision."

The butler shook his head. "No, my dear. The smartest decision was marrying you."

Amelia blushed. "Oh my. You are a flirt, Mr. Charles." He laughed and stood up escorting her out of the library to go up the stairs.

Amelia was painting outside early the next morning. She jerked her head with a light panic as Andrew kissed her neck. He laughed at her shock. "You're in the same place that I left you a few weeks ago."

Amelia relaxed and looked at him. "Didn't you know that I sleep here when you are out of town?"

He enjoyed her banter and kneeled beside her. "I have a surprise for you. I want to take you to a special place."

She shivered as the wind blew colder. "Today?"

Andrew took her arm and pulled her up from her blanket. "Yes, today. We will pack some blankets and a basket of food. It may be cold so dress warmly."

Amelia crinkled her nose. "Where is it?"

Andrew shook his head. "It's a surprise, so my lips are sealed. We must be on our way we are losing light. Hurry."

Amelia went upstairs and dressed warmly for her outing with Andrew. He had arranged for a carriage for just the two of them. Only one guard drove them and two guards would follow far behind them in a separate carriage for protection. He wanted their outing to be as normal as possible. He waited for her downstairs and assisted her into the carriage.

The drive to Edinburgh was long and a bit bumpy. Andrew entertained her with conversation and with wine, cheese, and some small cakes. "Do you enjoy music? I don't know if I ever asked you that or not."

Amelia nodded taking her attention away from the window and turned back to Andrew. "I do enjoy music. When I went to school, I took piano lessons and we would dance on weekends in our rooms."

Andrew smiled. "I must admit that I don't dance often, but I did learn to from some old acquaintances. Not quite the ballroom dancing that you would be accustomed too, but I learned those dances as well. I thought it would be good for my image." He lifted the corner of his mouth.

Amelia laughed out loud. "Oh yes, A moneylender must learn to ballroom dance."

Andrew kept a smile on his face. "Is that what you think I do for a living? Lend money?"

The smile faded from her face. "I thought… I mean, people owe you money. I do hear things. I guess I don't know what you do for your business. What would you expect me to say?"

Andrew studied her face. "I don't think anyone who knows us would ask you that question. Just tell them I am a businessman."

Amelia looked away out the window again. "Did you want to give me a hint of where we may be going?"

Andrew scooted over closer to Amelia and tickled her. "You are impossible in keeping patient." Amelia squirmed at his tickling and started to giggle as he held her in his arms. "I love to hear you laugh." He cupped her face and kissed her on the mouth. "You are so beautiful to me."

She batted her eyes. "You do like to tease me, Mr. Baird."

The carriage slowed and Andrew looked out the window. He turned to Amelia. "We are here. I will have to hide your eyes." He took a piece of cloth to put over her eyes.

Amelia took her head back. "My eyes? How will I walk?"

Andrew smirked. "You have to trust me. I will not let you fall."

Andrew led Amelia up a hill and she could hear the ocean roaring onto the beach. She could taste the salted sea air and it smelled like fish. Andrew held her arms, slowly guiding her into a building and up a spiral staircase to the top floor. They entered inside a door and Andrew took the cloth off. Amelia opened her eyes and saw a view of the ocean from a tower. It was the most beautiful picturesque view she had ever seen.

She looked at Andrew. "Oh, Andrew. This is beautiful. Are we in a tower with windows on all sides?"

Andrew smiled at her. "It's a lighthouse. It helps navigate ships with a beacon of light. I own it now and the land it sits on. I thought you could paint in this room."

Her heart beat rapidly in her chest. She looked around the small room and there was a desk, table, and small bed. Plenty of room to paint. The windows showed three different views of the ocean—a magnificent sight. "I don't know what to say. You surprise me sometimes, Andrew."

He came up behind her and put his arms around her waist. "I only want to make you happy, Amelia. I just wish you would let me."

Her resistance was melting. No one had ever done such a nice gesture in her life. Turning around, she looked at him in the face. "I am without words. I would love to paint in this room." She stepped away from him looking out a different window. "I feel like I am in the middle of the world up here."

He smiled and took out the wine, pouring her a glass. "Let's make a toast to happiness." She took the wine and toasted with him. After they drank, he took their glasses and put them to the side. Gathering her into his arms, he kissed her gently. She responded without pulling away, welcoming his touch, she wrapped her arms around his neck. He carried her to the small bed in the back of the lighthouse. Taking his time, he kissed her, lightly caressing her back. He slowly unlaced her gown, taking off her dress and laying her down beside him. They made love the next few hours as her body betrayed her enjoying his touch. Loathing him was turning to longing.

She found herself having feelings for him. "Andrew?"

He ran his finger gently down her arm. "Yes, love."

Searching his face, she took a moment to answer. "Thank you."

He reached over and kissed her. "I would deny you nothing if you would let me."

The ride back was full of contentment. There were few words spoken, but Amelia laid on his arm and fell asleep. He carried her up to their room and held her the rest of the night. The next morning, he woke her apologizing, but he had been pulled away for a few weeks, but promised to stay longer when he returned.

CHAPTER 15

AMELIA SPENT THE NEXT FEW days painting inside as the weather was dreadful. Andrew was away on business again, unsure when he could return. A part of her missed him although it was hard for her to admit. To keep herself from going stir-crazy, she went into the village and worked with her art teacher.

Beatrice and Alfred were getting closer. Amelia insisted they spend more time together giving Beatrice a Saturday night off. As much as she enjoyed her company, she knew the couple needed time together too.

After helping Beatrice dress, Amelia found herself alone. It had been a while since she didn't have Beatrice to spend time with. She felt lonely and decided to go to the library. Perhaps Mr. Charles would be up for a game of chess or she could at least find a book to read to pass the time. She was excited for Beatrice to come home so she could tell her about her time with Alfred.

Entering the library, she realized it was empty, Mr. Charles must still be working. She lit a candle to help move around the room. The books were a little unorganized and it took her some digging to find something to read. A movement by the side of the desk startled her. She held the candle out toward the desk and gasped as someone grabbed her from behind.

"Shh! It's me. Don't scream." Amelia recognized the voice immediately and quickly turned toward him. The heat of his body radiated against her, and she could smell a musky outdoor scent. She nearly lost her balance. "Billy? What are you doing here? Are you mad?" Amelia was astonished to see him.

He touched her face. "Do you have any idea what I have been through to find you? Is that any way to greet me?" He took the candle from her hand

and placed it on the desk. He embraced her, squeezing tightly. "I told you I would find you if you ever left me."

Closing her eyes, she breathed him in. She didn't let go of him and felt the tears burn in her eyes. He rubbed her back, and she trembled while a sob escaped. "I can't believe you are here."

He cupped her face. "Sally told me about your last visit. Forgive me for not being there to help you." He let her go and walked around the library touching some of the paintings and admiring the furniture.

He whistled. "I heard you married well but had no idea how well. Your husband must have a fortune." He stepped toward her and touched her face. "Does he treat you well? Sally told me you had no choice and was forced to marry him."

Amelia looked away and glanced toward the door. She hoped Mr. Charles would not interrupt them. "My father made the arrangements. He needed the money. I accepted it and did what I had to do for my family." That wasn't exactly the truth. Her feelings for Andrew were changing. It may have started out that way, but he was proving not to be cold and heartless.

He looked at her and ran his fingers over his stubbled chin showing a day or two of growth. "Do you want to be with him?"

Amelia looked down, unsure how she felt about Andrew. She whispered. "I hardly know."

He sat on top of the desk and raised his brow with a half-smile. "Do you think about me?"

Amelia felt herself swallow. "It doesn't matter. I am married now."

He took her hand and kissed it. "Amelia, it does matter. I love you."

She stared at him in disbelief. "Love?" No one had ever told her that.

He stood up from the desk. "Yes, I traveled all the way to Scotland to tell you that."

She turned away from him and walked toward the bookcase. He came up behind her leaning toward her ear. He whispered, "I also may have found your mother."

Amelia widened her eyes and she turned around to face him. "What? Are you serious?"

Those words took her breath away. Billy was the only one she told her secret too. She felt her mother was still alive and may be using a stage name. He had promised to find the truth for her.

He rubbed his lips together staring at her with excitement in his eyes. "Yes! A friend of mine thinks he knows her. Come away with me, and I will show you."

She gasped. "I can't run away with you. Are you mad?"

He smiled and kissed her cheek. "No, not mad. Just in love with you." He reached for her hands and held them up to his mouth kissing her knuckles. "I want you with me. We can have a good life together if you will give me a chance. Now, come on love, grab what you can, especially anything we can sell."

He released her hands and looked around the room for any valuables and opened the drawers in the desk. "I met a few friends on my way here that will help us take a boat to France. Where does your husband keep the cash?"

Lost in thought of her mother she didn't hear him for a few seconds. He asked her again for some cash, looking up at her and expecting an answer.

She looked up at him. "I have some pin money in my room. I don't know where he keeps his cash."

Billy walked over to her and pulled her waist against him. He leaned down touching her chin, brushing his lips against hers. She returned his kiss, familiar with his touch. She put her forehead against his. "You found my mother for me?"

He whispered in her ear. "I told you I would find her for you and I did."

Amelia's head was spinning as her eyes burned with tears at the possibility of finding her mother. Could it be possible that he really found her? Thinking about his offer and her situation made her chest feel heavy. She looked over towards the library door and eyed Andrew's coat on the hook. It reminded her of her husband and she hesitated, knowing she couldn't do it. She looked at Billy. "Wait! I can't go with you. I am married, Billy. It wasn't my choice, but I am still married. My husband is dangerous and will come after us. They call him Black Baird because of his reputation. I can't let anything happen to you."

Billy snorted, amused at her worry. "Amelia, I am not scared of your husband." He puffed out his chest. "He took what was going to be mine. I should be the one mad." He leaned over and gave her a quick peck on the lips. "Look, we don't have much time. The boat is leaving in the morning.

We can talk about your husband later." He took her arm. "Who knows, maybe he will annul the marriage once you are gone."

Amelia pulled back. "I don't know, Billy. I am frightened to leave with you."

He snapped at her in frustration. "I am leaving tonight with or without you Amelia. If you want to find your mother, then you will come. Hurry."

Amelia couldn't think straight. Billy charmed her from their very first meeting trying to woo her. She knew his adventures and stories might be a bit exaggerated, but he was the first boy she had ever kissed. Sally called him a small-town ruffian. But she fell for him all the same. Her heart was torn, but the desire to find her mother won the battle within her and she would take her chances. Besides, she couldn't bear the thought of him leaving and her never knowing if her mother was alive.

She bit her bottom lip. "Fine. I will be just one minute while I pack a bag." They heard the front doors open and Amelia gasped backing back into the library. "The guards are back inside. We can't get to my room right now. You will have to go without me, and I can meet you later."

Billy took her hand. "I won't leave you. We don't have time for you to get your stuff. But we can sell your wedding ring. That will help us once we get to France. Let's get out of here." Amelia took his hand and followed him out the side door from the library. They ran toward the bushes and away from the house.

Mrs. Haughton stood outside the cracked library doors. She was coming to get Amelia regarding the message she had received earlier—Andrew was on his way home and would arrive within a few hours. He had requested dinner with his wife. She smiled as she heard the whole conversation and witnessed the young couple's reunion. She went expediently to the guards to let them know of Amelia's betrayal and deception.

Bull was with the guards when Mrs. Haughton spoke of Amelia's departure. He called for all the guards to come to the entrance of the house. Within twenty minutes, fifteen men were waiting for orders. Mrs. Haughton told them that the couple was headed to France by boat. Bull sent the men to the docks to find Amelia and the man she left with.

Andrew arrived home a few hours later. He was surprised to find Bull waiting for him by the door when he entered the home. Bull's face looked grave and he struggled with his words. "Sir, there has been some disturbing news, and I must speak with you at once."

Andrew walked past him and looked around the house barely listening. "In a moment, Bull. I want to speak to Amelia first. I will meet you after dinner." Andrew walked up the stairs.

Bull shook his head. "Forgive me. It's about Mrs. Baird."

Andrew stopped climbing the stairs and slowly turned around. "What did you say?"

The front door opened and two guards walked in. Andrew looked around at the guards who entered the room noticing their sober expressions. "Would someone tell me what is going on? Where is my wife?" He walked back down the stairs.

Bull looked down unable to meet Andrew glare. "She is gone, sir. I have my best men looking for her." Bull looked up and watched Andrew's face turn red.

"What do you mean she is gone? Where did she go?" The vein in his temple began to throb with his anger.

Brian walked into the room and stepped between them. "Bull, tell us what happened from the beginning."

Bull nodded. "Mrs. Haughton came to us a few hours ago and heard Amelia speaking with a man in the library. They were making plans to leave Scotland. She heard them leave out the side door and came to tell us right away."

Andrew felt his world darken. "A man?" His rage consumed him as it built up in his chest. "She was with a man?"

Brian touched his shoulder. "Andrew, we need to find out the explanation. There could be a good reason why she left."

He glared at Brian. "Bull, bring Mrs. Haughton to me immediately." Bull left to find Mrs. Haughton.

Andrew paced in the drawing room as Mrs. Haughton entered. "Mrs. Haughton, please sit down and tell us the exact story of what you heard in the library."

Mrs. Haughton took a seat and lifted her chin. "Well, I was on my way to the library to tell Mrs. Baird about the message you sent regarding your early arrival. That's when I heard voices. I thought it peculiar and stood outside the library doors trying not to interrupt when I saw a young man embrace Mrs. Baird. You can imagine my surprise."

Andrew choked on his drink and coughed at his shock. He motioned with his hand for her to continue. She looked at Brian who nodded his head. She cleared her throat. "I heard him say that he came back for her. She was upset he had waited so long. That's when I saw him kiss her and told her that he would take her to France. I nearly lost my balance trying to hide behind the door. However, I continued to listen and he mentioned that she could cash in her wedding ring. She kissed him back and they left out the side doors. I knew that girl was trouble."

Andrew's breathing became rapid, and he walked to the wall punching a hole through it. His fist drew blood and Mrs. Haughton shrieked. Brian escorted her out of the drawing room and closed the door behind her. "Andrew, Bull has men looking for her down by the docks. We will find her."

Andrew knocked a vase off the side table and grabbed the linen tablecloth wrapping his hand with it. He bit back a retort and walked to the door. "I will be in my study. Bring me Amelia's maid. I want a full report of the men's findings within the hour."

CHAPTER 16

AMELIA'S MIND WAS RACING AS they took an unmarked carriage to the docks. Billy introduced her to his friend Adam who drove the carriage. He kept his eyes out the window making sure they were not followed but held on to her hand.

"Adam knows the truth, but we will have to tell others that we are married. That way we can share a cabin."

Amelia's nerves caused her hands to dampen. Billy was a bit reckless and she started having doubts about his ability to tell her the truth. She closed her eyes trying to relax. Andrew was not due back for a few more days. The thought of her husband dug into her chest. Betrayal was a complex emotion. She assured herself that he wouldn't be able to find her. A small part of her felt cowardly for leaving without saying goodbye or leaving a note.

She looked down at her dress. "I may need some essentials for our journey. I left with no clothing."

He eyed her body with his eyes. "I like you better without clothing." He laughed at the look on her face. "I am just teasing you. I will send Adam to retrieve something from his friend's house. He has a wife and can probably find you something."

Amelia looked away blushing. There hadn't been time to plan their escape and the desire in his eyes gave her room for pause. She was not sure what he would expect from her. Her only thoughts were about finding her mother. He rubbed her hands. "Amelia, forgive me for not rescuing you sooner. Was he terrible to you?"

She shook her head ignoring the tension in her body. "Not terrible. He was gentle with me. But he could be a tyrant to other people. He wanted his way at any cost." She didn't want to speak of him.

He kissed her head. "I know this is hard for you. You can trust me. When Sally told me you were married, I knew it was because I was not there to take you with me."

The carriage slowed and finally stopped. The doors opened and Adam told them to hurry. Billy escorted her through the back alley to a brown door. He opened it and it led to a staircase. Amelia could hear muffled music in the front of the building. They went upstairs to an office where two rough men sat behind a desk. "Billy, you're late." They looked at Amelia. "Is she the one you told us about?"

Billy nodded taking Amelia's hand. "Yes, this is my wife. We will be taking the boat in the morning. Charlie said we could sleep in the storage room. I have my stuff ready to go. You will be paid once we get to York."

The older man looked at Amelia and stroked his beard. "It will be rough traveling. You best get some rest. Just make sure I get paid."

Billy nodded and left the room. He showed her the storage room with blankets on the floor. Amelia hesitated as she watched Billy spread the blankets out for her. Adam knocked on the door and handed him a sack of food. "I will go ask Travis for some extra clothes for her." Billy thanked his friend, closing the door so they could be alone. He sat on the floor and patted the blanket beside him. Amelia sat down, unsure of how to act around him.

"Relax, don't you trust me?" He rubbed her hands taking them to his mouth to kiss. "I have waited a long time for you, Amelia."

Amelia's heart beat faster thinking of his intentions. "When did your friend see my mother last?"

He ignored her question and kissed her neck rubbing her arm. "Kiss me." She tensed her body. "Do you think he really saw her?"

He sighed in frustration and looked in her eyes. "Yes, I do. He said Dorothy Tress was using a stage name and working in France at a small theatre company. She was connected to your father at one time and fits the description." He pulled her against his chest. "Now, relax."

Another knock on the door interrupted them. Billy groaned annoyed at the distractions. He stood and answered the door seeing Adam again. "What?"

Adam stepped inside. "There are some rough men downstairs asking for a Mrs. Baird. Amelia Baird." He looked pass Billy to Amelia and his face grew pale. "Please tell me your husband is not Andrew Baird."

She looked down at the floor. "Yes, my husband is Andrew Baird."

His eyes widened. "Are you mad, Billy? You told me her name was Miss Abbott! You never told me the chit was married to Andrew Baird. Do you know what he will do to you? Do you know what he will do to me for helping you? We are dead men."

"I am not afraid of anyone," Billy growled at Adam.

Adam put up his hands. "I want no part in this. I am out of here." Adam looked down at Amelia. "You have no idea what you have done. You can get people killed. Is that what you want?"

Amelia's mouth fell open, not meaning anyone harm. Billy shoved Adam out the door and slammed it. He reached for Amelia. "We don't need him. Let's get out of here before he tells anyone where we are. I will find another way for us out of Scotland."

Amelia was shaking as she took his hand. They snuck down the back staircase and Amelia followed Billy out the door around the side of the building. He turned around. "I need to get us a horse and supplies. My business deal did not come through here, so we will need some money. Give me your wedding ring. I will find a way to sell it and come back for you."

She enlarged her eyes. "Where am I to stay to wait for you?"

He looked around the buildings and walked her down the street staying near the shadows. They came across some stables and there were a few carriages inside. He lifted her up to hide in one of the carriages and touched her face. "Don't fret, I will be back soon. You will be fine for a few hours. Now give me your ring, Love."

Amelia's shook her head "I can't. He would kill me." Her heart hurt to part with her wedding ring.

Billy took her hand. "Amelia, we have no choice. Trust me, you won't need it." He slid the ring off her finger cupping the ring in his hand.

A twinge of sadness overcame her. Andrew had given her a beautiful ring. Reluctantly, she looked at her bare finger, rubbing where the ring had been. She looked up at Billy. "Please hurry."

Billy nodded and took off down the street. She sat back down in the carriage covering her nose. It smelled of dirty clothes and the cushions were torn. She hoped that no one saw her come inside.

Time went by slowly as she waited for Billy's return. The quietness gave her time to reflect on her impulsive choices. Her thoughts turned to Andrew. Admittedly, he was not exactly the blackguard she had once thought. But what will happen when he finds out? Coming to terms with her decision, she drifted off to sleep and awoke to complete darkness. It took her a minute of panic to realize where she was. How long had she been asleep? Quickly, she opened the carriage door and climbed out thinking it must have been over a few hours by now. Where was Billy? She walked near the stable door and peeked outside. She saw no one. The dryness of the air made her thirsty. After a few moments debating with herself, she walked outside and snuck around the corner. A couple of people were walking by and she hid next to the stable. No one saw her.

After a few moments of silence, she ventured out near the tavern. Hoping there might be some water to drink, she walked to the back door peeking inside. Perhaps she could sneak into the back and look for something to drink. She had no money to buy anything. The tavern had patrons standing by the kitchen. Amelia took a step back into the shadows outside the door waiting for the opportunity to get some water.

Andrew seethed inside as his heart shattered. His hand was swollen from hitting things, but the hurt fed his anger. Thoughts of his childhood crept through his mind. Rejection was not new to him. Pushing the thoughts deep down inside, he remembered his mother disappearing days at a time and him looking for her in every broken-down establishment he came across. Finally finding her in a compromising position or with unsavory characters. He would beg her to come home. She had tried to be a good mother. But her addictions made it difficult. Her actions taught him to numb his heart and have no emotion toward anyone, especially women. Affection in his opinion was for weak-minded people.

His thoughts turned to Amelia. Remembering the first day he saw her and her laughing with the children playing games. Her natural beauty tore a hole in the ice he had built around himself. He earned the name Black Baird—but with her—he wanted to be a husband. To feel something he never experienced. He was in love with her. Now all he felt was anger at her betrayal. A rage inside him that he could not control.

Brian entered his study anxious to speak about his findings. "Andrew, we have some news. Her lady's maid came back to the house with Alfred. Apparently, they were together tonight and Mrs. Baird gave her the night off. She claims to know nothing. But we will send her in to speak with you. The men did find another man who may know of her whereabouts. Apparently, the man she ran away with had an accomplice only he didn't know she was your wife. Once he found out, he dumped the two of them and came to tell us everything. He is a petty criminal that hangs out at the docks. An Adam Reynolds. He wishes to speak to you."

Andrew's jaw flexed as he clamped down to grind his teeth. "Send him in."

Brian nodded. "As you wish." He motioned to the guards and they walked behind him. Andrew dismissed them all except for Bull and Brian. They stayed as a sign of force.

Adam entered with his head down. Andrew spoke through his teeth. "Take a seat, Mr. Reynolds."

Adam nervously sat down in the chair unsure of his surroundings. Andrew's stoic expression was hard to read. He stared at him for a few moments before speaking. "You assisted a man to take my wife away from me? Tell me, Mr. Reynolds—why I should allow you to leave here in one piece."

Adam's eyes showed fear. "Mr. Baird, please you have got to believe me. I didn't know she was your wife. I met this guy Billy a few years ago in London. We did some dirt together and both received a good payday. We kept in touch and he wrote me to say he was coming to Scotland. He had a lady friend here that he found out was a baron's daughter and married some rich guy. He wanted to get some money from her and take her to France. He said she was real pretty and could help him with some con job he was running. Billy didn't say her name was Baird, he said her name was Abbott."

Andrew looked at Brian and then back to Adam. "What do you know about Billy?"

Adam's hand fidgeted with his hat. "He act's tough, but a bit squirrely. He is married but doesn't see his wife much. She lives in Bath last, I heard. A few other women claim they have his babies in different cities. He runs a small gang in London and that's where he met Amelia about a year ago. He said she was friends with his cousin's girlfriend. A country girl named Sally. Not sure how a baron's daughter hung out with the likes of his group."

Andrew narrowed his eyes seething inside. "Where did you leave my wife?"

Adam shifted in his chair running his fingers through his hair. "At my friend Charlie's place. He owns a tavern by the docks and Billy made a deal with a couple of merchants to take him and Amelia to France. He was going to stay in their storage room for the night and take the ship in the morning."

A commotion outside the door interrupted them. Three guards ran inside the study. "We have Mrs. Baird contained in the carriage."

Andrew wrinkled his forehead questioning their response. "Contained?"

The guard took in a deep breath with resignation on his face. "Forgive me, Mr. Baird she tried to escape, and we had to restrain her."

Bull acknowledged the guards with a faint nod trying to intervene. "Where is the man she was with?"

One of the guards shrugged. "We left a group of men down by the docks to look for him."

Adam looked stunned and relieved at the same time. Andrew stood up intimidating the men around him. He cocked his brow and whispered with a low growl. "Bring her inside. I will meet her in my study in ten minutes."

Andrew stomped to the door of his study and whispered into Brian's ear. "Get rid of this nuisance."

Brian obeyed his orders and escorted Adam out of the house. Andrew straightened his cravat while walking upstairs to his chamber. He needed to calm himself and wash up. It had been a trying day.

Andrew entered his study eyeing Amelia sitting on a chair slumped over with her hands tied. Her long beautiful hair covered her face hiding her beauty. She was breathing heavily as she waited for her fate. Brian and Bull stood behind her waiting for instructions along with a few other guards near the door.

Andrew looked at all of them without expression. "Cut the ropes and untie her."

Bull hesitated. "Are you sure?"

Andrew gave him an annoyed look. "I am not afraid of my wife. Untie her at once."

Bull took out a knife and cut the ropes. She reached for her hands rubbing her wrists as she hid her expression under her unruly hair.

He took in a deep breath watching her shifting in her chair. "Leave us."

Brian hesitated. "I will stay in case you need assistance."

Andrew creased his brow. "I can handle my own wife. Leave us at once and close the door." The men obeyed leaving him alone with Amelia.

Andrew paced the floors absorbing the silence. Her deception cut him like a knife. He wanted to throttle her but kept his temper in check. He took a chair and dragged it across the floor in front of her taking a seat. The veins in his temple rose against his head as he tried to control his anger.

After a few moments of staring at her, he finally broke the silence. "Were you going somewhere?" He lifted his brow waiting for her to respond. After a moment he leaned over close to her face. He whispered, "You didn't think it proper to say goodbye?"

She made no movement or sound. He waited a few seconds.

In a mocking tone, he took an exaggerated breath. "Oh, Amelia. Tsk, tsk. Do you even know what you have done?" He taunted her sarcastically spitting out a laugh. "Was your life so bad? Did I beat you or hurt you? Did I not provide for you?"

She refused to look at him.

He stood up and walked to the bar making himself a drink. He took a hard swallow and wiped his mouth. Looking over his shoulder, he observed her head still down and her silence infuriated him. Unable to control his emotions, he threw the glass across the room hitting the wall watching it splinter into hundreds of pieces. Her body jerked at the sound of the glass breaking, and he finally felt some satisfaction. The satisfaction turned to fury and a ferocious sound came out of his mouth as his rage continued. "I was good to you! I cared about you. You tainted yourself and our marriage with a petty criminal who has a death wish."

He closed his eyes trying to take control of his temper. Her lack of reaction frustrated him even more. She gave no response to his tirade, so he tried a different approach. Composing himself, he sat back down in the chair leaning close to her. Taking in her faint rose smell, he whispered loudly. "Did you know he is married and has bastard children throughout

England? Oh yes, my dear. He planned to use you for financial gain, Amelia. Are you so naïve? You are pathetic!"

She snapped her head up in shock shaking her head, disagreeing with his accusation. Her defense of her lover enraged him further. He leaned back in the chair and crossed his arms. In a condensing tone, he continued his assessment. "Sweets, your lover lied to you and your few hours of fun at my expense have cost you everything. You will pay for your deception."

She looked away from him and refused to make eye contact.

He let out a fake laugh and reached for her chin forcing her to look at him. "I own you Amelia, and you will live only as long as I see fit. I have legal rights to do to you whatever I choose. You will know that the Black Baird reputation was not earned by my generosity." He threatened her squeezing her chin.

Amelia jerked her chin out of his grip and mumbled something while looking away from him.

Andrew clenched his fist. "What did you say?"

She lifted her head and stared at him refusing to cower at his strong words. "Do what you will. I hate you!"

He narrowed his eyes. "Don't test me. I think you will find me most accommodating."

She lifted her chin as her voice began to shake. "My father sold me to a ruthless man like I was nothing." She wiped a tear looking away from him. "Perhaps, I am not the bargain that you paid for? The truth is that you never even knew me." She sobbed letting out a breath as he stared at her with disbelief.

She snorted finding the courage to strike back with a feigned smile. "I cringed *every* time you touched me. Don't you understand? I have loathed you since I met you."

Her spiteful words affected him more than he could ever imagine. She was right, he never knew her at all. He hated her. Andrew stood up. "Enough! You will not speak so freely, madam. I will punish your insolence if you repeat such vile words again. For now, you will be locked in a room of my choosing and not let out until I say so. You are dismissed."

He went to the door and told Brian and Bull to escort her to the green room upstairs. She gave him no reaction and stood up when the guards grabbed her arms. Andrew yelled at Bull. "Bring me her maid and Alfred." He nodded and obeyed Andrew's order.

Beatrice had tears in her eyes as she watched them pull Amelia up the stairs. She was shaking as Brian escorted her into the study. Alfred followed behind them. Andrew had a sober expression and did not stand when she entered. "Have a seat. Both of you."

Andrew's jaw ticked with anger. "I will only ask you this question once. You will not lie to me." Beatrice nodded slowly trying to hold back tears.

"What did she tell you about her leaving? Did you help her plan?" He waited and watched her body language.

She looked at Alfred and back at Andrew. "I knew nothing, Mr. Baird. I promise you. I didn't know."

He looked at Alfred. "Alfred? What did Beatrice tell you?"

Alfred widened his eyes. "Nothing at all, Mr. Baird."

Andrew lost his patience. "I trust no one. You will both gather your belongings and leave my home."

Alfred put his head down and got out of his chair.

Beatrice cried. "Please, Mr. Baird. I will do a better job. I promise."

He shook his head. "My wife has lost the privilege of having a personal maid. She will no longer require your services. If you go quietly, I will provide you a reference and a month's salary."

Beatrice stared at him biting her bottom lip. "Yes, sir." She slowly walked away not looking back.

A few guards walked in. "We just returned from the docks. There is no sign of him. Rumor is that he sold your wedding ring and fled away from Scotland. We recovered the ring." They handed the ring to Andrew.

He held it in his hand trying to mask his anger. "Put the word out that when he is found, I want him brought to me alive."

They nodded. "As you wish, Mr. Baird."

Andrew held the ring on the tip of his finger swirling it around. Thoughts of Amelia plagued his mind as his hand squeezed the ring into his fist and he pounded the desk in his anger.

CHAPTER 17

MELIA ENTERED THE GREEN ROOM and the door promptly slammed behind her. She heard a lock and knew the reason why Andrew chose this room for her. She was locked in with only a small window that was high enough off the ground to give her no option of escape.

The bed was made with greenish and cream coverings, and there was a table and chair on the other side of the room. Exhaustion forced her to lie down on the bed as she fought not to sleep. Her mind would not stop thinking about the events that brought her to this place. Supposedly Billy was married? Could Andrew be lying? That would make her an adulterer or at least close to it. When did this happen? Why didn't Sally tell her? She shivered, but was too tired to start a fire.

She bent her legs holding them to her chest trying to keep warm. She was too numb to cry anymore. How her life would have been different if she had skipped Rachel's ball. Although she would probably be married to Edward, it was better than being a prisoner. Her husband was no longer her protector but her punisher. Her thoughts turned back to Billy. Truthfully, she was skeptical of Billy's motives. Perhaps Andrew was right? He had disappeared and left her there to fend for herself. The ring was a treasure and would have brought him a small fortune.

A knock on the door startled her as it creaked open. A maid she did not recognize came into the room. Sunshine streamed through the window, and a disoriented Amelia realized she must have fallen asleep. She was fully dressed and laying on the bed.

"Pardon me, miss. I brought you some eggs to break your fast." She curtsied and brought a tray placing it on the table. Amelia tried to adjust her eyes to the light and sat up on the bed.

"Where is Beatrice?" She wondered why she wasn't bringing her a tray. The maid looked down. "Mrs. Baird, Beatrice is no longer working for the household."

Amelia drew her eyebrows together. "Why ever not?"

The maid's flushed face told all she needed to know. Amelia flipped her hand toward the door. "Never mind. I am sure that it was my husband's order."

The maid said nothing and walked out the door. Amelia was not hungry and the smell of the food was making her sick. She looked at the corner of the room and saw a trunk with some clothes and a basin of water. She washed herself and changed into a nightdress. If she wasn't allowed to leave the chamber, then she would not dress for the day.

She walked around the room unable to sit idly by. The room was not large and had worn furnishings. There were a few paintings on the wall and some worn carpets on the floor. After a few hours, she was bored. The small window allowed some sunshine to come through, but she was unable to open it because it was too high up and out of her reach. Tears threatened to fall as she pondered her fate. It was worse than prison as prisoners could go out of their cells on occasion.

She crawled into bed hoping to sleep. At least in her dreams, she was free. A plight of a woman was historically oppressed by the men in her life. Her options were limited, and escape was her only thought. She would rather live poor with nothing than to be subject to a life of misery.

Andrew traveled out of town on business. Not wanting to speak to Amelia, he notified the staff he would be gone for a few weeks. He needed space from her to make final decisions on the state of their marriage. He would contact his solicitor to find out his options. Part of him wanted to make her pay dearly for her deception, and the whispers of his associates proved they thought as much. He was expected to punish her in a way befitting of a blackguard. Protecting his reputation as a ruthless businessman was key to building his empire. No one mentioned her name on their trip afraid of his wrath.

Dundee was a shipping town where Andrew owned a small cottage. He set up the rooms and hired a small staff. Brian accompanied him making inquiries with some business associates regarding some shipping partnerships. Their days were spent with local merchants discussing supply runs and their nights in a local gambling club. A few days after their arrival, Brian accepted an invitation to a dinner party by a prominent shipping owner. Andrew had reason to believe that he may need some help securing some contracts with some influential friends. A deal could be struck.

Brian accompanied him with a few of their guards to the man's home. He spared no expense and had plenty of entertainment. This was not like the formal dining parties of the aristocrats. Dinner guests were dressed in fashions and painted woman were on display. Tables were set up for games as brandy flowed freely. Mr. Bradley welcomed the group and offered special accommodations. Andrew was more interested in a private meeting, but he loosened up his cravat and took a glass of brandy.

"I have arranged some rooms for your group as my dining parties last most the night." A cynical laugh rumbled out of Mr. Bradley. Andrew lifted the side of his mouth in a smile accepting his hospitality. Brian left the group and took an arm of a woman near the tables. The rest of the group mingled as Andrew wiped his finger across the glass studying the various groups of guests.

"Andrew? How many years has it been?" A well-dressed man stood behind him. Andrew recognized him immediately and turned to embrace him.

"Jasper, my friend. It's been years. How is your family?" The older gentlemen cracked a smile. "My family is well, and my brother just finished college. Can you believe a blackguard like me sent his brother to a university?"

Andrew tilted his head. "Nonsense, you were my hero growing up. What about you? Last, I heard you were engaged to be married. Rumor had it that you were in the market for an heir."

The man laughed. "I heard the same rumor about you. How is your wife? I am a little offended I was not invited to your nuptials."

Andrew's eye twitched at the thought of his marriage Not wanting to explain his displeasure of the topic he tried to change subjects. "It was a small affair. We have settled in Scotland. How is Jack? I heard he had built a few factories in America."

Jasper shook his head. "Not good. I took him in after his dad passed away. My nephew is a dreamer. He lost his money trying to make deals with

McKenzie. I told him to go see you, but he said he owed you some money and would try to ship the goods another way. His factories were bought on credit, and when he lost his supplies at sea, he lost everything."

Andrew took a drink. "He was like family to me, practically my stepbrother for a few years. My mother loved his father. I would have helped him. His father taught me a lot about how to survive the streets. I owe him."

Jasper nodded and patted his shoulder. "Your mother would have been proud of you. I think about her all the time. Did you know that I introduced her to my brother? She was not perfect Andrew, but did the best she could."

Andrew's throat tightened as he tried to mask his emotions. Jasper was a special friend of his mother. He became like an Uncle to Andrew. His brother George lived with his mother for a few years before he died and did a lot of the dirty work while Jasper was the brains of the operation. They focused on petty gang activity which Jasper invested the profits in some estates up north. When their operations started to lose money, Jasper pulled out and lived off the rents of his tenants. George was murdered and shortly afterward Andrew's mother died. The water supply in Glasgow was not clean and cholera ran rapid. It claimed his mother and many other neighbors. Cholera and smallpox took many that year. Andrew took over the operations at a very early age and built it back up to a criminal empire. Jasper kept in touch, but sold off his interests to Andrew and practically disappeared from the streets.

Andrew smiled, "Tell me what brings you to Dundee?"

Jasper's smile widened as he started shaking his head with humor. "Can you believe it's a woman? My previous engagement ended a few years ago and I met Mrs. Sellars in London. I heard you took the prettiest woman, so I settled for second best." There was amusement in his eyes. He patted Andrew on the shoulder. "Tell me about your bride. Who caught the Black Baird and brought him up to scratch?"

Andrew took a drink and inhaled a deep breath. His thoughts turned to Amelia. His chest constricted at her deception and he took a moment before answering. "It was business. You know how I feel about women. She is very beautiful but nothing more. I needed an heir."

Jasper studied his face drawing his eyebrow together. "Perhaps you will find more than that. Let us toast to your marriage. I hope I will get to meet her one day."

Andrew hid his discomfort and toasted with his old friend. He noticed his once smooth skin covered in fine lines and the gray hairs hiding the golden locks that once defined his appearance. Andrew remembered the first time he saw him. It was raining outside the day he pulled up in a new carriage in front of their home. He exited with his mother and was dressed in the height of fashion. He walked with a golden cane more for appearance reasons than for help walking. He gave Andrew and his brother a new coin and sweets. Jasper owned the gambling hall where his mother worked. Her boyfriend was his brother. Although George and his mother had a turbulent relationship, Andrew learned a lot from him.

Jasper whispered, "Your mind seems occupied. I hope you will find time to relax. You have made the business bigger than we ever thought possible."

Andrew stopped his woolgathering and looked at Jasper. "It's all I know."

Jasper started to refute his friend but was interrupted by Brian. Brian embraced Jasper. The two of them spoke for a few moments and joined a few others at a card table. Andrew's mind was occupied and he decided to call it a night. He thanked his host and was led to a room by the butler.

He entered the chamber that was richly furnished with gold tapestries and blue coverings. He went to the water closet and undressed himself, washing in the basin. He put on his robe and walked back eyeing some movement on the bed. As he got closer, he walked around the four-poster bed seeing a beautiful painted woman lying in the middle. She wore a nightdress of silk that barely covered her voluptuous body. She smiled and pulled the pins out of her hair while staring at Andrew.

"I am a gift from Mr. Bradley." She moved seductively on the bed inviting Andrew to join her.

Andrew's body reacted, and he wanted her. Holding back from the temptation, he composed himself and held out his hand. She took it stepping off the bed. Her smell intoxicated him, and he ran his fingers through her hair. It was shorter than Amelia's and not as silky. Her face was painted, and she was pretty but not naturally beautiful. Her skin did not entice him, and he held her back from rubbing against him. He leaned down to speak closer to her face. "I am flattered that I could have your company tonight, but I am married. Please thank Mr. Bradley for the thought, but I will have to decline."

She pushed out her bottom lip to protest, expertly moving her shoulders to expose parts of her breast. "You should never return a gift."

His lip twitched at her presumptions. He whispered in her ear as he closed her robe for her. "I sleep alone. Please show yourself out."

She looked down at her hands and shrugged her shoulders. "If you change your mind, I will be at the end of the hall."

Andrew watched her leave and locked the door behind her. He leaned against the wall shaking his head. He was growing soft. It had been days that he had been without a woman and all his body craved was his disobedient wife. She invaded his thoughts. He assured himself that all he needed was time away from her. Time to remember her deception and let his hate consume his heart.

Andrew's trip ended a few days early and he headed back to his estate. It would take a few days to reach his home and decide Amelia's fate. He would not allow her to live with him. She would be sent away. Preferably stripped of all her assets and forced to fend for herself. His generosity was over.

CHAPTER 18

THEY ARRIVED LATE IN THE evening. There was an unmarked carriage near the front door. When Andrew entered his home, he noticed a sober look on Mr. Charles' face.

"Mr. Baird, you have arrived early. You must have missed the missive we sent out yesterday."

Andrew raised his brow. "What is it, Mr. Charles?"

The butler straightened his shoulders. "It's Mrs. Baird. She has taken ill, and the physician is with her now. He will wish to speak to you."

Andrew's heart pounded. Unable to mask his emotions he climbed the stairs to speak to the doctor. The doctor was leaving the green room with a sober look on his face. Andrew stopped him. "Doctor, I am Mr. Baird. I am anxious to hear about my wife."

The doctor nodded at Andrew. "Mr. Baird, I am Doctor Bailey. Is there somewhere we can go and speak in private?"

Andrew showed him to the next chamber which had a private sitting area.

"Mr. Baird, my understanding is that you have been out of town. I have examined your wife and have news of her condition." The doctor spoke matter-of-factly as Andrew shifted in his chair.

The doctor continued. "After speaking to your wife, I realize this may not be a happy occasion. She has severe morning sickness and was completely out of sorts that she may be with child."

Andrew's face drained of blood. He looked like he may faint, and the doctor drew his brow with concern as he reached for him. "Mr. Baird, do you need my assistance? You look like you may pass out."

Andrew let out a breath. "I am well. How far along?"

The doctor rubbed his lips together. "I would say around two months, maybe a little more." Andrew felt a twinge of relief. Part of him hoped nothing had happened that night of her escape with the lowlife Billy. Andrew realized the doctor was still staring at him. He sat up straight. "Thank you, Doctor. If you will excuse me."

The doctor stood up. "Of course. I will be by tomorrow to check on her."

Andrew stood at the closed door and dismissed the guards. He opened the door and saw her lying on the bed with her back to him. His head was spinning, and he had no idea what he would do now that she was with child. He walked to the bed and sat down.

"Amelia?" He watched her body tense at the sound of his voice. She turned her body to face him but remained lying down.

She whispered, "You're back? You spoke to the doctor?"

Andrew nodded watching her close her eyes. They sat in silence for a few moments.

"Is it mine?" Andrew couldn't help but ask.

Her eyes opened, and a look of disgust came over her. Even pale and disheveled he found her irritatingly beautiful. He glared at her response. "It's a fair question. You were alone with your lover for hours."

Amelia sat up propping herself against the pillow. She sighed deeply. "He was not my lover. Unfortunately, the baby is yours."

He looked away from her. "This poses a problem. I was hoping to be rid of you and your infidelity." He expected a smart retort back, but instead, her eyes reddened. His heart squeezed tightly as he fought with himself not to comfort her.

She took a deep breath as her voice trembled. "I did not have *relations* with him."

Andrew breathed a sigh of relief as his voice caught in his throat. "I still don't understand. Why would you do it? Why would you leave with him?" He searched her face briefly letting down his guard.

She looked away from him whispering low. "I was confused. He was talking so fast and told me he loved me."

Andrew's heart sank, and anger filled his belly. "Love?"

She wiped a tear that came down her cheek. A whisper escaped her breath. "No one has ever loved me."

He stared at her unable to move, his pride softening at her confession. "How can you say that? We are married, Amelia."

She made eye contact with him. Powerless to decipher his meaning, she continued, "My father despised me. My stepmother always told me I was a burden. I was forced into *this* marriage. I used to dream that my mother would show up and help me." She took a deep breath as a sob escaped. "Billy said he found my mother for me."

Andrew's emotions played in his head, confused by her story. "I don't understand. I thought your mother died."

She wiped her nose with her hand. "I found a letter in my father's things. It was from his solicitor regarding my mother. It was not very clear, but I don't think she is dead. Billy traveled the world and I knew her rumored stage name was Dorothy Tress. I asked him if he could make inquiries and find her. Perhaps she has been wanting to meet me and love me too. He told me he might have found her, and I had to go with him to find out if it was truly her."

Andrew closed his eyes. "Are you that naïve? He was using you Amelia, and now you have lost everything." He paced in front of the bed contemplating how he would handle their new circumstances.

Running his fingers through his hair, he sagged his shoulders. "Given that you're with child, our marriage will not end immediately. My child will not be a bastard. For now, you will be stripped of all pin money and assets."

Amelia's eyes grew moist as she peeked through her eyelashes watching her husband give out his punishment.

Determined to show his authority in the matter he cleared his throat. "You will be allowed a modest living in a small cottage I own in Dundee. We will live apart. No visitors, guests, or letters will be permitted. After the baby is born, I will decide your fate. If you break any rules, you will be locked away in an institution and won't see your baby."

She sat up in the bed, her colorless cheeks turned pink with anger. "I will be a prisoner?"

Andrew shook his head trying to drag his eyes away from her. Pride would not allow him to forgive. Softening a bit, he explained, "Not a prisoner. I will permit you to have run of the house and one supervised walk outside each day. It's the life you chose when you deceived me."

She sighed exhaustedly and turned away from him. "Please go away, Andrew. I am not feeling well."

He stared at the bed not wanting to leave. Though, he would not lower himself to comfort her. Reminding himself of her deception, he held back his feelings. His reputation proceeded itself, and he would be determined not to give in to momentary weakness.

CHAPTER 19

THE NEXT MORNING ONE OF the maids pulled the curtains open allowing the sunshine to disrupt Amelia's sleep. The maid placed dry toast and water beside her bed and woke her.

"Mrs. Baird, I have been told to dress you for your journey north. A carriage has been prepared and your escort awaits you. Are you well enough to sit up?"

Amelia sat up and covered her mouth motioning for the chamber pot. The maid quickly ran and held it in front of her so she could vomit. Amelia's insides squeezed at the dry heaving of any contents left in her stomach. She worried how the baby could survive if she could not hold down any food. After wiping her mouth, she felt better and took a sip of water. "Where is my husband?"

The maid fidgeted with her travel dress and looked away from Amelia. "Forgive me, Mistress. I am not supposed to speak of your husband with you. I could lose my position."

Amelia closed her eyes trying to brace herself as she stood up from the bed. "That is ridiculous."

The maid looked away and poured some water into a basin. "Would you like to wash up before you dress?"

Amelia walked to the basin and washed her face. She refused the maid's help and brushed her long hair leaving it down on purpose to annoy anyone who thought it was not proper. She wanted to have some control of her own life.

Leaving her room, she climbed down the staircase welcoming any change of scenery. Locked up in the same room for several days had taken a toll on her.

Mr. Charles met her at the end of the stairs and smiled. "I wish you a safe journey, Mrs. Baird. I will miss you."

Amelia stared at him and looked away without saying a word, not knowing who she could trust. She curiously looked around for her husband but did not see him. Maybe it was better this way.

Realism hit her when she walked outside. She was leaving. There were four carriages lined up waiting to depart. Two of them held guards for protection and one was for her luggage. Amelia boarded the middle carriage awaiting her journey to her new life.

Andrew watched Amelia leave from the window of an abandoned bedchamber on the third floor. Her long hair wrapped around her body as the wind blew. It was pure nonsense that she would wear her hair in such a fashion. He rolled his eyes in annoyance and continued watching her carriage pull away. Her departure should help him get her out of his mind. She consumed his thoughts, and he needed a diversion to keep his mind focused.

A maid stood in the doorway. "Mr. Baird, she has departed."

Andrew continued looking out the window, watching the carriage get smaller as it pulled away. Without looking at the maid he spoke, "Thank you. If you will tell the cook that I plan to eat out tonight."

The maid gave a curtsey. "As you wish."

Amelia traveled most of the day stopping at an inn to rest that night. They would arrive mid-morning the following day. Amelia was escorted to her room by Bull who insisted she take a tray to her room and not indulge in the dining room with the staff. Amelia accepted his direction and stayed in her room. She contemplated escape as this would probably be her best opportunity, but her stomach sickness would not permit her to imagine the consequences. She was trapped for now and would not risk her child's future. After she ate some bland tasting soup, she read a book provided by the innkeeper's wife. It was nice to be entertained even if it was only a book.

The next day she awoke early and was sick again before consuming her breakfast. The carriage ride was bumpier, and the roads were miserable. They reached the cottage late in the afternoon due to having to stop several times for Amelia to relieve herself. She could only imagine the tongues wagging with complaints among the men.

The stone cottage was bigger than Amelia imagined. Greenery ran up the sides running ragged over the stones. There were two floors and a few gardens that welcomed her eye. Her husband had promised her that she could take a walk a day, and she looked forward to sitting outside. The men carried her trunk to a bedroom on the landing. A few newly-hired servants welcomed her. Bull met with them privately giving them explicit instructions from Andrew.

Amelia enjoyed her newfound freedom. She was no longer locked in her room but was allowed access to the small library and study. She dined in the dining room alone as the men took to town to eat their dinner. She didn't mind that she was alone. It was better than a tray in her room.

The men left the next day and Amelia was left with only two guards that were local from the area. There were two footmen and three maids—more than enough in Amelia's opinion. She walked around the estate and took in the fresh air. Mrs. Palmer was the main housekeeper and had a soft nature. Amelia liked her and asked her to purchase some paper and paints. She gave her a few coins she had hidden in one of her dresses and Mrs. Palmer obliged her. Painting for Amelia was her escape and she spent most of her days in the garden. A walk a day turned into hours in the garden. No one questioned her time spent outdoors.

Andrew left the chamber and found Brian in the dining room with a few of his men. The light banter ceased as Andrew entered with a scowl on his face. He filled his plate with some eggs and took a seat. The silence felt louder than a tavern after a festival. Andrew looked up sizing up his companions. "What is on our schedule today?"

The men looked at Brian to answer as he was like a brother to Andrew and well respected. They knew Andrew's calm demeanor could be a facade. After all, his wife was found with another man and everyone knew it. His ruthless reputation cowered when it came to his wife and some were talking about it. It was only a matter of time before he would punish someone. Only Brian could speak to him as an equal without fear of retribution.

Brian cleared his throat. "Martin says Henry's obtained his payment and is ready to make a deal. John and a few of the others took off to the docks to meet with him. A few of his warehouses were part of the deal and I thought we could check them out. One of the properties includes a small opera house mostly for locals." Andrew nodded as he took a bite of his eggs. Brian leaned toward him and whispered, "I can take care of business today if you would rather rest."

Andrew narrowed his eyes. "What do you mean?"

Brian sighed exhaustedly. "Andrew, you look awful. I bet you didn't sleep at all last night."

Andrew swished his hand. "Nonsense. I am fine. I will be ready within the hour." He got up from the table and went to freshen up in his room.

Andrew entered the Tree Lounge taking in the familiar scent of sweat and liquor. It was bustling with customers which always gave him a bit of satisfaction. He straightened his jacket and headed to his table in the back. Jean had it available for him just in case he stopped by. He had just finished up some collections and needed to unwind hoping to keep his mind from wandering. His night had been successful as he recovered a few loans with interest and some property that was put up for collateral. He usually enjoyed attending the high roller collection meetings. It normally involved spoiled aristocrats that were out of their league displaying their pompous attitudes—always thinking they were better than the common man and referring to themselves as betters. The tables had turned and now Andrew's name was no longer associated with criminals, but business elite. Although his methods had been questioned, he was able to stay out of jail. His businesses were legal although questionable in certain circles.

Jean was working and came to greet him. Andrew's mood was solemn, and he gave her a guarded grin hoping she would not bring up any questions about his wife.

"What will it be, boys?" She smiled as a waitress came over to take their order. Jean patted Andrew on the shoulder. "May we speak privately? In the office?"

Andrew stood up reluctantly and headed to the back office. Jean lit a lantern and closed the door behind them. "Andrew, you look horrible. I am worried for you." She sat down motioning him to take the seat across from her.

Andrew sat down. "Thank you for the compliment." He tried to make light of the conversation.

He saw her purse her lips together and leaned back in his chair.

She crinkled her forehead. "What is this I hear about Amelia? You sent her away to have your baby?"

He flexed his jaw in anger. "I don't wish to talk to you about my wife." He let out a sigh and looked away. "Now, let's talk business. Brian wants to add on to the tavern by taking out the bakery next door."

Jean shook her head. "Andrew, I am not just your employee. I am your friend. Since we were kids, I have watched over you. While others feared you, I did not... Don't take this burden by yourself. Talk to me."

Andrew looked down and paused in silence. "What do you want me to say? You were right about her. I never knew her at all!"

Jean shook her head and reached her hand out, touching his arm. "It's not about me being right. Did she tell you why she left with that man? I didn't take her as the type to run away. There had to be a reason why she would risk losing you."

Andrew shrugged his shoulders as his nostrils flared. "The lass is a selfish whore. I was good to her and tried so hard to gain her affection. I never cared about anyone like I cared for her. I am just so angry... I feel like punching something."

Jean took a deep breath. "Calm down! Are you sure she didn't give you some explanation that you could understand?"

Andrew chewed on his fingernail thinking about her. "It's hard to tell with all her deceptions. She gave some ridiculous reason." He laughed mockingly, "She said no one has ever loved her. Can you believe that? Supposedly, the petty ruffian is the only person who ever told her those words."

Andrew shook his head. "He lied to her and told her that her mother was really alive, and she had to leave me to go see her. Now she comes back pregnant and how am I to know if it's mine?"

Jean closed her eyes. "Was she an innocent when you married her?"

Andrew drew the lines on his forehead together then nodded his head.

Jean looked at him with compassion. "Andrew, I believe this is your child and you must take responsibility for the child and the mother. You know how hard it is to grow up without a parent. I believe Amelia is a broken young woman who feels betrayed by those who should love her. She craves for someone to love her and doesn't feel that from you. Being nice to someone is not the same thing as loving them. I know you provided for her, but did you love her?"

Andrew looked down at his lap. "What difference does it make? Love is a weak emotion and now I can't stand to look at her."

Jean narrowed her eyes studying him. "You're hurting, but so is she. Can you imagine how scared she must be all alone with the possibility of having her baby taken away from her? You abandoned her when you were supposed to be her protector. You must forgive her. I don't believe she was intimate with this other man. He was a con artist that tricked a naïve young woman. Andrew, don't live the rest of your life hating her. Give yourself a chance to be happy."

Andrew stood up dismissing her. "I can't discuss this with you. This is my business. My life. I don't wish to speak of it ever again." He turned around and walked out the door.

CHAPTER 20

AFTER A FEW MONTHS, AMELIA settled into her new life. She was friendly with the housekeeping staff keeping close guard of her secrets. The friendlier she was—the less they watched her. Her painting occupied most her afternoons, not much different than her time spent in the country as a child.

One day she felt the ground rumble and looked up startled to see a floppy-eared dog attacking her with kisses. Amelia laughed out loud and embraced the furry creature. A few moments later she heard a horse and saw a man jump off. "Forgive me, Miss. Beans! Stop licking the young woman!"

Amelia smiled enjoying the welcome. "It's okay. I fancy animals. You precious boy!"

A stocky man took the dog from Amelia and two more horses came up beside them. A young woman with dark hair dismounted and her companion did as well.

The woman petted the dog. "Forgive us for intruding on your privacy. We didn't realize anyone was staying at the cottage and usually don't come up this far on our rides."

Amelia held up her hand. "It's quite all right. I enjoy the company."

The young woman stood beside her companion. "My name is Mrs. Brooks, but please call me Judith. This is my husband, Sam Brooks and his brother Joseph."

Amelia petted the dog. "My name is Amelia, and we recently moved to the cottage."

The men bowed. Sam looked at Amelia's painting before she could hide it. "Do you like painting? That is a great portrait of the landscape."

Amelia blushed at the compliment. "I suppose I do like to paint a little."

Judith slanted her head studying the painting. "You have a lot of talent and I would love to see more of your work. Do you accept visitors?"

Amelia's smile faded, and a panicky feeling overcame her. "Forgive me. I need to be on my way at once."

Judith touched her arm. "No, please forgive me. I shouldn't have tried to impose on you."

Amelia was embarrassed at her reaction to a requested visit. The truth is that she longed to have a friend. "Please, I would love for you to come to my home. It's just that I am not allowed any visitors." Not able to make eye contact due to the absurdity of her statement, she wrung her hands looking away.

Judith's eyes widened. "Are you a servant? We apologize we thought you were the mistress of this manor."

Amelia's thoughts were interrupted by the housekeeper. "Mrs. Baird? Your lunch is prepared." Amelia turned around. "I will be there in a moment." The housekeeper waited a few seconds and then walked away.

Sam's face went white. "Did she call you, Mrs. Baird?"

Amelia looked away trying to mask her apprehension. "Yes, my name is Amelia Baird."

Sam looked at Joseph and he rubbed his lips together. "Are you related to Andrew Baird?"

Amelia was silent pausing before she spoke. "Yes, he is my husband."

Their demeanor changed instantly. Sam motioned for Joseph meeting his eyes with a look of understanding. Judith looked confused as her husband put his hand on her back moving her to the horses. "We must get back. Thank you for helping us with our dog."

The men went to mount and Amelia spoke for the first time. "Judith, please if you could do me one favor?" Judith looked back at Sam who shook his head. He lifted Judith up on her saddle. Amelia walked beside her. "Please, if you could wait one moment. I have a letter that I need mailed. I would be indebted to your kindness."

Judith looked back at her husband and brother-in-law who were already walking their horses away from them. Judith looked back and whispered, "Meet me here same time tomorrow and I will take your letter."

Amelia closed her eyes and mouthed the words: "Thank you."

She went inside quickly to eat lunch as the housekeeper was already suspicious. Upon entering the home, Amelia could see the housekeeper's mouth formed into a straight line of disapproval. "Mrs. Baird, I am under strict orders that you are to have no visitors."

Amelia looked back at the housekeeper irritated at being reprimanded by a servant. "Mrs. Palmer, please remember your place. They were not visitors, but lost neighbors. I will not be rude."

The housekeeper sighed and walked away. Amelia told the cook she would take a tray to her room. She wanted a chance to check on the letters hidden for Sally and Rachel. She needed to find the information that Billy knew about her mother. Sally was her only hope. If her mother was alive, perhaps she could find her.

Amelia went for a walk in the gardens the next day before lunch hoping that Judith would keep her word. She concealed the letters under her skirt. Amelia avoided Mrs. Palmer by sneaking out the study doors and going around the back of the house. Hopefully she would not realize the ruse. Amelia had told the staff she was under the weather and not painting in the garden that day.

She waited near the trees and finally heard a horse come closer as she came out of hiding. True to her word, Judith rode alone and smiled when seeing Amelia. Judith stayed on her horse stopping near Amelia. "I was hoping I would see you. I can't stay long. Sam would kill me if he knew I was here."

Amelia nodded her head handing her the letters. "I can't send them from here. If they could send a letter back to you to respond, I would be grateful."

Judith bit her bottom lip. "I will see what I can do." She looked at the letters and tucked them into her bag. She grabbed the reins and looked back at Amelia. "Sam told me about your husband. Talking with you makes me wonder if it could be true? Are you in danger?"

Amelia looked down at the ground. Not wanting to confide in a stranger of her circumstances, she hid her feelings. "I am well and thank you again for your help."

Judith looked at her for a few seconds. "I wish you well, Amelia. If I receive a response, I will find you."

CHAPTER 21

AMELIA'S FEET HURT, AND SHE found it difficult to walk. It had been months since she gave the letters to Judith. There was still no reply from Sally or Rachel. Her feet were swelling, and her doctor warned her to keep to her bed. It was difficult to lie down all day. She was bored, and there were only so many books she could read. Sleeping was difficult as she couldn't get comfortable. The staff tried to appease her but only made her more miserable. It has been several months since she saw Andrew, almost forgetting she was married. Only his guards came a few times to check on the status of the manor and to give Mrs. Palmer money for the household.

She missed Mr. Charles and his amusing stories. Hopefully he was doing well. She worried that Andrew might take her transgressions out on him. Mr. Charles was like the father she never had, and Andrew may not believe he had no part in her deception. Her thoughts turned to Beatrice and Alfred. One of the guards mentioned their marriage when he didn't realize that Amelia was listening. There was some self-satisfaction that her weeks of efforts to encourage their courting had paid off. At least some people married for love and could live happily. Andrew tried to control every aspect of her life taking away her friendships and spying on her with his paid help.

Amelia spent most of her time sitting in a chair in the nursery—a small chamber beside her room. She painted pictures of ducks and ponies on the walls with bright colors. Mrs. Palmer purchased paint for her when there were leftover household funds, and she was grateful for the housekeeper's kindness.

Amelia stacked the bookshelves with a few children's books she received from Mrs. Palmer. Once she knew if it was a girl or boy, she could decorate more. Mrs. Palmer made her a few baby blankets and gave her two baby gowns. Their friendship grew as Amelia depended on her good graces and advice during her pregnancy. Mrs. Palmer raised two brothers and three sisters outside of Glasgow. Her mother had taken ill with fever and never recovered. Her father had died in a carriage accident. All her siblings were married, and she found a job as a housekeeper after she was widowed at the age of eight and twenty. She never had children but helped deliver many of her nieces and nephews. Amelia would be happy to have her around when she delivered her own baby.

A few weeks before the doctor said she was due Amelia started having sharp pains. She notified the housekeeper and a doctor was promptly called. Her heart rate increased and sweat beaded against her forehead as she braced for more pain. It was relentless, and she felt the pain would be more than she could bear. Falling into unconsciousness, she willed the pain away through tears and screams.

Andrew's carriage pulled up in front of the cottage and was accompanied by Brian and many guards. He had arranged for them to stay at the inn in town but wanted to check on Amelia. Her due date was close and the last letter he received was that she was experiencing some difficulty with swelling and mobility. He hid his concerns and replied with indifference when anyone asked about her upcoming birth. Rumors whispered throughout the staff regarding the status of Andrew's marriage.

One of the footmen came to the door as Andrew opened it. "Mr. Baird! They are with her now."

A look of concern crossed Andrew's face. "What has happened?"

The housemaid went down the stairs carrying a few towels with evidence of blood. Eyeing Mr. Baird, she hesitated and replied, "The other doctor is examining her."

His chest felt heavy and the walls felt as they were closing in on him. *Why did the sheets have blood on them?* Struggling to keep the panic out of his voice, he asked, "Why? Is she ill?"

Mrs. Palmer came down the stairs with a stoic expression. Recognizing Andrew, she stopped her descent and addressed him. "Mr. Baird? I am glad you are here, Amelia went into labor this morning a few weeks early. The doctor has been with her for several hours and is worried about her. She is not doing well and keeps losing consciousness. He said it is the loss of blood and if she doesn't deliver soon…"

His heart pounded against his chest "The baby?"

Mrs. Palmer looked away distressed. "I do not know. He sent a footman earlier for another doctor he knows that could help. He is with her now."

Andrew walked past her up the stairs and stood outside Amelia's bedroom door. He overheard the doctor's low voices discussing Amelia like she wasn't in the room. He opened the door, "Doctors? I am Mr. Baird."

The older doctor pushed his spectacles up the bridge of his nose. "Mr. Baird, we meet at last. I wish it were under better circumstances. I am Dr. Carlyle, and this is my associate Dr. Brenham. May we speak outside?"

Andrew nodded and stepped out of the room with the doctors. He watched the doctor take in a deep breath finding it difficult to look him in the eye. "Mr. Baird, there is no easy way to say this. Your wife is in grave danger. If she doesn't deliver soon, she may die. She is bleeding and the baby is breech. It happens sometimes when the baby is early and has not turned yet. Dr. Brenham has some experience of this in his past. His mother was a midwife and he will try to turn the baby. She is exhausted and in extreme pain. We are getting her ready for the procedure and will leave you a few moments alone with your wife."

On the outside Andrew hid his emotions, but inside his stomach was twisting. He hated and loved her at the same time. The doctors left him alone and he entered the room eyeing her unmoving body on the bed. Afraid she was unconscious, he took a few steps toward the bed and saw her eyes open slowly, a look of confusion showed on her face. "Andrew?" The weakness in her voice made his chest constrict. She looked frail and had lost all color. Sweat had drenched her hair and her eyes drooped.

"Don't talk, Amelia. You need to save your strength. The doctors are going to try to save you and the baby." He sat on the bed next to her.

Amelia's eyes filled with tears. "Andrew, please listen to me."

He looked away and felt her hand touch his. Surprised she would touch him, he swallowed his pride and gripped her hand looking in her eyes seeing pain and desperation.

She whispered, "I know you hate me."

He sat in shock watching her close her eyes struggling with her voice.

"But please don't tell the baby I was a bad person. Please tell my baby good stories about me." She was losing her breath between sobs and her face contorted with pain.

Andrew found it hard to speak. "Amelia..."

She shook her head. "No, please listen." She tried to sit up moaning in pain. "I don't think I will live through this, Andrew. It hurts so terribly. But I want our baby to survive. I told the doctor to save the baby. But before I die, I need you to know the truth. And I hope you can forgive me one day."

Andrew wanted her to rest, but finally hearing the truth piqued his curiosity. Pushing aside his selfishness, he replied, "Amelia, please save your strength."

She cried out grabbing his hand tighter and shifting in the bed. "No. Please listen to me. I wanted to hate you. I thought you were like my father and I never gave you a chance because my heart was closed." Sobs slurred her speech as she tried to catch her breath. "I was wrong." Her eyes closed and then there was silence.

He thought she fell asleep. But after a moment she took a deep breath struggling to speak. "You are a good husband. So gentle and you showed me so much kindness. I wanted you to know that I didn't mean the words I told you that day. I liked your touch. Please forgive me, Andrew." Her voice was strained and she let out a moan.

Andrew couldn't take seeing her in pain any longer and stood up taking his hand away from her grip. "Amelia, we must get the doctor."

She closed her eyes losing consciousness again.

Andrew stood over her unable to leave. Years of hiding his emotions had not prepared him for this. Taking a moment, he reached over and kissed her on the forehead. She was asleep. Emotions weighed heavily on his chest, and he whispered, "You are my heart, Amelia." He walked out the door, so the doctors could check on her.

The servants brought up a few chairs and Brian joined him outside of her room. Bull brought up some brandy and sat with them beside her door. It was hard for Andrew to speak. "You may both go to the inn. It will be a long night."

They watched five servants enter the room to help the doctors. Andrew could hear her moaning loudly.

Brian put his hand on his shoulder. "I am here for the night. I won't leave you."

Bull shook his head. "Neither will I."

Andrew ran his fingers through his hair. "I have never felt so helpless."

Brian raised his brow. "Did you speak to her?"

Andrew nodded his head unable to speak. His thoughts turned to her last words.

Screams shook the men and Andrew stood up reaching for the door. Brian grabbed his shoulder. "Let the doctor's do their job. You can't help her."

Andrew dropped his head to his chest. His sadness turned to anger, and he punched a hole in the wall. Brian took his handkerchief and wrapped his bloody hand. "You won't be any good to her if you don't keep calm. She will need you."

Andrew's face was red and he grabbed Brian's collar. "Need me? What if she dies?"

Brian took his hand away and embraced him. It was a display of affection foreign to the men. "I know we are not the most religious men, but maybe we can ask someone from the church to visit?"

Mrs. Palmer came out of the room visibly shaken and out of breath. "Mr. Baird, the doctor asked me to tell you that the baby has turned. Amelia is ready to deliver. It could be a long night and he recommends you get some rest."

Andrew took a deep breath. "How is she? I heard her screaming."

Mrs. Palmer tried to reassure him. "The doctor said the procedure of turning the baby is more painful than delivery for a lot of women. She is exhausted and fainted from the pain. He needs to revive her to push the baby out."

Andrew looked at Brian. "She is so frail. How much more can she take?"

Brian handed him a glass of brandy. "She is young and strong. You must believe she will be okay."

Mrs. Palmer pressed her lips together. "The maids have been praying for her. We believe that she will come through this."

Andrew took a seat looking down at the floor. "If you could give me a few moments alone."

Brian motioned for the group to leave. He looked back at Andrew. "We will be downstairs. If you hear anything let us know." Andrew nodded not looking at this friend.

Andrew's mind raced with thoughts and suppressed feelings for his wife. He tried to block out the moans and cries coming from the room. At least he knew she was alive when he could hear her. He longed to hold her and give her comfort. The hate in his heart was melting, and only his pride kept him from declaring to her how he felt.

"Mr. Baird!" The doctor's voice rang out.

Andrew was disoriented and realized he had fallen asleep in the chair. He stood up quickly almost knocking the doctor over. "Forgive me for falling asleep. How is she?"

The doctor smiled. "You have a son, and he is doing fine. They are cleaning him up now."

Andrew's heart busted with joy—yet a nagging feeling came over him. "How is my wife?"

The doctor tilted his head. "She is resting and will be the rest of the day. I gave her a hefty dose of sleeping medicine. Amelia suffered some bleeding. But we believe we got it stopped. Dr. Brenham is quite versed in women's health and believes she will recover. She will be very sore and weak for a few days and I recommend bed rest." He patted him on the back. "And I recommend you get some bed rest too."

Andrew smiled. "Thank you, Doctor." The door opened and one of the maids held a small baby swaddled in a blue blanket. She handed the baby to Andrew. He gently took him and kissed his forehead. "Oh, my son. You are a little fighter."

Brian came up the stairs with Bull. "Congratulations. Baby Baird has made his arrival." Brian touched the baby's toes. "Aren't you a handsome one?" They smiled ear to ear cooing at him. "What name have you for him?"

Andrew shrugged. "I will speak to Amelia when she wakes. If you will excuse me, I want to see her."

Andrew entered the room as two women servants were cleaning up the mess. The doctor was checking her heart. She laid still in a deep sleep. Her hair was knotted, and her face was pale. The doctor smiled. "Her heart is strong, and the bleeding has not come back. I will check on her tomorrow. I suggest a wet nurse for a few days until she can regain her strength."

Andrew looked at the housekeeper. She spoke up at the doctor's request. "It's been arranged, and the wet nurse is already downstairs. Mrs. Baird requested not to hire one, but given the circumstances, we will take your direction."

Andrew looked at her. "Keep the nurse for now until Mrs. Baird has recovered."

The housekeeper smiled. "May I take him for a while? The wet nurse is in the drawing room waiting for instruction. I will let her know to come up at once."

Andrew kissed him again and handed him to the housekeeper. "Please bring him back in a few hours. I want Amelia to see him as soon as she wakes."

The housekeeper smiled. "As you wish." As she walked out the door, Andrew noticed her wink at Brian who looked away with a smirk on his face.

CHAPTER 22

MELIA WOKE UP ADJUSTING HER eyes to the lighting in the room. She was dizzy and disoriented and felt a bit nauseous. She bent over the bed and was thankful there was a chamber pot on the floor, she let out the contents that were still in her stomach. After recovering and wiping her mouth, she surveyed the room realizing she was alone. Her body felt weak and her legs hurt. Gathering her thoughts, she touched her stomach realizing that she was no longer pregnant and remembered the night before. Where was her baby? She began to call out for a servant and saw that the door to the room was opening. To her surprise, in the doorway stood her husband who held a tiny bundle in his arms.

"You're awake?" He walked to the bed with relief etched on his face. He sat on the bed and scooted his body next to her causing the bed to dip low. His eyes left hers temporarily to look at the bundle in his arms. He held the baby up for her to see and she felt her face light up with happiness. "The doctors will be happy you woke—you gave the household quite a scare." He loosened the blanket placing the baby nearer to her face. "You gave birth to a beautiful son."

Amelia looked down at her beautiful baby with dark hair and pink skin. Her eyes filled with tears as she reached for him. Lifting him up, she held him close to her chest. She let out a coo and closed her eyes, relishing in the baby's smell.

Andrew could not suppress his joy. Admiration along with joy was all that could describe his elation of having a son. Noticing how vulnerable his wife looked, he offered his arms to take the baby. His lips parted forming a sentiment, but he quickly closed them. He affectionately soothed the baby who was beginning to stir. "We have no name for him."

Amelia glanced at her son. "Do you have a family name you would like to use?"

Andrew shrugged his shoulders. "Not anyone that I know that would be worthy. I want him to have a strong name. Not Andrew, but something with meaning."

Amelia thought for a few moments. "What about a king's name? Edward or Henry?"

Andrew smirked with amusement mixed with a bad taste in his mouth. "Those were English Kings. He needs a strong Scottish name." He looked down at his son. "What about Robert?"

Amelia narrowed her eyes playfully. "You do remember I am English?" A small chuckled escaped her lips. "No matter, I like the name Robert. But I think he should have a bit of his father in his name. What about Robert Andrew Baird?"

He smiled proudly. "A very strong name indeed."

There was a knock on the door and the nurse entered. "Forgive me—I didn't know that Mrs. Baird had awakened yet. It's time for the baby to eat."

Amelia's face straightened showing her unwillingness to let her baby out of her sight. She glanced at Andrew with a look that said she was ready to do battle if necessary. Andrew looked at her reassuringly and handed the baby to the wet nurse, Mrs. Franklin. "Please bring him back once you are finished."

She left the room and he turned to Amelia. "It's only until you are feeling better. I hope you understand."

Amelia bit back a retort. "I am feeling fine."

Unapologetically, Andrew took a stance. "Amelia, even the doctors said you are not ready to feed Robert. Our decision to have a nurse was based on doctor's orders."

Amelia pushed out her bottom lip as if weighing her options. "Andrew, I do understand that he needed nourishment while I was resting. I just hope you understand that I didn't have a mother growing up. I want to take care of my baby and make sure he knows that I love him. That I will not leave him like my mother left me."

Andrew stared at her for a moment before responding. "Amelia, he will know you're his mother even if you have a nurse help you. I think it's best to keep one on staff." He paced the floor in front of her bed.

She didn't want to argue. "As you wish."

Andrew snapped his head in surprise at her obedience. Not knowing how to respond to her submissive behavior, he cleared his throat. "Very well. The doctor will be by later today. He insists that you stay in bed for a few days. Your body went through a shock and you will need to regain your strength."

Amelia stared at him defeated. "I will stay in bed, but I do want my baby to stay with me for a while."

Andrew agreed. "Of course. If you will excuse me, I have some business to attend too."

Andrew found Brian and a few others in the drawing room. They all congratulated him again. After a briefing on the day's agenda, they left for the inn, so they could meet with a few business associates. Andrew wanted to keep Amelia's residence free from any unsavory men who asked for a meeting.

Andrew met with some of his men upon his arrival at the inn. Congratulations and well-wishers for the new father went around the group, and their smiles were contagious. Mr. Bradley was waiting in the dining parlor and asked Andrew to have a private luncheon with him. A few well-dressed men from London were accompanying him and they had waited all night for his return.

"Forgive me. My delay could not be avoided. My son came a few weeks early. My wife was in labor last night."

Mr. Bradley raised his brow. "A likely excuse." He laughed loudly echoing across the room. "I am jesting and wish you the best. I didn't realize you were married until recently. She must be a remarkable woman to be married to the famous Black Baird and for you to return my precious gift the night of my dinner party."

Andrew studied his face, his demeanor changing from friend to businessman. He didn't like his tone. "Your hospitality was appreciated. I find the older I get, the more refined my taste."

The men looked at each other, shifting in their chairs. "Mr. Baird, let me introduce you to two of my associates—Mr. Keller and Mr. Bryant."

The men nodded. Mr. Bryant cleared his throat. "We are well familiar with your name, Mr. Baird. It's a pleasure to finally meet you."

Andrew leaned back in his chair not responding and taking control of the meeting. "What is it that I can do for you, Mr. Bradley?"

He looked at his associates. "Well to be frank, we need your strong arm with one of your business associates. I wish to protect my investment. A few months ago, I gave Keller and Bryant a large amount of revenue to help build two factories in England." He looked around the table and whispered closer to Andrew. "I know you are acquainted with a Mr. Fuller in London. He holds the deed to the property that we built two of our factories on. There was a misunderstanding and we thought the property belonged to a Mr. Drier who sold us the rights. The buildings are now finished, the equipment is installed, and we are ready to begin production." He became angry spitting as he spoke. "It is now gathering dust!" He balled his fist and pounded on the table. "Come to find out, it was a forgery and now Mr. Fuller is refusing to sell us the property. We would pay double the amount, but he still refuses. Meanwhile, our investment loses money every day. There is no way to run the factories if we don't own the property or if we could at least rent it. He is refusing us access to our own buildings."

Andrew was good friends with Mr. Ron Fuller and the man did owe him plenty of favors. Not to mention, Andrew's knowledge of Ron's involvement in a delicate matter could give them what they wanted. However, Andrew had no incentive to help Mr. Bradley. He decided to have some fun with the man. Trying to suppress a laugh from the irony of the situation. "Mr. Bradley, am I to believe that you and your partners purchased property from a forgery without checking into it further? Did you have a solicitor help you?"

Mr. Bradley's face turned red and he tried to loosen his cravat. He looked down at the table and barely whispered, "We used his solicitor."

Andrew drew his brow in confusion. "Did you just say you used his solicitor without checking references? Why didn't you consult yours?"

Mr. Bradley lifted his chin trying to defend himself. "Mine was out of the country and we didn't want to wait. It was an unbelievable deal."

Andrew laughed out loud. "Unbelievable indeed."

Andrew lifted his head and gestured for Brian to join them. Mr. Bradley tightened his hand around his glass causing his knuckles to turn white.

Brian pulled out a chair at the table. "Gentlemen," he said, keeping the mood polite. He accepted a glass from the waitress and Andrew took one as well.

After taking a drink, Andrew looked at Mr. Bradley. "I can appreciate your dilemma and although I am acquainted with Mr. Fuller, I am unable to help you."

Andrew gave Brian a conspicuous nod of unspoken words between them. The meeting may take a turn in the wrong direction, and he wanted Brian to be prepared.

"Pardon me, Mr. Baird. I was under a different perception. Surely you have some influence over Mr. Fuller?"

Andrew smirked. "I am a businessman. I do have influence over Mr. Fuller and plan to use that influence. He seems to be the new owner of two factories waiting to be operated. I am sure I can convince Mr. Fuller to operate the factories with my investment. I thank you for the tip."

Mr. Bradley's face turned pale. "Are you jesting?"

Andrew's smiled faded. "I never jest about business. If you will excuse me, I have other meetings I must attend too."

Mr. Keller scowled at Mr. Bradley. He turned to Andrew. "Mr. Baird, I invested my life savings in this factory and know I can make it work. If I can't be part owner, would you consider hiring me to run the factory? Perhaps give me a small percentage to help recover a little of my money."

Andrew rubbed his lips together. "How do I know your qualifications?"

Mr. Keller showed Andrew his hands. "I have the hands of a worker not a businessman. My investment came from challenging work and a small inheritance from my aunt. Give me a trial run, and I won't let you down."

Andrew looked at Brian. "What do you think?"

Brian lifted the corner of his mouth. "Mr. Bryant? What about your investment?"

Mr. Bryant looked down at the floor. "I was to do the books. I would still like to work in the factory."

Andrew glared at Mr. Bradley. "Well, Mr. Bradley do not let it be said that Andrew Baird is an unreasonable man. I will give you each ten percent and I will receive fifty percent of the profits. The other twenty percent will go to other investors that Brian will coordinate."

Mr. Bradley stood up fuming. "You're a crook. You bastard."

Andrew drew his head back in feigned shock. In a mocking tone, he addressed the table. "Tsk, tsk. Mr. Bradley, I take offense. Regarding my business practices, they are all quite legal. I assure you that I am not a crook. Before our deal is complete you will sign over your shares as well as Mr. Keller's and Bryant's. My solicitor will be in contact and he does come with references. Ten percent is very generous of me considering I could take your investment and give you nothing. My generosity will only go so far, and I will take offense at any more name-calling."

Andrew laughed out loud as the men left the inn. "May all our deals today be so prudent."

Brian shook his head and drank the rest of his brandy. He excused himself and walked over to the table. He handed Andrew some paperwork to review. "We have a small crowd that would like to speak to you today."

Andrew leaned back in his chair in the private dining room. "I don't have all day. I want to spend some time with my son."

He nodded. "I will see who takes priority and send the others on their way."

Andrew took a drink, reviewing the papers.

Brian walked into the main dining area and reviewed the matters personally before he allowed people to see Andrew. A woman approached him claiming that her husband had lost their land to Andrew and she felt he was cheated. She wanted to speak to him on her husband's behalf. Brian was tired of the trivial problems that junior guards could not handle.

He took a new guard, Lawrence, out of the room. "Lawrence, I want you to deal with the petty women who come here on behalf of their husbands, fathers, or brothers. There are no excuses for nonpayment. Her husband borrowed money he did not repay. No one will see Andrew unless I say so. Do you understand?"

Lawrence's face paled as Brian's orders were as good as Andrew's. "Yes, sir." Lawrence escorted the few women waiting to see Andrew out the front door.

Bull had a few men who wanted extensions on their loans and claimed to have a personal relationship with Andrew. Brian recognized one from Edinburgh but the rest he had never seen and knew that Andrew wouldn't want to be bothered. Brian looked at Bull, speaking loud enough for all to hear. "We don't give extensions. It's bad business. The collateral will be taken from anyone who does not pay today." He walked away refusing to hear their excuses and closed the door behind him.

Andrew smirked at his friend. "You are getting ruthless in your old age."

Brian shook his head. "You're one to talk. You have a son now, and your age will start to show."

Andrew signed the papers and handed them to Brian. "If there is nothing else, I will take a horse back to the cottage. I will be back for dinner tonight. See if you can arrange a meeting with Mr. Ryley. I hear he is one of Mr. Bailey's biggest adversaries and competitors. We may partner with some factories he is building in York."

Brian lifted the corner of his mouth. "How much did it bother you when he called you a crook?"

Andrew glared at Brian before forming a smile. "It's been years since I have been called that name."

Brian laughed and sat down. "Are you sure about dinner? I thought you might want to have dinner with your wife tonight."

Andrew's face changed to a stoic expression. "She is the mother of my child. That is all. I will not be dining with her."

Brian stared at Andrew, "Andrew, it's me your talking too. I have never spoken to you about her, but I think…"

Andrew stood up. "Don't think. It's not a subject I will discuss. If you will excuse me, I am going out the back."

CHAPTER 23

AMELIA STARED AT HER SON studying his little features. He was looking into the light holding her fingers. She tried to feed him earlier and after some awkward moments, finally got him to eat. Hopefully the wet nurse could get him to eat a little more. She felt content for the first time in months. His dark hair curled at the ends and Amelia laughed as she ran her finger through his hair pulling the little curls and watching them bounce back. Her heart warmed as he looked at her. She cooed and smiled at him giving him feather-like kisses all over his cheeks.

"How is he?" The deep voice woke her from her woolgathering. She turned her eyes and found Andrew standing in the doorway.

Amelia looked away staring at her son as she answered him. "Come and see." He walked to the edge of the bed seemingly hesitant to get too close to Amelia.

Andrew gazed at the baby and a smile formed on his face. "He already looks bigger."

Amelia laughed out loud. "You just saw him this morning. I am sure he is the same."

Andrew reached out and picked him up. "If he is anything like me, he will grow fast and soon have to carry me around."

Andrew kissed his son on the forehead. "How are you today?" He rocked him in his arms and kept smiling at him. The rocking eventually caused the baby to slowly close his eyes and before long he was asleep. Andrew kissed him again and laid him beside Amelia.

"I will come see baby Robert tomorrow." He turned around to leave.

Amelia's heart fell into her stomach. "You're leaving?"

Andrew turned around. "Yes, I have meetings and dinner planned out. I have a room at the inn."

Amelia looked at him confused. She finally blurted out. "I don't understand. This is your home."

Andrew drew his head back. "Home? No, this is not my home. This is your home. I provided it for you to raise our son. I don't live here—my home is in Edinburgh. I also have a residence in France and London that I will be visiting soon to check on my brother."

Amelia's eyes widened at his confession. "May I go with you to London?" she pleaded with him.

"No, the baby is too young to travel."

Andrew rubbed the stubble on his chin. "Listen, Amelia. Our agreement has not changed. I will provide you a home and a small living. You will be a mother to our son, and I will visit when I can. We will remain married in name only for his sake. In return, you will act properly and not engage in any questionable behavior. If you fail to keep your end of our bargain, then I will take our son away from you. Am I clear?"

Amelia's head was spinning. She will live as a prisoner, and it was legal. "What about you?"

Andrew tightened his lips. "What about me?"

Amelia lifted her chin. "Your questionable behavior?"

Andrew straightened his jacket. "I am no longer your concern. You lost the right to ask me about my whereabouts when you left me for that man. I know you have apologized, but I don't know if I can ever forgive you." He left the room not looking back.

She lost her breath, not able to control her sobs. Looking at her baby, her heart burned with such emptiness. Her husband was not physically abusive, but his words cut through her like a knife. What hurt the most was that they were true.

She picked up baby Robert and held him close to her chest. Trying to compose herself, she stood up from her bed and walked near the window. Holding her son close brought thoughts of her own mother. She imagined her mother holding her, hoping to never let her go. Memories of her father leaning down to speak to her flooded her mind. It was foggy, but she remembered the man with a funny hat telling her that she was to stay with her nurse Miss Mildred. She could not come with him, and her mother had gone to heaven. She didn't really understand what being dead meant. How cruel and matter-of-factly he spoke to her as a child.

A knock on the door interrupted her thoughts. "Mrs. Baird, I have come to take the baby for the night. Are you in need of any assistance?"

Amelia shook her head kissing Robert one last time before handing him to the nurse. She laid back down on the bed trying to fall asleep.

The next day Amelia overslept and quickly got up to feed the baby. She went to the nursery seeing the nurse holding him. "I apologize I overslept. Has he eaten yet?"

The nurse smiled. "He ate once, but could probably eat again." She handed the baby to Amelia who sat in the chair to feed Robert. The nurse cleaned up the room and looked over at Amelia. "Mr. Baird stopped by early this morning. He told me he wished to say goodbye to his son."

Amelia looked up at her. "Goodbye?"

The nurse looked down. "I am sorry Mrs. Baird, I thought you knew. He said he was going back to Edinburgh."

Amelia's eyes filled with tears as she tried to look away from the nurse.

The nurse rubbed her lips together unsure if she should say anything. "Mrs. Baird, forgive me if I speak out of turn. It's just that you are such a beautiful young girl full of love and compassion. I am having trouble watching you suffer at the expense of your husband." Amelia's shocked face must have scared the nurse. "Forgive me. It was not my place to say anything."

"No, please. It's quite all right. It's just that no one has shown me such kindness in a long time. My husband is not as bad as he seems. His reputation is exaggerated." Amelia managed to smile.

Mrs. Franklin smiled back at her. "My husband says I speak too freely sometimes."

Amelia drew her eyebrows together. "I have never asked about your family. Where are you from?"

Mrs. Franklin held up her hand. "No worries. I come from Dundee, we live in a cottage not too far from here. My baby is already two and can eat on her own. It was time for her to stop needing me for her nourishment. My husband is unable to work right now due to a broken arm. This extra money will help, so he won't be too upset. I would like to visit him on Sunday if that is acceptable to you?"

Amelia smiled. "Of course. Please stay overnight with your family. I will be fine."

A little over a month later, Robert was looking up at his mother. Cooing was a new favorite pastime. He was getting big and was the absolute joy of her life. Andrew had not seen him since he left that morning after he was born.

Mrs. Franklin, the wet nurse, had become a close friend and Amelia enjoyed her company. They planned a picnic and loaded up the basket with bread, cheese, wine, and apples. The walk through the gardens was pleasant. The temperature was mild, and Amelia thought it would be good to get the baby outdoors for fresh air.

"You should go home for a few days to spend some time with your daughter. The weather is so enjoyable nowadays."

Mrs. Franklin smiled. "My mother is watching her this week. I may go home on Sunday again provided you agree."

Amelia smiled. "Of course."

Amelia spread out a blanket and put the basket on top. Robert cuddled between the ladies. A few minutes later, a small rabbit snuck up beside Mrs. Franklin, touching her hand. She jerked her hand away and ran from the blanket screaming down the hill. Amelia was giggling as the baby watched her in interest. Exhausted, she came back up the hill and sat on the blanket beside Amelia. The look on Mrs. Franklin's face made Amelia laugh loudly trying to catch her breath. She held her stomach as her shoulders were shaking. She hadn't laughed this hard or enjoyed herself in such a long time.

After they ate their lunch, they heard a sound coming from the woods. Looking up, they saw Andrew walking toward their blanket. He looked over at them. "Hello, Amelia. Are you well?"

Amelia looked up a bit disoriented. "Andrew? What a surprise." She composed herself on the blanket. "Are you lost? I'm surprised you remembered you had a family."

Andrew looked between the two of them and closed his eyes. "Will you excuse us, Mrs. Franklin?"

She stood up wiping her skirt. "Of course. I will be inside the nursery if you should need me."

Andrew sat down beside the baby taking him into his arm ignoring Amelia's sarcastic words. Instead he put his full attention on his son. "Look at you! You have gotten so big."

Robert squirmed in his father's arms and started to whimper. Amelia crinkled her nose. "He doesn't know you." She reached for the baby and Andrew turned away from her. "Of course, he knows me, I am his father."

She took her hands away. "I know you're his father, but you're holding him too tightly. He is uncomfortable." The baby was crying harder, and Amelia's heart fell. "Please, Andrew! Let me hold him."

Andrew held the baby in one hand and grabbed Amelia's wrist with the other. "Stop it! I will not hurt him." He pushed her arms away rocking the baby as he cried and eventually fell asleep.

Amelia looked at him with concern. She held her wrist in her hand rubbing it looking away with watering eyes.

After a few moments, he broke his stare from the baby and looked at her. "Amelia, you will stop this loathing every time I am around you. We will be civil, or I will not see you on my visits."

Amelia's voice was shaking. "Loathing? Are you jesting? You leave your child for weeks, and when you return, I have to appease your mood swings."

The baby stirred and she whispered loudly, "Look, I already apologized for my wrong decision—I wish it never happened. I can't change it!" Taking in a deep breath, she touched his arm that held the baby. "I don't wish to live like this. Do you care about me at all?"

Andrew studied his wife's face in silence. It was the first time in their acquaintance that she had asked him such a personal question about his feelings for her. He had longed at one time to confess his affection and have it returned. But he didn't trust her and had to guard his heart.

He whispered locking her eyes with his. "You're the mother of my son, and I hold *that* in high regard. But with everything we have been through, you are now like an employee who takes care of my son. I can't see you as anything more than that." He lied.

Amelia's face turned deep red showing sadness mixed with anger. She stood up facing Andrew. "If that is all Mr. Baird, may I take my son to the nursery?"

He looked at her standing in front of him noticing how her womanly curves had accentuated more lusciously since having a child. It stirred up feelings in his body that he wanted to ignore, and he had to look away. She addressed him formally as Mr. Baird, and although it annoyed him, he would not correct her. His feelings for her had not changed—and no matter how hard he wanted to dismiss them, she still moved him like no other. He bent down and kissed the baby and handed him to Amelia. She took the baby and walked away from Andrew without saying a word.

Andrew worked in the small study for the rest of the afternoon choosing not to return to the inn. He would never admit it to his men, but he wanted to be close to her and Robert.

Before dinner, he went up to the nursery and spent some time with Robert. Amelia stayed in her room not wanting to speak to Andrew. As dinnertime approached, Brian, Bull and a few other guards joined Andrew in the dining room. They waited for Amelia.

Growing annoyed, he whispered to the housekeeper. "Mrs. Palmer, could you tell my wife that dinner is ready and we await her presence?"

Her face grew white. "Forgive me, Mr. Baird. Mrs. Baird took a tray to her room thirty minutes ago when I told her you were here dining with some friends."

Andrew clenched his jaw having to force the words out of his mouth. "Did she say anything else?"

The housekeeper clutched the folds of her gown in fear. "Um… She said something peculiar about being an employee and not dining with her betters when Mr. Baird was at home. I didn't understand her, but she shut the door in my face before I could ask any other questions, so I went to fetch her tray."

Andrew looked away from the housekeeper and motioned to the footman. He addressed his friends. "Amelia will not be joining us this evening. I have asked the footman to serve our first course." The men began to speak louder about a few of the women in the tavern next to the inn. Andrew didn't engage in the conversation and instead stared at his plate taking a drink of wine lost in his thoughts.

Brian addressed him. "Andrew, tell them about the time you watched old lady Rhonda's cats."

Andrew looked up with a smile on his face. "You mean the cat lady?"

He knew what Brian was trying to do with getting his mind thinking about something else and lightening the mood. "Yes, she even looked like her cats growing up."

Andrew smiled at the memory. "She always had many cats coming in and out of her home. She treated them like her children. One day she offered me some money to watch them for her. I was only around one and three and thought it would be easy money. I made Brian and Ian help me. My little brother left the kitchen window open in her house and all the cats disappeared. We ran all over the street trying to find the cats before she got home. I had to climb trees, crawl under carriages, go into people's homes, and chase cats down the street. I had scratches, bites, and probably fleas by the time we finished collecting them all and putting them back inside her house." He shook his head looking at Brian.

Bull smiled. "What happened when she returned home?"

Andrew tilted his head. "She refused to pay me because she said they were a mess and had been outside. I don't know how she knew, but somehow she did." Andrew leaned back in his chair. "But she did pay me all right. It was the beginning of the respect that I demanded."

Brian laughed. "She even paid with interest."

They laughed together not indulging on how Andrew got paid. They knew of his reputation and chose to keep quiet.

Dinner concluded shortly afterward. Andrew went upstairs to check on Robert. He was sleeping, and the nurse was out of the room. Andrew touched his son's face as his heart clenched seeing how fragile he looked sleeping so peacefully. He left him alone and went down the hallway. Stopping in front of Amelia's door, he contemplated if he should open it or not. He had no idea what he would even say. After a few moments, he chose to leave her alone and went back to the inn with his friends.

After being there for a little while and not being able to enjoy himself, he went back to the cottage and slept in the chair beside the crib. Watching his son sleep tugged at his heart. Never an emotional man, his chest ached to protect him.

The next morning Amelia awoke early and was startled to find Andrew asleep with Robert in his arms. Her eyes watered watching them together and thoughts of what could have been. Mrs. Franklin went into town to visit her family, and Amelia needed to feed the baby. Not wanting to wake him, she carefully removed the baby from his arms.

Amelia hummed quietly as she rocked back and forth until she heard a noise coming from her husband. She looked up stunned to see Andrew awake and staring at her breast. Embarrassed at being exposed, she reached for a blanket to cover herself. "I didn't know you were awake."

Andrew shook his head at her and smirked. "It's okay, it's only me. I have seen you naked."

Amelia looked away trying to cover her breast. "I don't think it's proper for you to watch me feed Robert. After all, I am only your employee."

Andrew smirked playfully, "True. But some employers exercise such rights. We could engage in an arrangement if you desire."

She glared at him and threw a linen at his head. He ducked in surprise at her playful behavior and laughed. Amelia tried to keep a straight face but laughed too. It was the first time since she moved to Dundee that she laughed with him. "You must be jesting."

She took Robert from her chest and wiped his mouth carefully ensuring that a blanket covered her from exposing herself any more than she already had. She held him to burp him and handed him to Andrew. Turning away from Andrew, she adjusted her gown giving him a glimpse of her back.

Andrew tried to look away but couldn't help noticing her smooth back and perfectly curved neck. Desire for her was affecting him. When she faced him again, completely dressed and covered, he couldn't help but feel a bit disappointment in his gut.

Andrew kissed his son on the cheek and handed him back to Amelia. He had to get out of there quickly, or he would lose control. "I must go back to Edinburgh. I will be back soon to visit."

Amelia looked down at Robert ignoring Andrew. Andrew bent over to kiss him one more time while she held him. Her scent invaded his nose causing him to remember their closeness. He turned away and walked out the door before he could do something that he would regret.

He found Mrs. Palmer in the kitchen. "I have some money for her art supplies. You have kept our secret?"

Mrs. Palmer nodded. "Yes, sir. She thinks we have some extra money left over each month from the household accounts. She has no idea that you bought her the paints. I still don't know why you keep it hidden that you buy these things for her."

Andrew took the money out of his pocket. "I will give you some extra this month, so she can get some more paper as well. Maybe buy her a few frames." Mrs. Palmer nodded taking the money from him.

He put on his hat and looked at Mrs. Palmer. "Painting makes her happy. And for some reason that I can't explain, that makes me happy."

CHAPTER 24

A FEW WEEKS LATER, THE AIR grew colder than Amelia thought possible. The northern climate combined with the sea air made the outdoors almost unbearable at times. She kept baby Robert wrapped in blankets near the fire most of the day. Her meals consisted of hot soups or teas trying to stay warm. Amelia spent most of her time painting in the attic when she wasn't playing with Robert. Mrs. Palmer arranged a small workspace for her to indulge in her favorite activity. Her drawings were mostly of snow-capped mountains or raging seas. Her art distracted her from her loneliness as she looked out the small window into the whiteness of the snow.

"Mrs. Baird, you must come at once. It's baby Robert."

Amelia dropped her paintbrush and ran down the attic stairs.

"Forgive me for scaring you, he is well. We just noticed that he is blowing bubbles." Mrs. Palmer covered her mouth with the back of her hand as she laughed. "I think he scared himself."

Amelia let the relief fill her veins. As she came further into the room, she saw Mrs. Franklin lying with him on the blanket next to the fire.

"Oh, Mrs. Baird. Please watch him when I lay him on his stomach."

Amelia attentively watched as Robert pushed bubbles out of his mouth. He widened his little eyes at his newfound ability. Amelia's heart melted as she went and picked him up. "Look at you, my big boy."

The three women laughed together as they played with Robert on the floor.

Amelia's heart ached a bit at not being able to share this with Andrew. But she quickly pushed thoughts of him out of her mind. She needed to accept her role as a sole provider for her son. After all, many widows could provide a proper upbringing for their children when their fathers were not there to help. Why should she be any different? Andrew was not dead, but had made his choice to leave. She would not beg him to change his mind.

A few more weeks passed and some of the bitter chilly air subsided. Amelia took small walks outside during the afternoon's trying not to go mad indoors. She wished she could ride in the countryside, but didn't want to push her luck with the stable staff. One day on her way back to the house, she noticed a lone horse with a black carriage. Not recognizing the marking, she went through the front door to inquire about their guest.

Mrs. Palmer approached her and whispered. "You have a guest, Mrs. Baird. She didn't state her business but said she had an important matter to discuss with you and would wait in the drawing room. I put her in there and shut the door not to alert the guards. We don't want loose lips speaking to Mr. Baird." She winked at Amelia who smiled back.

She opened the door and was surprised to see Judith. "Amelia, I am so happy to see you. Forgive me for not coming sooner. We took a trip abroad, and your return letters came without my knowledge. We came back few weeks ago, but with the severe weather, I have not been able to come. I wanted to bring them to you posthaste."

Amelia looked down at the letters. Two were marked over three months ago and one was two weeks ago. "I don't know what to say. I had lost hope. Thank you so much!"

Judith smiled and sat back down. "I know you said you were not allowed visitors, but with the awful weather I was afraid I would not catch you outdoors and hoped to take my chances."

She took a drink of tea that Mrs. Palmer had served. "If anyone asks, I am also part of the city society and call upon wealthy residence for charitable donations. We have plenty of opportunities to give to the less fortunate. Perhaps you and your husband would like to be part of our small group?" She smiled and winked.

Amelia winked back. "My husband is out of town. However, when he arrives, I will ask him to donate."

She put down her teacup as her smile faded. "How are you, Amelia? I must admit that I have thought about you a lot since we last met. My husband warned me to stay away. I don't think it's fair to judge you by your husband. Some women have no choice who they marry."

Amelia's heart burned at the chance to have a friend—one that Andrew didn't know and have an influence upon. "I am well and had a beautiful baby boy who is resting upstairs. I do understand your husband's concern, but to be fair my husband and I live separate lives. We barely see each other and do not share the same friends."

Judith studied her face. "That must be a remarkable story and once you trust me more, I hope you will tell me. For now, I must go. However, I will be back to see about my donation." She smiled as she put on her bonnet and cloak.

Amelia nodded her head. "Of course. I will let me husband know. He likes to appear to be a generous businessman. A donation would help in that pursuit."

Judith put her hand on Amelia's shoulder and squeezed it reassuringly before bidding her a good day with a promise to return soon.

Amelia went to her chamber as Robert was sleeping. She locked the chamber door and pulled out the letters as she lay on her bed.

The first letter was from Rachel dated four months ago.

My Dearest Friend,

It's been so long since I last spoke to you. I have sent a few letters that were returned to me. I went and saw your stepmother who didn't have a clue as to your well-being. She put on a nice show with tea and pleasantries, but I saw right through her. I was very relieved to get your letter and to learn a way to keep in contact with you. I should have known that you would be unable to communicate with me freely once you married that man.

There is nothing to forgive, my friend. I can't imagine making the sacrifices that you have made. Please know you will always have a friend in me.

Sincerely,
Rachel

The next one was from Sally dated three months ago.

Dear Amelia,

I told you Billy was a sweet-talker. He should not have left you in that carriage alone. I have not spoken to him since I told him about

you marrying that Scottish fellow and moving to Edinburgh. He was
mad when I told him where you were. If I hear from him, I will write
you again. Chuck said Billy was looking for your mother—not sure if
he found her or not. Be careful who you trust, Amelia.

> *Your friend,*
> *Sally*

Amelia ripped open the last one dated six weeks ago.

Dear Amelia,

We saw Billy yesterday. He came into town with a few new guys he
met in York. He said you had left him. He came back to the carriage
and you were gone. He said he had no choice but to leave with the
money he got from your ring because your husband had many people
trying to kill him. He said your husband is ruthless with lots of money.
Does he hurt you, Amelia?

Billy told Chuck that he did find your mother and she is in a
traveling show. She changed her name to Mary Brady and will be in
Edinburgh on March 17th for the show called Blue Birds. Billy said he
might try to make it to the show since you're locked away. If he can, he
will tell her how to find you.

> *Your Friend,*
> *Sally*

Amelia clutched the letter to her chest. Her mother would be in Edinburgh, and her name was Mary Brady. Tears formed in her eyes at the prospect of seeing her mother. The date was a few days away, and tough decisions had to be made. She did not trust Billy to speak to her mother despite what he told Sally. This was her one chance to find out for herself if her mother was alive and find out why she left her that fateful day. Was she forced to give her up? Did she try to find her?

A knock on the door interrupted her thoughts. Mrs. Franklin came in and saw Amelia crying. "Mrs. Baird, what is the matter?"

She tried to hide the letters under her skirt and wiped away her tears. "I am well. Just a bit melancholy I suppose."

Mrs. Franklin bit her bottom lip unsure if she should pry. "Mrs. Baird, was it the visitor that came to see you this morning? I helped keep the guards at bay. If you want to talk about it, I promise I am a good listener."

Amelia's shoulders shook as she put her face into her hands. "It was about my mother."

Mrs. Franklin tilted her head. "I am not sure I understand?"

Amelia took a deep breath. "I was told when I was a little girl that my mother died. But servants whispered that my mother had left my father in the middle of the night." Amelia wiped her face with her hands fidgeting with the blanket on the bed. Mrs. Franklin handed her a handkerchief.

"Do you think she is alive?" Mrs. Franklin sat beside her on the bed.

"I hardly know. When I was a little, I dreamed of her coming for me—especially when I moved to London to live with my father. He was cruel and indifferent at the same time. He assured me she had died and was buried in France, so I was unable to visit her gravesite. I believed him for a while but always hoped it was a mistake and that she would come for me. I imagined that she would tell me that my father kept her away from me. All he told me was that they were married briefly and she died. He married my stepmother shortly afterward. I don't think that is true. He must have threatened my mother to stay away from me. I want her to know that it is safe now that I am grown. We can be together."

Mrs. Franklin pressed her lips together. "What about your husband?"

Amelia's face looked pale. "I will speak to him—maybe he will allow her to visit. But I haven't the time right now. The visitor brought me a letter from a friend who told me she will be in Edinburgh in a few days. She is in a traveling show from Paris. I need to find her."

Mrs. Franklin asked in a concern way, "Do you think your husband will allow you to go?"

Amelia looked away not able to answer her question. Mrs. Franklin asked, "Amelia, do you think you have time to get to Edinburgh and see your mother and then get back before he comes home again?"

Amelia widened her eyes. "Mrs. Franklin, please listen carefully. I would never ask you to do anything that could cause you problems."

Mrs. Franklin reached for her hand. "I want to help you as you have helped me."

Amelia looked down at her hands considering her idea. She took a deep breath, "I will leave in two days. It will take me at least a day and a half to get to Edinburgh. I could take the mail coach and dress as a servant. Once I find my mother, I will convince her to come back to Dundee with me. I should be back within a few travel days. I will need you to take care of Robert. Tell the staff I am in my room or the attic. Andrew waited at least a month the last time he visited. If I leave soon, I shall be back before he returns. I will have to let Mrs. Palmer know the truth."

Mrs. Franklin shook her head. "I think you should not tell her. I will tell her once you are gone. That way she will be forced to keep your secret and won't be able to stop you. She won't like it, but she won't betray you either." She reached over and hugged Amelia. Amelia cried in her arms, glad she had someone in her life that would help her.

CHAPTER 25

ANDREW RECLINED IN THE CHAIR looking over papers in his study. He had just arrived home from Glasgow. It had brought back a lot of memories from his childhood being in the area. He normally sent his men to conduct business there, but he wanted to stay busy and keep his mind off Amelia and Robert. The baby had her eyes and looking at him was like looking at her. It tore his heart, and he found it more tolerable to stay away.

Brian entered the study. "It's been a long day and the men want to go to the Tree Lounge. Jean has a new singer performing tonight. The men saw her perform in London and they say she is quite beautiful."

Andrew grunted. "They think any woman on stage in beautiful if she gives them the time of day."

Brian smiled. "It won't hurt to check it out. Perhaps I will get lucky."

Andrew put the papers on his desk away and put on his coat. The men loaded the carriage and were on their way. Andrew looked out the window thinking about his son. One day he would explain to him why he had to stay away. Perhaps when he got older, he would take him in the summers when he wasn't in school and teach him about life. He didn't want his son to take over his business as it was—possibly parts of the legitimate side in shipping and factories. He would send him to Oxford to learn about business from professors instead of criminals.

The carriage slowed to a stop, and the men entered the Tree Lounge. Jean had their usual table ready for them and drinks were served quickly. She winked at Andrew and hugged him. "Good to see you tonight. I will talk to you later as we are very busy. Miss Briar is here, and the place is going mad. I will introduce you after the first show. She is doing two tonight. Greg made a stage in the corner and Katie will play the piano."

Andrew removed his coat. "It sounds like you have everything under control. Barns will come by tomorrow to collect the profits." Jean nodded and was distracted by more people coming into the tavern. She left the group to see to some waitresses.

The men enjoyed their drinks as the crowds pushed into the room. Every table was taken, and more chairs were set up along the walls near the stage. The room's heat was stifling with the smell of body odor and perfume. Miss Briar entered from the back office, and the crowds cheered and whistled. Andrew turned to look at the painted face woman with long white blond hair. She wore most of her hair down with only one side pinned up in a barrette. Her tight-fitting gold gown showed off her voluptuous curves and left little to the imagination. She walked to the stage with an exaggerated sway of her hips attracting nearly every man in the tavern.

The rough, throaty sound of her voice brought chills to the audience as she performed three songs. Her attention was on Andrew's table in most of her verses. She did play with the audience with a seductive smile and skillful body language. After the set, she returned to the back office as the crowd ordered more drinks waiting for the second set of songs.

Jean took Andrew and a few of his men to the back office to meet Miss Briar. She was sitting in the chair behind the desk and stood when they entered the room. Jean smiled at her. "Miss Briar, I would like to introduce you to the owner of the Tree Lounge, Mr. Baird and his associates."

She arched her back showing off her plunging neckline and smiled at the men. "Nice to meet all of you. Please call me Vivian."

Brian took her hand and kissed it. "I am Brian and it's a pleasure, Vivian." She narrowed her eyes. "Aren't you a charmer?"

She looked at Andrew. "I have heard a lot about you, Mr. Baird. The infamous Black Baird. I was hoping to meet you tonight." She held out her hand to him.

He smiled as he took her hand and kissed it. "Don't believe everything you hear."

She stared at him like he was the only man in the room. "Did you enjoy my show?"

He looked at his men. "Did you enjoy her show?"

They all nodded, and Bull spoke up. "You're a great singer. We saw you in London when you were there."

She broke her stare from Andrew and looked at the men. "I thought I recognized such handsome men."

They all blushed as she flirted. She turned her focus back to Andrew. "Mr. Baird, do you mind if I call you Andrew?"

He smiled. "As you wish."

She licked the top of her teeth not breaking her stare from him. "You know Andrew—you are the reason why I played at the Tree Lounge tonight. You're a hard man to meet socially. I was hoping after the show we could get to know each other better?"

The men looked at him with a bit of jealousy in their eyes.

Jean's smile faded as she replied, "The second set should start in just a moment. Perhaps you men should take your seats."

The men walked out of the room and Vivian reached for Andrew's arm. "Andrew, please think about having a drink with me tonight."

He took her hand and kissed it again. "I look forward to hearing you sing again." He left the room without answering her question.

Brian stared at Andrew as he took his seat. Andrew looked over at him annoyed. "What's amiss?"

Brian snorted. "Your luck astonishes me."

Andrew creased his brow. "Why? Because of the singer?"

Brian let out a sigh. "You will be thoroughly entertained. Lucky dog."

Andrew flipped his hand. "I don't have time for that type of entertainment. I have a lot of work to do."

Brian took a drink and shook his head. "What is wrong with you?"

Andrew opened his mouth, leaning his head back. "What makes you ask that?"

Brian rolled his eyes. "Andrew, you have a beautiful, willing woman who is practically giving you an invitation to sleep with her, and you have work to do?"

Andrew stared at him not saying a word.

Brian took another drink. "I know what this is about." He looked at the men who were engrossed in their own conversations then leaned over and whispered. "It's a shame you don't do anything about it and choose to stay miserable."

Andrew glared at Brian. "You seem to be full of knowledge tonight. Why don't you tell me how I should live my life?"

Whistles sounded throughout the room again and a few cheers as Vivian made her way to the stage. She stopped at the table and blew the men a kiss while she walked to the piano. Andrew looked away and took a drink.

Brian stood up. "May I speak to you in private?"

Andrew stood and followed Brian to the back office. Jean noticed the two and Brian gestured that they needed some privacy. She nodded her understanding as the piano music started.

Brian sat down on the chair behind the desk and Andrew sat in the other chair by the door. He looked at Brian. "What is all of this about?"

Brian replied. "It's about you not trusting me and deceiving yourself."

Andrew was puzzled by his oldest friend who was closer to him than his own brother. He stared at him. "I don't understand?"

Brian leaned back in his chair. "You are wasting your life. You're in love with your wife and can't see past your own pride to allow yourself to be happy. Yes, she made a mistake. Not a fatal one. You haven't been with another woman since you met her. Beautiful women throw themselves at you, but you push them away because of her. You are only punishing yourself. You have a blessing of a beautiful son that you never see because you're mad at your wife. You're a bad father, Andrew!"

Andrew's mouth widened, and he glared at Brian.

Brian held up his hand, his face turning red. He loosened his cravat. "I never thought I would say that. But it's been too long and she has suffered enough. I don't think she would make the same mistake *ever* again. Your home is wherever your family is. I can handle things. I helped you build this business. You don't trust me to run it in your absence? Go home."

Andrew's chest hurt at the emotions he felt. No one dare spoke to him that way. Only Brian had the guts and he did it with apprehension.

A few seconds of awkward silence came over the room. He finally stood up, "You're wrong. I do trust you, Brian. It's just difficult for me to talk about Amelia." He rubbed his forehead with his hand. "I don't know if I have the strength to forgive her. Perhaps that is a weakness of mine."

Brian looked up at him shocked by his vulnerability. "I have known you most my life. You are a different person when you are around her. She has brought out your human side." He chuckled as he stood up and walked over to him. "Forgiving her doesn't make what she did right. It gives you a chance to be happy as a husband and father. Hating her is only making you miserable. Besides, I know you're in love with her even though you try to stay away. I have never heard you use the word, but it's obvious to me."

Andrew looked down as he straightened his jacket. "If you will excuse me, I will call it a night. I have to get home and pack as I will be leaving early tomorrow morning." He winked and patted Brian on the back. "I will tell the men you are in charge. I want to take a few weeks off."

Brian cracked a smile. "I have one more favor to ask of you."

Andrew raised his brow and Brian opened the door letting the music soar into the room. He whispered, "Perhaps you could be a little rude to our Miss Briar when you say goodbye? That way I can console her after you leave as being the blackguard that you are."

Andrew laughed out loud as they walked out of the room.

Amelia took a few pounds she had hidden and sewed them into her petticoat. That would be enough to get the stagecoach tickets back to Dundee and a few nights at the inn. She didn't want to carry it in her reticule just in case she was robbed on the stagecoach. It wasn't unheard of to be a part of highway robberies. Mrs. Franklin had brought her an old gown to wear. It was gray and a little worn around the collar. She gave her a dark bonnet and old shoes to fit the part of a servant.

"You're naturally beautiful, Amelia. My suggestion is to hide it as much as possible." She helped Amelia tie her hair up in a tight bun hidden under the bonnet. She gave her an old worn cloak with a hood that could obscure some of Amelia's face.

"I purchased the ticket yesterday to Edinburgh with the money you had left from Mr. Baird this month. Mrs. Palmer left the money in a bowl in her room. I told her you requested some supplies and I was going to town. Not exactly a lie. I will pack you a few snacks, and I think you should bring a piece of jewelry in case you need to sell it."

Amelia nodded and took a bracelet Andrew had given her. She put it in her cloak pocket. "Thank you, Mrs. Franklin. I don't know what I would do without your help. I feel horrible leaving Robert."

Mrs. Franklin touched her arm. "He will be fine. I will spend lots of time with him. You will be home within a few days. Now we must go before Mrs. Palmer returns. She is at Mrs. Burton's purchasing kitchen supplies.

I can stall her for a while after she returns. That should give you plenty of time to get to the coach. My husband is waiting for you with our cart on the corner of Birch Street. He will take you where you need to be."

Amelia nodded and kissed Robert goodbye. She took her bag and went to meet Mrs. Franklin's husband. He was a short man with black hair and a crooked front tooth. Amelia was hesitant, but he was friendly and took her to the coach. Amelia tried to pay him, but he refused and instead wished her well on her journey.

The stagecoach was packed full. Amelia sat by the window so she could look outside. A young woman sat beside her with an older man next to her. Amelia couldn't figure out if they were married or father and daughter. Across from her was a middle-aged man dressed as a soldier. Amelia wondered why he didn't have his own horse but kept her opinions to herself. Beside him were two older men who introduced themselves as blacksmiths.

The ride was mostly in silence before they stopped at the inn. It was already their third stop and Amelia realized that riding in a stagecoach took a lot longer than a private carriage. She rented a room for the night. Not wanting to spend any more money, she had some bread in her bag that she ate for dinner.

The inn was loud in the middle of the night. She could hear the piano and tables moving across the floor. The noise reminded Amelia of her trip from London when she first married Andrew. A smile came across her face at the way he looked at her. Always strong in front of his men yet so gentle with her behind closed doors. If people only knew how long they waited to consummate their marriage due to her nervousness. What other man did she know that would have waited to exercise their husbandly rights? Her chest burned with the loss of his favor. Andrew could be a good man although she didn't want to see it in the beginning. His words and actions could be harsh, yet she understood him.

Her thoughts turned to Robert—she missed him terribly and hoped Mrs. Franklin was taking care of him the way that she would. Would he be crying for her? Tears escaped her eyes as she fell asleep dreaming of her baby.

Andrew arrived in Dundee early in the morning. He was anxious to speak to Amelia. There was much to say and he was finally ready to have a conversation. The house was quiet when he entered the front door. It was unlocked and no one came as he stood in the doorway. He could hear some movement in the kitchen and entered to inquire the staff about his wife.

Mrs. Palmer grabbed her chest. "Mr. Baird, you startled me!"

He crinkled his brow. "Yes, Mrs. Palmer. I came this morning to see my wife and son. Are they well? I just wanted to get a glass of water first. I am parched from my journey. I have a few guards in the stable. If you could prepare some food for us, that would be much appreciated."

Mrs. Palmer's turned white. She stood mesmerized by his words unable to speak. He looked at her peculiarly. "Are you well? You look ill."

Mrs. Franklin entered the kitchen carrying Robert. When she saw Andrew, she gasped loudly. "Mr. Baird?"

He looked at her and a smile came across his face. "He is huge. I have been away too long." He walked over and took Robert out of her arms. Holding him close, he kissed him on the forehead. "I missed you, my son."

Both women looked at each other and back at Andrew. He put his face in his son's neck and laughed. "Where is Amelia? I wish to speak to her." He headed toward the servant staircase assuming Amelia was upstairs.

Mrs. Palmer let out a breath. "Forgive us, Mr. Baird."

Andrew looked at both of them still holding Robert in his arms. "For what?"

She looked at Mrs. Franklin who looked like she was going to faint. "Um... She is away from the house."

Andrew shrugged his shoulders not understanding. "Where is she?"

Mrs. Franklin rubbed her lips together. "Mrs. Baird said she would be back in a few days. She hated leaving Robert, but it was regarding a family member. She left yesterday."

Andrew's face turned red as he tried to keep his temper under control. "Mrs. Franklin, do you like working in my home?"

She nodded her head as she fidgeted with the baby blanket she was holding.

Andrew looked at Mrs. Palmer. "Do you enjoy working for me?"

She bit the inside of her cheek. "Yes, sir."

He adjusted Robert in his arms. "Then stop talking in circles and tell me what is going on with my wife or both of you will be dismissed today with no references."

Mrs. Palmer started speaking first. "Mrs. Baird received a letter about her mother and read it to Mrs. Franklin. I was away from the home shopping when they planned her trip. I found out after Amelia was gone."

"What about the guards? They didn't see her leave?" He was growing impatient and the tone of his voice reflected his annoyance.

Mrs. Franklin's voice caught in her throat. "No, Mr. Baird. I didn't tell them she left. Mrs. Baird didn't want to leave Robert. I volunteered to watch him and she was only to be gone for a few days. Her mother was found in Edinburgh at a small playhouse. The play was called *Blue Birds*. She found out her mother changed her name to Mary Brady. She was only going to be in Edinburgh for one day. It was her only chance to find out it if her mother was really alive."

Andrew gritted his teeth. "Who was the letter from?" He braced himself for her answer. Hoping it would not be Billy as his forgiveness could only go so far.

Mrs. Franklin took a second to remember. "It was a woman named Sally, I believe. Amelia knew her from London."

Andrew took a deep breath and handed Robert back to Mrs. Franklin.

"I will travel back to Edinburgh at once. The horses are tired and we will need to fetch some fresh ones to make our journey. If she returns before I get back, make sure she doesn't leave again. Are we clear?"

Mrs. Palmer replied. "Yes sir, Mr. Baird."

Andrew kissed Robert. "Please pack us a few baskets of food. I want to travel until it gets dark so I can reach Edinburgh by tomorrow evening."

CHAPTER 26

T HE NEXT DAY THEY LEFT early. Amelia was famished and ate two apples and a boiled egg to break her fast. The group squeezed into the stagecoach making their way to Edinburgh. Amelia was hoping she could find the small theatre quickly so she could find her mother and get back to Dundee. She also didn't want to be spotted by any of Andrew's employees or friends. Dressed in servant clothes gave her a certain amount of protection and peace of mind.

They arrived late in the evening in front of an inn. Amelia secured a room spending more of her dwindling money. She stayed in there the rest of the night to not attract the attentions of the other guests.

The next morning, she changed to a more suitable gown, not wanting to greet her mother in servant clothing. She folded the clothes in her bag for her return trip. She hoped that she could catch the stagecoach the following day, so she didn't have much time.

The sidewalks were busy with the day's business. Smoke filled the city and animal scents filled the air. Amelia kept her head down looking for the theatre. A few men made some suggestive comments as she walked down the streets. She ignored them and kept walking hoping they would not try to stop her. An unescorted female could become a target in a city. After a few hours, she relented and went into a candle store to ask for directions.

A very tall man with blond hair greeted her. "Are you needing any assistance, Miss?" Amelia didn't want to appear rude and thought to buy something small for his trouble.

"Yes, I am. I wish to purchase some candles." Amelia dug into her reticule upset that she had to spend some of her money. She had to make sure she had enough to buy the tickets back to Dundee.

The man smiled largely. "I am Mr. Johnson. I would be pleased to assist you. Please have a seat." He helped her to the counter to look at different selections of candles that he thought she would like.

"Mr. Johnson, I thank you for your help." She picked a few candles that were not expensive and finished paying as he wrapped them up in a bag. She smiled. "I must go to the theatre now and visit a friend of mine while I am in town. If you could be so kind to give me the directions."

He patted her arm. "Miss, you really should have an escort in the city. It's about time for me to take my lunch. I could escort you there."

Amelia smiled. "That would be very kind of you."

Mr. Johnson strolled with her through the city.

He took her to the theatre and she thanked him for the assistance. The front doors were locked until the show later that night. She walked around the theatre trying to find an entrance. Unable to find any help, she walked to the bakery across the street from the theatre. Perhaps something to drink or eat would help her pass the time until the theater opened. It would be a few more hours before they started selling tickets.

Taking a seat by the window, she watched the activity flurry around her. Merchants sold flowers and trinkets out on the cobblestone sidewalk. Vegetable and fruit stands proved to be popular among the locals. Children ran up and down the streets—some looking for their parents and other begging for money. Amelia studied each customer as they came in to order their drinks and treats. She hid behind her cloak to obscure her identity. The smells in the bakery made her mouth water. Cinnamon and sugar filled the air with sweetness. Memories of her childhood baking with her governess filled her mind.

A touch on her arm surprised her as she turned her head to find the culprit. A heaviness came over her as she recognized the man behind a worn hat and spectacles. "Billy?"

The corner of his mouth turned upward. "I knew you would come." He sat at the table next to hers looking a different direction to appear nonchalant. He leaned over behind him and whispered, "We must be discreet so wait a moment and then meet me around back. There is an abandoned store next to a dress shop. The side door is unlocked." He stood up and moved through the front door not looking back and went around the building.

Amelia waited a few moments and walked out the doors going around the side between the stores to the back. She noticed a dress shop across the street and walked to the side until she found a door. She turned the knob and it opened. She walked in looking for Billy when she heard the door slam behind her.

Billy stood beside her without his hat and spectacles. "We meet again, love."

She took a step away from him. "Are you mad?"

He slanted his head. "Is that any way to thank me? I am the one who found your mother. I knew if I gave that message to Sally, you would come. You found a way, didn't you?" He put his hand around her waist pulling her closer.

She put her hands on his chest pushing him away. "Billy, stop. You have ruined my life." She broke away from him. "You left me there with *nothing*. You took my wedding ring and now my husband hates me. The only reason why I have a place to live is because I was pregnant."

Billy creased his forehead. "Pregnant?" He eyed her body checking out her stomach. He shook his head, "It's not my fault! I told you to wait in the carriage. It's *your* fault they found you. Don't blame me. I told you I would take care of you and you didn't trust me."

He grabbed her hands squeezing them. "Don't you understand that I had to leave? Your husband was trying to kill me. I had no choice."

Amelia pulled her hands out of his grip and took a step away. "It doesn't matter. I am only here to see my mother."

Billy took a step toward her and touched her face. "I thought about you every day."

Amelia met his eyes with hers. "I was told you were married. Is that true?"

Billy took his hand away and looked down. "In name only. We never loved each other. You're the one I want to be with."

Amelia sighed heavily at the realization of who he really was. No longer was she infatuated with the man. "I can't, Billy. After you left me, I realized that I was wrong. I was married and now I have a baby. He hates me, but I still can't be with you. I have too much to lose."

Billy stared at her. "Don't say that. We can work it out."

She shook her head. "No, I won't lose my child. Please, if you care about me, just leave me alone."

He stared at her without saying a word. After a moment, he shook his head. "We could have been great together Amelia. You and me traveling the world."

She looked away. "You will always be a dreamer, Billy. Trust me, I am not the girl you think I am. I need stability. Please, move aside. I must go."

He reached for her and pulled her next to his chest. She tried to push away, but he held her tighter.

He kissed her on the forehead and finally released her. "I hope you find what you are looking for." He walked out the door and shut it behind him.

Amelia stared at the door for a few moments before letting a tear come down her face. Billy may have been her first love, but he was not her future. She was happy that he was not her husband. Her thoughts turned to her mother and finding out the truth. Then she would have to figure out how to get her husband back.

The theatre doors were open and Amelia paid for a ticket. She snuck around to the side doors finding her way to the back behind the curtains. A few dressing rooms were locked and stage hands were busy with the set. The costume props and wardrobe were in a back room and Amelia couldn't help but to touch the beautiful gowns.

"Are you working in costumes?" A voice echoed across the room.

Amelia quickly took her hand away from the dress. "Forgive me—I was looking for a woman." She noticed the man narrowed his eyes at her deciding if she was going to be trouble.

"Who may that be?" He took a few steps in her direction. Amelia dropped her shoulders trying to mask her nerves.

"Miss Mary Brady." Amelia trembled a little at his large stature towering over her. He rubbed his chin and stared at her from head to toe. "Who may you be? We don't allow guests back here."

Amelia lifted her chin. "I am her daughter."

The man cracked a smile. "Mary Brady doesn't have children."

Amelia rubbed her lips together. "Sir, I am her daughter. If you could tell her I am here to see her, I would be most grateful."

The man touched Amelia's chin turning her face from right to left. Amelia swallowed hard willing herself not to jerk away. He dropped his hand to his side. "You do look like her, only a better version." He raised his brow checking out her body. "You would look good on stage. Have you considered the theatre?"

Amelia wanted to cover herself as his eyes drank her in. She stepped away from him trying to keep her senses.

Not wanting to upset him, she played along hoping to gather information about her mother. "Perhaps it's something we could discuss later. If it's not too much trouble, could you escort me to my mother?"

He snorted and held out his elbow. "I would love to escort a beautiful woman."

She took his arm hoping that his flirtation would end. They walked through some paths of wood boxes full of stage props to a few rooms in the back. He turned to Amelia. "Wait here, and I will get her for you." Amelia nodded as he disappeared through the door.

Amelia's heart was pounding through her chest. Her mother was on the other side of that door and she was going to see her for the first time. Her whole life she had prayed for this moment. The door opened and the man lifted his chin toward the door. "She is getting dressed for her performance and claims she has no daughter."

Amelia's heart hurt and she looked down. The man touched her hand. "You look too much like her not to be hers. Go on in. I will give you a few minutes."

Amelia looked up and whispered, "Thank you." She reached for the door, closing her eyes.

The room was small and smelled of flowers. They lined the tables and curtains covered the small windows. It was dark, but the candlelight allowed her to see a woman brushing her hair looking at herself in a looking glass.

Amelia cleared her throat. "Miss Brady?"

The woman stopped brushing her hair and looked to Amelia. She stared at her for a few moments. "You shouldn't have come."

Amelia's bottom lip began to tremble. "I thought about you my whole life. They told me you were dead."

The woman took a deep breath. "Those were my wishes."

Heaviness came over Amelia as she tried to digest what the woman had just told her. She shook her head. "Why?"

Her mother walked across the room and gestured to a chair. Amelia sat down and she sat in the chair across from her. Soaking in her appearance the woman spoke, "Amelia, is that what they still call you?"

Amelia nodded.

"It was not my wish to be found. I was young when I found out I was with child. Your father was rich and a gambler. He would occasionally visit my family's inn on his way out of town. My family were innkeepers. That is where I learned to sing and dance."

She took a moment and rubbed her hands together. Cracking a smile, she looked at Amelia in the eyes. "He took my innocence. I was so naïve and believed everything he told me. I soon learned that I was going to have his baby. He left me alone when I told him. I never wanted children. I wanted to travel the world and become an actress."

Amelia looked down at her hands in her lap. Her mother was nothing as she imagined and it was breaking her heart. "What happened?"

Her mother leaned back in the chair. She took a bottle of brandy off the table, drinking it without pouring it into a glass. "I had you. My parents kicked me out of their home when they found out I was with child and I lived with one of my sister's until you were born. I found out where he lived and took you to his house. He had become a baron. I didn't even know he was a baron's son. I found out through some men who knew him. I interrupted a garden party with him and his family." She laughed out loud. "You can imagine the shock on his face."

She took another drink wiping her mouth with the back of her hand. "His mother—your grandmother—was mortified. She offered me money to leave immediately. I took her money, but left you too."

Amelia's face burned. "You left me there?"

She shrugged her shoulders. "I told you that I wanted to be an actress. I couldn't have a kid hanging around. Besides, you were better off with them. I told the old bat to tell you that I died."

Amelia's tears streamed down her cheeks. "I was not better off with them. Do you have any idea how hard my life has been?"

Her mother's smile faded. "Poor little rich girl. You probably never wanted for a thing. I know they kept you. I checked back a few weeks later."

Amelia's voice quivered. "My grandmother died before I knew her. My father ignored me for most of my childhood, blaming me for being born." She rubbed her lips together wondering if her mother was listening. She wiped her face. "When I was twelve, he lost his country house and I moved to the city. My stepmother resented me."

Her mother rolled her eyes leaning back in her chair. "She was jealous."

Amelia nodded and lifted the corner of her mouth. "She deserved him. He lost his fortune and was being sent to a debtor's prison. He blamed me for everything that went wrong in his life. I used to dream that you would rescue me. That you loved me. I found the box. It was all I had of you."

She narrowed her eyes. "Box?"

Amelia pinched the bridge of her nose trying to stop it from running. "The box that said Amelia Rose. It had an old rose, locket, and a chain inside of it."

Her mother's face creased with bewilderment. "The box was a gift from my sister when you were born. I didn't realize they would keep it. I gave it to the servants that day. The locket was a gift from your father. He gave it to me the day he used me along with the rose. I gave it all back to him as I wanted to forget him."

Amelia's body trembled thinking about how her childhood dreams had been based on falsehoods. The box held no regards of her past, only bad memories that her mother gave away.

She looked at Amelia with no expression on her face. "I think you read too many books with happy endings." She closed her eyes and sighed. "Amelia, I don't mean to hurt your feelings. Honestly, I put you out of my mind years ago and never spoke of you again. I may have given birth to you, but I am not your mother. You are a stranger to me."

Amelia's head felt dizzy as the world crashed around her. Never had she felt so defeated. She tried to compose herself and stood up. "Forgive me for taking up your time today. It has been enlightening." She walked to the door.

Her mother called after her, but she closed the door and kept walking until she reached the side of the building that led to the outside. After letting herself out, she leaned against the building and sobbed. A strange man approached her. "Miss, may I assist you?"

Amelia caught her breath. "Could you call me a hack, sir?"

He nodded and showed her to the front, calling for a ride.

Andrew went to the theatre after the performance. He searched the crowds not finding Amelia. He walked into drawing room near the box office as actors were conversing with important guests after the show. One of the stage managers recognized him and quickly came to greet him.

"Mr. Baird, it's a pleasure you could join us tonight. I would have reserved you a special seat had I known you would be in town." He bowed and stood in front of him. A few of the waitresses whispered to the actresses of his presence.

"It's quite all right, Mr. Samberg. It was unexpected." He smiled at the man as a woman approached the group.

"Mr. Baird, how nice of you to visit with us. Can I get you a drink?"

Andrew smiled. "Yes, as a matter of fact. A brandy would be nice."

The woman smiled. "Of course. May I also introduce you to Laura Myers and Janice Kilpatrick? They are the stars of tonight's performance."

The women smiled holding out their hands for Andrew to kiss them. He obliged and took their hands to his mouth. "I am sorry I missed the show. I came afterward."

Laura rubbed his arm. "Would you like to join me for a drink?"

Andrew smiled. "I would, but need to take care of some business first."

She stuck out her bottom lip to pout. "I will take you up on that."

Andrew rubbed his nose with his finger. "I am looking for a woman named Mary."

The girl looked at her friend. "Why? She is a little old for you. We would be better company."

He raised his brow. "I am sure you would. This is another matter. She may have some information that I am interested in obtaining."

Janice took a drink. "She is probably in the back over there next to those boxes. I will go get her."

Andrew accepted a drink from the waitress and engaged in conversation with Laura. A few minutes later Janice appeared with an older woman who had the same eyes as Amelia. He had no doubt that this was her mother. She was still very attractive and worked her image with the help of cosmetics and tight-fitting gowns.

"Mr. Baird, it's nice to meet you. Janice has told me good things about you." She smiled and stood in front of him.

He smiled at her flirtatious nature. If she only knew that he was her son–in–law. "May we speak over there privately?"

She motioned toward the boxes and they stepped away from the others.

Andrew leaned over and whispered. "I am looking for a girl that may have come to see you. Her name is Amelia."

"Amelia? I buried that name years ago, yet it keeps coming up today." Pinching her cheeks for more color, she turned to face Andrew. "Mr. Baird, you are out of luck. It seems your friend has left."

Andrew straightened his mouth. "Do you know where she went?"

A man came over to Mary before she could answer. "John wants to see you."

She nodded. "Tell him I will be there in a moment." She looked at Andrew. "Mr. Baird, I must go."

Andrew grabbed her arm as she tried to leave him. "I am not finished with you." He looked at the man. "Tell John I will send Miss Brady when I am finished with her."

The man's eyes widened. "Yes, Mr. Baird."

She looked at him jerking her arm out of his grip. "Do people always do what you say?"

He straightened his jacket. "Don't be coy with me, Miss Brady. I am losing my patience."

She laughed. "Okay, tough guy. Why are you looking for her? Does she owe you money?"

Andrew lifted the corner of his mouth. "I give her money without pay back. It's my responsibility."

Miss Brady crinkled her brow. "Does she work for you?"

Andrew's face hardened at her attempt to be evasive. "Where is she? I won't ask you again."

She shrugged her shoulders. "I do not know. She thought I could be someone I am not and ran out of here."

Andrew's jaw flexed as he tried to remain calm. "What did you say to her?"

She watched his reaction. "I can see she told you about me. I told her that having a baby and being a mother was not the same. I gave her away and never looked back. She told me her life was hard and she thought I would rescue her. Hard? She doesn't know what hard is and grew up with privilege. She should thank me."

Andrew narrowed his eyes. "You don't know her at all. Don't pretend to know what her life was like. Do one good thing for her and tell me where she is."

She shook her head and let out a huff. "Who is she to you?"

Andrew tilted his head. "She is my wife."

Her mouth dropped open. "I had no idea." She smirked. "I bet her father had a heart attack. I would have loved to have seen that." She fidgeted with her gloves pulling them tighter on her hands. "Mr. Baird, I would tell you where she went if I knew. Amelia ran out of here crying and that is the last time I saw her."

Andrew looked annoyed as Mary walked away. He turned around as a man approached him. "Mr. Baird? May I have word in private?"

Andrew walked with him by the side doorway. He looked down with a bit of a shudder showing his nervousness. "Forgive me for intruding on your conversation. I overheard you say that you were looking for that girl."

Andrew creased his eyebrows. "Yes, her name is Amelia."

The man looked away finding it hard to make eye contact. "She was crying and I helped her find a hack. Real pretty girl she was. I heard her tell the driver to take her to McNown Street. She said she wanted to see the entire world. Hope she doesn't get herself into trouble."

Suddenly he knew where she was going. It had to be the lighthouse, it was near McNown Street and she could see the entire world. "Thank you, sir."

He tried to put some cash into his hand, but the man refused. "I am just happy that she has someone to look after her. Seemed like a good girl."

Andrew found his horse and went to find her.

The lighting on the streets was sporadic and darkness lurked on corners causing Andrew to go slowly through the cobblestone walkways. The lighthouse he owned was a good hour away at this pace. He wanted to get to her as fast as he could. She must be distraught at finding her mother in such a state. Who could blame her for running out of the theatre?

He reached the lighthouse with emptiness in his chest. The doors were locked and the key was in his home in Edinburgh. He hoped she found a way inside as the chill of the night would be too much for her. After inspecting the tower, he noticed the side window was broken. A smile crept across his face as he eyed a faint light in the upstairs window. Someone was inside and he had a feeling it was Amelia. He reached through the broken window and opened the door. Not too safe, but he would fix it later and replace the window.

He climbed the stairs reaching the second floor. He saw her lying on the bed with her back to the door. Not wanting to scare her he whispered, "Amelia?"

She gasped loudly and scooted across the bed frightened at the figure taking up the doorway. She looked closer trying to decipher who the figure was. "Andrew?"

He smiled and stepped toward her leaning down to sit on the bed. Upon closer inspection of his wife, he could see her swollen eyes and tear-stained face. Her hair tumbled down out of her braid, and she was shivering. He reached for a blanket and wrapped it around her.

She pulled it up to her chin. "Thank you." Not sure of his mood, she stuttered, "How...? What are you doing here? I promise you that I was coming back. Please don't be angry with me. I was not running away only trying to find my mother. There was no time to get your permission." Fresh tears welled up in her eyes.

He reached for her hand. "Shh. Amelia. I am not angry with you."

She wrinkled her brow confused by his kindness. "I don't understand. How did you find me?"

He let go of her hand and stood up closing the door trying to get some heat into the room.

"I went to Dundee. Mrs. Franklin reluctantly told me where you went." He turned to look at her as her face twisted in bewilderment.

She rubbed her lips together. "I was so sure that my mother would be happy to see me. I imagined that she would welcome me with open arms as her long-lost daughter." A sob came out as she tried to continue. "I thought my horrible father kept her away from me."

She snorted, looking back up at Andrew. "Turns out that he had more honor than she did. Can you believe that? The only reason he acknowledged me was because she dropped me off to him in front of my grandmother. It was her that made him provide for me. An unloved child that was a burden. My grandmother must have arranged the fake papers that showed my parents were married for my protection. They were never married. I am a bastard. I now understand why my father treated me so poorly. He didn't want me and I reminded him of his mistake. He could never love me. She could never love me. No one could ever love me." Sobs came out as she put her hands over her face.

Andrew came to the bed and sat down again and embraced her. "Don't say that. I love you."

Amelia froze. Unsure of his words, she snuggled against his chest unable to see his face. Trying to compose herself she pulled back from his embrace. "What did you say?"

He touched her face wiping the tears and brushing her hair back with his hand. "It doesn't matter if your parents loved you. You are loved, Amelia. I love you."

She closed her eyes basking in the feelings that went through her. "Say it again."

He smiled and kissed her on the forehead. "I love you."

She reached out her arms and squeezed him tightly around his neck laying her cheek on his chest. "I love you, too."

He held her in his embrace for a few moments. Neither of them saying anything. She finally broke their hold. "I thought you would never say those words. That you would never forgive me."

Andrew looked down. "You hurt me, Amelia. I never thought I would allow anyone to hurt me since I was a kid—I had a heart of stone to survive. They used to say I had ice in my veins. But the day I saw you dancing with those kids and looking so beautiful, the ice melted. You betrayed me and I thought I could never forgive you. But I learned that sometimes love is more important than all things—even vengeance. You make me want to be a better person. I love you and our son. I want us to be a family. It tore my heart out when I thought I might lose you."

She touched his face and whispered, "Make love to me, Andrew."

He leaned down and kissed her softly. Pulling her closer to his chest as he deepened the kiss. She responded by opening her mouth and her body responded to his touch. For the first time, she initiated her own touching removing his coat and loosening his cravat. He unlaced her gown as she explored his body, not breaking from the kiss. He leaned her back on to the bed and took off her gown, then finished undressing himself, excited that she wanted him as much as he wanted her. Their lovemaking was intense. She lay in his arms afterward as they slowly recovered. He didn't want to let her go.

He ran his fingers through her hair. "I have something for you."

She leaned back to look at his face. "I have everything I need."

He shook his head. "No, this is something I hope you will want." He scooted from under her and took his pants off the floor. He put his hand in the pocket taking out the ring.

She gasped. "It's my wedding ring. How did you get it back?"

He grinned, rubbing her hand. "One of my guards found it the night you left. I have been keeping it for you. Waiting for a time that you would want it back."

She put her hand out and Andrew slid the ring on her finger. "I will never take it off."

He bent down and kissed her.

She held her hand out looking at her ring. "I can't believe I have it back."

He watched her closely. "I want to start over, Amelia. I want us to be married again. This time for love."

She looked surprised at his confession. "A love match? I like the sound of that." She reached up and kissed him on the cheek.

Andrew slipped out of bed and bent down on his knees taking her hands. Amelia sat up, drawing her brow, confused by his action.

"Amelia, will you marry me again? I don't want you to say yes out of obligation or because you are afraid you will lose any money. If your answer is no, I will give you a divorce and you can keep the cottage and the money I gave your father along with a hefty settlement. It was wrong of me to make the deal with your father without considering your feelings. If you say yes to me, I will try to be the best husband for you. I want it to be your choice."

She put her hand over her face, nodding her head and catching her breath. "Yes, yes, yes, I will marry you again."

He reached for her pulling her closer to him. She was shaking with tears of joy.

He squeezed her tightly. "It's freezing in here. I say we get dressed and go stay at the inn down the road. Tomorrow we can go back to Dundee and get Robert. I want us to be a family. A real family. There is a chapel on our estate in Edinburgh, and I want to say our vows again as soon as possible."

She touched his face. "I do too."

Amelia dressed in a beautiful lacy cream-colored gown. She held red roses that Andrew had given her that morning. She wore the diamond necklace from their picnic highlighted by cream gloves and a few flowers in her hair. No longer nervous, but excited to say her vows again.

Andrew waited for her in the chapel. Mr. Charles served as her escort to give her away. They had gathered their friends and servants for another wedding. Amelia was overjoyed to see Beatrice and Alfred. Andrew had spoken to the couple and asked them to join in the festivities. Alfred accepted his position back and Beatrice remained as Amelia's friend rather than her employee. Andrew provided them a hunting lodge to live in on the estate. Mrs. Franklin held Robert during the ceremony while Mrs. Palmer assured them that there were plenty of apple tarts for their wedding breakfast.

Amelia said her vows with love in her heart, and Andrew declared his love for her in front of all the guests. The couple was congratulated by well-wishers and wished a lifetime of happiness.

Jean hit her glass with her spoon. "May I say my heartfelt congratulations to the bride and groom? I am so happy I could be at this wedding, since I was not invited to the other one." She smiled and winked at the couple. "However, there seems to be something missing. Only one more wish could make this wedding perfect."

Andrew's smile faded. "What would that be?"

A deep voice came from the back the crowd. "Me! Do you think I would let you guys celebrate without me again?" All the heads turned and Ian entered with a wide smile.

The couple stood up and hugged him. Ian laughed and walked over to Mrs. Franklin. He lifted Robert from her lap. "Now, I have fallen behind in my duties as an uncle and have some catching up to do if I am to corrupt him to be the finest kid in the nursery."

Amelia laughed at his silliness and looked around the room realizing her life had come full circle. Her dreams had changed. Her parents were not what she had hoped they would be. But these people at this wedding breakfast were her family now. They loved her and she loved them. And she couldn't be happier.

EPILOGUE

A MELIA ENTERED THE DRAWING ROOM eyeing Mr. Charles on the floor trying to find a chess piece. "Robert! Stop throwing the chess pieces, or he will not teach you to play anymore."

"Mama, I want to play with the pieces in my fort." Robert jumped off the chair and ran over to Amelia with chess pieces in each one of his chubby hands. He held up his hands for her to carry him.

A deep voice rumbled behind him. "Robert, your mother can't pick you up. She is getting ready to have another baby, and you are too heavy now."

Amelia looked up at her husband. "I didn't hear you come in."

He walked over and kissed her stomach. "How do you feel, love?"

She stretched her back. "My ankles are swollen, and I look awful. Rachel invited us to dinner, but I'm not sure I am up for it."

He embraced her. "You look beautiful. But I don't want you to push yourself too much. Come and sit on the settee. I told the doctor we would be staying in London until after you deliver. I like the doctors here better. I want to make sure that you have the best medical care."

Mr. Charles stood up and straightened his jacket. "Mr. and Mrs. Baird, may I suggest we wait another year before young master Robert will be ready to play chess."

Both Amelia and Andrew laughed. Andrew sat beside his wife rubbing her stomach. "I agree."

Robert crossed his arms. "I can play chess, Papa."

He reached over and pulled his son on his lap. "Of course, you can. If you use the pieces for toys. Chess is a game for big boys. Perhaps we can play a different game?" He squeezed him and sat him between Amelia and himself.

Amelia rubbed her son's head and looked over at Andrew. "I thought you were working this afternoon."

Andrew touched her face as Robert wiggled between them unable to sit still. He hopped off the settee and ran to his toys by the fireplace.

"I told Brian I wanted to spend the afternoon with you. He handles most of the day-to-day business now. Perhaps when he finally takes a wife, I will help him out more than I do now. But Robert may be big enough to take over before that happens." He chuckled.

Amelia smirked rubbing her stomach. "Or this one could be a girl and she can take over your business."

Andrew took both of her hands laughing. He kissed her on the mouth. "As you wish, my dear. As you wish."

THE END

ABOUT THE AUTHOR

GG Shalton has been writing short stories most of her life. Often entertaining friends and family. At their encouragement she wrote her first novel in 2016 for publication. Although, she received her Bachelor's degree in Business Management, her real passion is history. Her fascination with different time periods is the inspiration for most her stories. GG is an avid reader and can often be found in various hiding places around her home enjoying a good book. She loves happy endings and most of her free time is spent developing story lines and writing. She is married to a wonderful husband who inspires her to pursue her passion. They met while both of them served in the US Navy. Her heart belongs to her two sons who both promise that one day they may read one of her books. She thanks Jesus for her multiple blessings each day, especially the gift of storytelling.

Authorggshalton@gmail.com.
https://www.facebook.com/gigi.shalton.7

Made in United States
Orlando, FL
13 March 2024

44711257R00125